James Patterson is one of the best-known and biggest-selling writers of all time. He is the author of some of the most popular series of the past decade — the Alex Cross, Women's Murder Club and Detective Michael Bennett novels — and he has written many other number one bestsellers including romance novels and stand-alone thrillers. He lives in Florida with his wife and son.

James is passionate about encouraging children to read. Inspired by his own son who was a reluctant reader, he also writes a range of books specifically for young readers. James has formed a partnership with the National Literacy Trust, an independent, UK-based charity that changes lives through literacy. In 2010, he was voted Author of the Year at the Children's Choice Book Awards in New York.

KILL ALEX CROSS

The President's son and daughter have been abducted from their school . . . Detective Alex Cross is on the scene from the outset, yet he's shunted to the fringes of the investigation. Someone powerful doesn't want Cross too close. A deadly contagion in the DC water supply threatens the capital, and Alex sees the most devastating attack on the United States looming. Working flat-out on the abduction, this massive assault now pushes Cross over the edge. Time passes. The chances of finding the children alive diminish. In an emotional private meeting, the First Lady asks Alex to please save her kids. But, despite the highest security clearance, he gets no closer to the kidnapper — and Alex makes a desperate decision that goes against everything he believes in.

JAMES PATTERSON

KILL ALEX CROSS

Complete and Unabridged

CHARNWOOD
Leicester

First published in Great Britain in 2011 by
Century
The Random House Group Limited
London

First Charnwood Edition
published 2012
by arrangement with
The Random House Group Limited
London

The moral right of the author has been asserted

This novel is a work of fiction. Names and characters
are the product of the author's imagination and any
resemblance to actual persons, living or dead,
is entirely coincidental.

British Library CIP Data

Patterson, James, *1947* –
    Kill Alex Cross.
    1. Cross, Alex (Fictitious character)- -Fiction.
    2. Police- -Washington (D.C.)- -Fiction.
    3. Suspense fiction. 4. Large type books.
    I. Title
    813.6–dc23

    ISBN 978–1–4448–1232–9

Published by
F. A. Thorpe (Publishing)
Anstey, Leicestershire

Set by Words & Graphics Ltd.
Anstey, Leicestershire
Printed and bound in Great Britain by
T. J. International Ltd., Padstow, Cornwall

This book is printed on acid-free paper

For Steve Bowen, Leopoldo Gout,
Stuart Manashil, and Bill Block —
the Four Musketeers

Book One

UNACCOUNTED FOR

1

It began with President Coyle's children, Ethan and Zoe, both high-profile personalities since they had arrived in Washington, and probably even before that.

Twelve-year-old Ethan Coyle thought he had gotten used to living under the microscope and in the public eye. So Ethan hardly noticed anymore the news cameramen perpetually camped outside the Branaff School gates, and he didn't worry the way he used to if some kid he didn't know tried to snap his picture in the hall, or the gymnasium, or even the boys' bathroom.

Sometimes, Ethan even pretended he was invisible. It was kind of babyish, kind of b.s., but who cared. It helped. One of the more personable Secret Service guys had actually suggested it. He told Ethan that Chelsea Clinton used to do the same thing. Who knew if that was true?

But when Ethan saw Ryan Townsend headed his way that morning, he only *wished* he could disappear.

Ryan Townsend always had it in for him, and that wasn't just Ethan's paranoia talking. He had the purplish and yellowing bruises to prove it — the kind that a good hard punch or muscle squeeze can leave behind.

'Wuzzup, *Coyle the Boil?*' Townsend said, charging up on him in the hall with that look on his face. 'The Boil havin' a bad day already?'

Ethan knew better than to answer his tormenter and torturer. He cut a hard left toward the lockers instead — but that was his first mistake. Now there was nowhere to go, and he felt a sharp, nauseating jab to the side of his leg. He'd been kicked! Townsend barely even slowed down as he passed. He called these little incidents 'drive-bys.'

The thing Ethan *didn't* do was yell out, or stumble in pain. That was the deal he'd made with himself: don't let anyone see what you're feeling inside.

Instead, he dropped his books and knelt down to pick them back up again. It was a total wuss move, but at least he could take the weight off his leg for a second without letting the whole world know he was Ryan Townsend's punching and kicking dummy.

Except this time, someone else did see — and it wasn't the Secret Service.

Ethan was stuffing graph paper back into his math folder when he heard a familiar voice.

'Hey, Ryan? Wuzzup with *you?*'

He looked up just in time to see his fourteen-year-old sister, Zoe, stepping right into Townsend's path.

'I saw that,' she said. 'You thought I wouldn't?'

Townsend cocked his head of blond curls to the side. 'I don't know what the hell you're talking about. Why don't you just mind your own — '

Out of nowhere, a heavy yellow textbook came up fast in both of Zoe's hands.

She swung hard, and clocked Townsend with it, right across the middle of his face. The bully's nose spurted red and he stumbled backward. It was great!

That was as far as things progressed before Secret Service got to them. Agent Findlay held Zoe back, and Agent Musgrove wedged himself between Ethan and Townsend. A crowd of sixth, seventh, and eighth graders had already stopped to watch, like this was some new reality TV show — *The President's Kids*.

'You total *losers!*' Townsend shouted at Ethan and Zoe, even as blood dripped down over his Branaff tie and white button-down shirt. 'What a couple of chumps. You need your loyal SS bodyguards to protect you!'

'Oh yeah? Tell that to my algebra book,' Zoe yelled back. 'And stay away from my brother! You're bigger and older than him, you jerk. You shithead!'

For his part, Ethan was still hovering by the lockers, half of his stuff scattered on the floor. And for a second or two there, he found himself pretending he was part of the crowd — just some kid nobody had ever heard of, standing there, watching all of this craziness happen to someone else.

Yeah, Ethan thought. *Maybe in my next lifetime.*

2

Agent Findlay quickly and efficiently hustled Ethan and Zoe away from the gawkers, and worse, the kids with their iPhones raised: *Hello, YouTube!* In a matter of seconds, he'd disappeared with them into the otherwise empty grand lecture hall off the main foyer.

The Branaff School had once been the Branaff Estate, until ownership had transferred to a Quaker educational trust. It was said among the kids that the grounds were haunted, not by good people who had died here, but by the disgruntled Branaff descendants who'd been evicted to make room for the private school.

Ethan didn't buy into any of that crap, but he'd always found the main lecture hall to be supercreepy — with its old-time oil portraits looking down disapprovingly on everybody who happened to pass through.

'You know, the president's going to have to hear about this, Zoe. The fight, your language back there,' Agent Findlay said. 'Not to mention Headmaster Skillings — '

'No doubt, so just do your job,' Zoe answered with a shrug and a frown. She put a hand on top of her brother's head. 'You okay, Eth?'

'I'm fine,' he said, pushing her off. 'Physically, anyway.' His dignity was another question, but that was too complicated for him to think about right now.

'In that case, let's keep this parade moving,' Findlay told them. 'You guys have assembly in five.'

'Got it,' said Zoe with a dismissive wave. 'Like we were going to forget assembly, right?'

The morning's guest speaker was Isabelle Morris, a senior fellow with the DC International Policy Institute and also an alum of the Branaff School. Unlike most of the kids he knew, Ethan was actually looking forward to Ms. Morris's talk about her experiences in the Middle East. Someday he hoped to work at the UN himself. Why not? He had pretty good connections, right?

'Can you give us a teeny-tiny second?' Zoe asked. 'I want to talk to my brother — *alone*.'

'I said I'm fine. It's cool,' Ethan insisted, but his sister cut him off with a glare.

'He tells me things he won't say to you,' Zoe went on, answering Findlay's skeptical look. 'And private conversations aren't exactly easy to come by around here, if you know what I mean. No offense meant.'

'None taken.' Findlay looked down at his watch. 'Okay,' he said. 'Two minutes is all I can give you.'

'Two minutes, it is. We'll be right out, I promise,' Zoe said, and closed the heavy wooden door behind him as he left.

Without a word to Ethan, she cut between the rows of old desk seats and headed to the back of the room. She hopped up on the heating register under the windows.

Then Zoe reached inside her blue and gray

uniform jacket and took out a small black lacquered case. Ethan recognized it right away. His sister had bought it in Beijing this past summer, on a trip to China with their parents.

'I'm all about a ciggie right now,' Zoe whispered. Then she grinned wickedly. 'Come with?'

Ethan looked back at the door. 'I actually don't want to miss this assembly,' he said, but Zoe just rolled her eyes.

'Oh, *please*. Blah, blah, blah, Middle East, blah, blah. You can watch it on CNN any hour of the week,' she said. 'But how often do you get a chance to ditch Secret Service? *Come on!*'

It was a totally no-win situation for him and Ethan knew it. He was either going to look like a wimp — again — or he was going to miss the assembly speech he'd been looking forward to all week.

'You shouldn't smoke,' he said lamely.

'Yeah, well you shouldn't weenie out so much,' Zoe answered. 'Then maybe assholes like Ryan Townsend wouldn't be all over you all the time.'

'That's just because Dad's the president,' Ethan said. 'That's all, right?'

'No. It's because you're a geek,' Zoe said. 'You don't see Spunk-Punk messing with me, do you?' She opened the window, effortlessly pulled herself through, and dropped to the ground outside. Zoe thought she was another Angelina Jolie. 'If you're not coming, at least give me a minute to get away. Okay, Grandma?'

The next second, Zoe was gone.

Ethan looked over his shoulder one more

time. Then he did the only thing he could to maintain his last shreds of dignity. He followed his sister out the lecture hall window — and into trouble he couldn't even begin to imagine.

No one could.

3

As soon as the door to the lecture hall slammed shut behind Agent Clay Findlay, he checked the knob — *still unlocked*. Then he checked the sweep hand on his stainless-steel Breitling. 'I'm giving them another forty-five seconds,' he said into the mike at his cuff. 'After that, we've got T. Rex going to assembly and Twilight headed to the principal's office.'

Word from the president and First Lady had been to allow Ethan and Zoe as normal a school experience as possible, including their own conflicts — within reason. That was easier said than done, of course. Zoe Coyle didn't always operate within reason. In fact, she usually didn't. Zoe wasn't a bad kid. But she was a kid. Willful. And smart, and devoted to her younger brother.

'I'm probably going to get reamed for this,' Findlay radioed quietly. 'Tell you what, though. That Ryan Townsend kid's a little prick. Not that you heard it here.'

'Like father, like son,' Musgrove radioed back. 'Kid got what he was asking for, and more. Zoe really clocked the little shithead.'

There was some low laughter on the line. Ryan Townsend's daddy was the House minority whip and a rabid opponent of virtually every move President Coyle ever made or even thought about. Sometimes the Branaff School could feel like Little Washington. Which it kind of was.

10

Findlay checked his watch again. Two minutes exactly. End of recess for the Coyle kids. Now back to work for everybody.

'All right, ladies and gentlemen, we're on the move,' he said into his mike. Then he knocked twice on the lecture hall door and pushed it open.

'Time's up, guys. You ready to . . . *goddamnit*.'

The room was empty.

No. No. No. Not this. Goddamn those kids. Goddamn Zoe!

Findlay's pulse spiked to a new high, at least for today. His eyes leapt to the multipaned windows along the back wall.

Even as he moved toward them, he was opening all channels on his transmitter to address the Joint Ops Center as well as his on-site team.

'Command, this is Apex One. Twilight and T. Rex are unaccounted for.' His voice was urgent but flat. There would be no panicking. 'I repeat, both protectees are unaccounted for.'

When he reached the windows, they were all pulled down to the sill, but one of them had been left unlatched. A quick scan of the grounds outside showed nothing but plush green playing fields all the way to the south fence.

'Findlay? What's going on?'

Musgrove was there now, standing in the doorway from the hall.

'They must have snuck outside,' Findlay said. 'I'm going to kill her. I really am. Long overdue.' This thing had Zoe written all over it. It was probably her idea of a big game, or a joke on her keepers.

11

'Command, Apex One,' he radioed again. 'Twilight and T. Rex are still unaccounted for. I need an immediate lock-down on all exits, inside and out — '

All at once, a commotion broke out on the line. Findlay heard shouting, and the grating sound of metal on metal. Then two gunshots.

'Command, this is Apex Five!' Another voice blared over the radio now. 'We've got a gray panel van. Just evaded us at the east gate. It's proceeding south on Wisconsin at high speed. Sixty, seventy miles an hour! *Request immediate backup!*'

4

MPD Patrol Sergeant Bobby Hatfield had just spotted a gray van, doing at least sixty through downtown Georgetown, when the emergency call came from dispatch. 'All units, patrol area two-oh-six. Possible armed kidnap in progress. Two kids. That's *two!* We have a gray panel van, traveling at high speed, south on Wisconsin, Northwest. Secret Service is in pursuit. Requesting backup! Please turn to channel twenty-three.'

Hatfield fired up his siren and pulled a fast three-point turn just as a telltale black Yukon went racing by. As soon as he got onto the dedicated channel, he could hear Secret Service broadcasting the chase.

'We are proceeding south. Plates are DC, tag number DMS eight-two-three — '

'Secret Service, this is MPD unit two-oh-six,' Hatfield cut in. 'I'm coming right up on your back.'

'Copy that, MPD.'

Hatfield accelerated as the Yukon fell back and let him take the lead. Already, the speedometer was pushing toward seventy, and his adrenaline was going off the charts. There was a whole lot more that could go wrong here than right.

At M Street, the van careened left, almost looked like it might tip.

It took the corner too wide and sideswiped two parked cars without stopping. Hatfield coasted into the turn — slow in, fast out, was the

13

drill — and punched it as soon as he was pointed in the right direction. It gained him some ground on the van, but not enough.

'Suspect headed east on M,' he called in. 'This guy's flying. Where's the damn backup? C'mon people!'

When they came to Pennsylvania Avenue just before Rock Creek, the van peeled off to the right. It was a wider street now, and whoever was doing the driving picked up even more speed, weaving dangerously across the bridge.

Hatfield blinked hard to keep his vision from tunneling. There were cars and pedestrians everywhere. The whole scene couldn't possibly be more confusing.

This thing is not going to end well. He could feel it everywhere in his body.

At Twenty-eighth Street, a second marked unit finally fell in behind. Hatfield recognized James Walsh's voice as he took over radio communication. Walsh was a pal of his on the force, but also a tormenter.

'How you doing, Robert?'

'Fuck you, how am I doing?'

'Continuing southeast on Pennsylvania,' Walsh went on. 'Suspect's driving is extremely erratic . . . seems to be a single occupant, but it's hard to tell. We're going to hit Washington Circle any second now and — oh, shit! Bobby, look out! Look out!'

As the van came into the rotary, it cut left instead of right, straight into oncoming traffic. Cars and cabs swerved to get out of the way.

It was like the parting of the Red Sea from

where Hatfield was sitting — and there, on the other side of the gap, was a city bus, too big to avoid. The bus driver cut hard to the right, but it was no good.

All he did was give the van a solid wall to run into!

Hatfield slammed his brakes and sent his own car into a hard skid. Even then, his eyes never came off the van.

It crashed, head-on at full speed, right into the Neiman Marcus ad on the side of the bus. The front end crumpled like an accordion. Glass flew everywhere and the van's back wheels lifted a good foot off the ground before the whole mess finally came to a sliding stop.

Hatfield was out of his car right away, with Walsh running up behind him. Miraculously, it looked like the bus had been out of service — nobody but the driver on board. But Washington Circle was a tangle of stopped cars and rear-end collisions.

Within seconds, another half-dozen marked units had converged on the spot.

Uniformed officers were suddenly everywhere, but Hatfield was the first to reach the back door of the van. Its gray metal panels were buckled inward and the chrome handle was smashed to shit.

His heart was still thudding from the chase and he could feel the blood pounding in his ears. This wasn't over yet. What the hell were they about to find on the other side of that door? Armed gunmen? Dead men?

Even worse — *dead kids?*

15

5

At the time of the first incident in the chain of events, I didn't know it was the president's son and daughter who were missing. All I'd heard on my radio was 'possible kidnap.' That's all any of us knew at that point.

I'd been driving east on K Street at the time and I was off duty. The location given put me less than two blocks from the crash site and I got over to Washington Circle even before the EMTs. I had to help if I could.

I was there in less than sixty seconds. A uniformed cop scurried behind me, unspooling a roll of yellow tape as I headed toward the smashed-up van.

The first thing I noticed was the wide-open back door. Second, that there was no sign of any kidnap victim here at all.

And third — Secret Service were everywhere! Some of them in the usual dark suits, others in preppy blazers, knit ties, dress shirts, and khakis. They looked like schoolteachers, but the corkscrew wires behind their ears told another story.

I badged my way over to the van to see inside for myself. The driver was pinned to his seat where the engine block had come all the way through in the crash. He was covered in blood below some obvious trauma around his midsection. His right arm was sticking up and out in a way that arms weren't meant to go.

The guy looked to be midthirties, curly black hair, a sketchy beard with soul patch that was as slight and pathetic as he was.

But where was the victim? Had this whole thing been a hoax? An intentional diversion? Already, I was starting to think so, and the possibility sent a rush of adrenaline through me. *A diversion from what? What else had happened at that school?*

'Is he cogent?' I asked the tweed-clad agent next to me.

'Hard to say,' he answered. 'He's out of it. Maybe shock. We don't even know if he speaks English.'

'And no sign of the missing kid?' I said.

The agent just shook his head, then held up two fingers. '*Two* missing kids.'

This was turning into déjà vu for me — the worst kind. Some years back, I'd worked with Secret Service on another double kidnapping, perpetrated by a monster named Gary Soneji. Only one of the two children had survived. In fact, I'd barely made it myself. John Sampson had saved my life.

I flashed my badge some more, then leaned in through the shattered driver's-side window.

'Police. Where are the kids?' I asked the guy, straight up. By default, I had to assume he knew something. This was no time to equivocate.

He was panting in quick shallow breaths, and his face was blank — like his body knew how much pain he was in, but his brain didn't exactly get it.

His pupils were huge, too. He had some of the signs of PCP, but this guy had just navigated a high-speed chase through the city. I'd never seen anyone on angel dust who could do that.

When he didn't answer — not a word or a nod or a grunt — I tried again.

'You hearing me?' I shouted. 'Tell me where the two kids are! If you want us to help you out of there.'

The ambulance was here now and two EMTs were at my shoulder, trying to push me out of the way. I wasn't moving anywhere.

I heard a hydraulic motor fire up somewhere behind me, too. That was for the spreader tool — the Jaws of Life — and this guy was definitely going to need it. But not until I got my answer.

'What do you know?' I said. 'Are you working for someone? Just tell me where the kids are!'

Something in the driver's face changed then. His breath was still shallow, but the corners of his mouth turned up and his eyes crinkled, like someone had told him a joke no one else could hear or maybe understand. When he finally spit out an answer, a spray of blood came with it, all over the mangled steering wheel and column.

'*What kids, man?*' he said.

6

The rescue team used a hurst tool to cut the posts flanking the van's windshield and door, then a halogen bar to peel the roof back like a can of sardines. It's amazing to watch, but usually you're rooting for the person trapped inside. Not so much this time. Actually, not at all.

While they lowered in a chain to pull back the engine and get our empty-eyed friend out of there, I tried to get a quick lowdown from the Secret Service agent I'd been speaking with, Clay Findlay.

'So, who are these missing kids?' I asked him, but he just shook his head. He wasn't going to tell me, was he? What was that about? 'Listen,' I said. 'I've had experience on this kind of thing — '

'I know who you are,' he said, cutting me off again. 'You're Alex Cross. You're MPD.'

My reputation precedes me more and more these days, but that can cut both ways. It didn't seem to be helping right now.

'We've already got all MPD units on alert,' Findlay said, 'so why don't you go check in with your lieutenant. See where he could use you? Obviously, I've got my hands full here. I've had some experience in these quarters, too, Detective.'

I didn't like the brush-off. It was a mistake for

somebody who claimed to have experience. Every passing minute meant those kids were a little farther out of our reach. Findlay should have known that. Even worse, maybe he did.

'You see that guy?' I said. I pointed over at the driver. They had a protective collar around his neck and were finally making some headway getting him out. 'That's an MPD arrest. You understand me? I'm going to talk to him as soon as I can, with or without your involvement. If you want to wait your turn, fine, but just so you know — once they get him to the ER, he's going to be sedated and tubed up for God knows how long. So it might be a while before you get your interview.'

Findlay stared hard at me. I watched his jaw work back and forth, heard a cracking noise. He knew I had jurisdiction here, that I had him if I wanted to go that way.

'It's Zoe and Ethan Coyle,' he said finally. 'You'll hear about it soon enough. They disappeared from the Branaff School about twenty minutes ago.'

I was stunned into silence. Knocked back on my heels. The enormity of this — the implications — started to fall on me at once. 'What else is happening on your end?' I asked in a lowered voice.

'The school's locked down,' Findlay said. 'Every available Secret Service agent is either there or on the way.'

'Could they still turn up over there?' I asked.

He shook his head. 'We'd have found them by now. No way they're still on the campus.'

20

'Any idea how someone could have gotten them out of there?'

Again, he paused. I got the impression he was editing himself as he went forward. The other thing I didn't know yet was that Findlay was lead agent on Ethan and Zoe's protective detail. This was all on his head. *The president's children.*

'Not really. It just happened,' he answered. 'There's an underground passage. Used to connect the main house with some of the service buildings. Way back when it was the Branaff Estate. We keep it all closed off now, but kids still break in there sometimes. Smoke a cigarette, grope each other. Believe me, if Ethan and Zoe were in that tunnel before, they aren't anymore.'

The van driver was out on a gurney now, hooked up to a nasogastric tube and IV. As they wheeled him to the back of the ambulance and loaded him up, Findlay and I fell in behind the procession.

My badge was out again. So were his creds.

'Hey!' one of the medics yelled at us as we climbed in. 'You can't — '

'We're coming with him,' I said, and closed the ambulance doors. No further discussion. 'Let's go.'

7

My mind was working even faster now, probably too fast. So was my pulse. And I couldn't catch my breath either.

The president's kids.

George Washington University Hospital was only a few blocks from the crash site so this was going to have to be quick. While the EMTs worked over our suspect and radioed in his vitals, I leaned in as close as I could to get his attention.

'What's your name?' I said.

I had to ask a couple of times before he finally responded.

'Ray?' He said it like a question.

'Okay, Ray. I'm Alex. You with me here?'

He was flat on his back and staring at the ceiling. I ran a finger back and forth in front of his eyes to get him to look at me.

'What are you on, Ray? You know what you took?'

His expression was as distant as ever. 'Just a drink of water,' he said finally.

'Don't give him anything!' one of the medics barked at me.

'*I'm not,*' I said. ''Drink of water' is PCP. That's what he thinks he took.'

'Thinks?' Agent Findlay asked.

'Something heavily anesthetic, anyway. Probably some kind of nose cocktail.' And I was

22

guessing he didn't mix it himself.

'Who got you the van, Ray?' I said. 'Who put you up to this? There's somebody else, right?'

'Anyone, anyone,' he said. 'Five hundred bucks and a little drink of water.'

'*Five hundred bucks?*' Findlay looked like he was ready to tear the guy's face off. 'Do you have any idea what kind of shit storm you just landed in — for five hundred dollars?'

Ray wasn't listening to the Secret Service agent, though. He was looking around now, like he'd just figured out where he was. When he got down to his own midsection, and the blood soaking through the heavy gauze dressing, he just grinned. 'This is some good shit,' he said.

'Ray?' I tried again. 'Ray? You said something about 'anyone.' What did you mean by that?'

'No,' he said, twitching away. 'Anyone, anyone.' The fingers on his left hand started moving rapidly; it looked like he was playing scales on a piano.

Findlay and I looked at each other. Whoever had put Ray up to this knew what they were doing. Now, while the trail to the kids was warmest, the one person we had in custody was virtually useless. We were wasting precious time on this guy. That was exactly what the kidnapper wanted, wasn't it?

'We're here!' the ambulance driver yelled back. 'Interview's over.' The other two stood up and started getting Ray ready to go.

'Who's anyone?' I tried one more time. 'What do you mean by that, Ray?'

'An-y-one. An-y-one,' he said again, tapping a

different finger on each syllable — and I realized it wasn't like he was playing a piano. It was like he was hitting keys on a keyboard. Then I had another idea.

N-E-1-N-E-1.

'Is that a screen name?' I asked. 'Did somebody find you online, Ray?'

'Watch out, guys!'

The back of the ambulance opened from the outside. Findlay and I had to jump out first to get out of the way.

An emergency medical team was already waiting, along with an incongruous crowd of gray suits off to one side.

It wasn't just any crowd, either. Findlay stopped short on the pavement, and I almost knocked into him.

'Sir?' he said to one of the suits.

Right there in front of us was the secretary of Homeland Security himself, Phil Ribillini.

'Detective Cross,' Ribillini said with a curt nod. We'd met once before, back when I was with the FBI and he was with Defense. There were no pleasantries today. 'We'll need a statement from you right away,' he said. 'But my people will take it from there. Has to be that way.'

In other words, I wasn't going any farther with the prisoner. All I could do was watch as they wheeled Ray inside through the automatic sliders and out of sight.

But that wasn't the bad part. The clock kept ticking on those two missing kids.

8

Dr. Hala Al Dossari was twenty-nine years old, slender and attractive, humorous when it was useful, very bright, with a photographic memory. Her husband, Tariq, was thirty-nine, pudgy everywhere, and hopelessly in love with his wife. They looked like they had everything to live for, but in reality, the Al Dossaris were prepared to die at any time. Probably sooner rather than later. That was their mission.

Hala snuck a sideways glance at her watch. They had been warned repeatedly about the dangers of Dulles Airport. The International Arrivals area was one of the most scrutinized in the world. Besides the armed security and usual customs agents, the terminal was staffed with a well-trained team of behavior detection officers — BDOs. The purpose of these police devils was to scan the incoming crowds for anything considered beyond the norm.

Too much sweat on the brow could get you pulled out of line here.

So could rapid eye movement.

Or a nervous gait.

Or a cranky BDO.

'Almost through,' Hala said, giving her husband's hand a reassuring squeeze. 'Not much longer. Give me a smile. Americans love a nice smile.'

'*Inshallah*,' he answered.

'Tariq, please — *a smile*. Just show your teeth for the surveillance cameras.'

Finally, he did as he was told. It was a stiff-jawed attempt — but a smile, anyway. So far, so good. Another minute or so and they would be perfectly safe.

Passport control had gone by without incident. Baggage claim, other than feeling like a cattle yard, had been fine. Now they were down to luggage screening, one final queue to wait in before they could truly say they'd arrived safely in Washington.

But everything had suddenly slowed to a crawl. This was a nightmare.

In fact, Hala realized, *the line had completely stopped*.

A couple of uniformed TSA agents were unhooking the stanchion belt up ahead, motioning for two people to step out of line. It was another couple — also Saudi, also in Western dress.

'Sir? Ma'am? Could you come with us, please?'

'What for?' the other man asked, immediately on the defensive. 'We haven't done anything wrong. Why should we lose our rightful place in the queue?'

His accent was Najdi, Hala noticed. The same as theirs.

But who were these people? Could this just be a coincidence? One look at Tariq's worried face and she knew he was wrestling with the same questions. Was their American mission about to be compromised before it had even begun?

26

More American security personnel hurried over now. A husky black female officer took the Saudi woman firmly by the arm.

'*Farouk!*' the woman screamed for her husband. Then she yelled at the security police. 'Leave us alone! Take your dirty hands off me!'

As Hala watched the husband, her heart skipped. *He was reaching for something in his pocket.* One of the guards tried to pull his arm away. But the man pushed back hard. The guard went down on his ass.

Two more officers rushed forward. There was a violent scuffle. The police threw the Saudi man to the floor. Jumped on his back. But he fought and got one hand free. The next moment, he'd stuffed something into his mouth.

And that's when Hala knew — this was no coincidence. She had a potassium cyanide capsule in her pocket as well. So did Tariq.

Whatever this couple had done to tip off the authorities, there was nothing the Al Dossaris could do for them now. Their only obligation at this point was to avoid detection. Above all, they mustn't be captured, too.

And they wouldn't be. Not if they kept their heads, Hala knew. Service to the cause was everything. Their mission could change the world. But first, they had to make it out of here alive. The Family was depending on them. Their mission here meant everything.

Tariq grasped her hand tighter. His own hand was wet with sweat. 'I love you, Hala,' he whispered. 'I love you so much!'

9

'This guy just ate something!' One of the TSA officers shouted to his partners. He held down the struggling, writhing husband while another guard tried to force the man's mouth open.

Hala saw the stream of blood run down over his chin. That meant he'd bitten through the capsule's rubber coating, into the glass bead inside. Her heart was thundering now. As a doctor, she knew all too well about the effects of potassium cyanide on the body. It was going to be horrible, absolutely awful to witness. Especially with a capsule right there in her own pocket.

Almost immediately, the man began to convulse. His torso bucked slowly, his legs kicking back and forth. It was an instinctive but ultimately useless response. While the oxygen built up to dangerous levels in his blood, less and less of it would reach his vital organs, including the lungs. The panic alone would be excruciating. The terrible burning inside.

The man's young wife collapsed at his feet next. A trickle of blood ran down her chin, too. Then more blood, from her nose.

'Something's wrong!' the female guard yelled. 'Call emergency services! We need a doctor right now!'

Border Protection was doing its best to maintain order, but panic had begun to take over the arrivals hall. People started bottlenecking toward the screening stations. Frantic voices echoed against the high ceiling. Two-way radios crackled everywhere.

'Tariq?' Hala said. He was standing perfectly still, even as other travelers pushed past them. 'Tariq? We have to go. *Right now.*'

His eyes seemed to be locked on the other couple, dying there on the terminal floor.

'That could have been us,' he whispered.

'*But it wasn't,*' Hala said. 'Move. Now! Keep the pill in your hand, just in case. And speak nothing but English until we are out of here.'

Tariq nodded. His wife was also his superior. Slowly, he tore his eyes away from the two suffering martyrs. Hala hooked her arm firmly into his and turned to go. Then she pulled him forward like a stubborn animal.

A moment later, the Al Dossaris had allowed themselves to be swallowed up in the crowd. People around them were crying. A young girl vomited right there on the floor. Then they were clamoring for the exits, just like anyone else. Only after they were clear of the security guards did they put away the cyanide pills.

They had made it to America.

10

After I gave my statement at the hospital, I headed back to the Branaff School. I called Bree and told her what had happened and that I'd miss dinner. She got it, which is the nice thing about being married to another cop.

A solid double line of MPD cruisers was parked up and down Wisconsin Avenue when I got there. This was as bad a crime scene as I'd ever witnessed.

The press had already been cordoned off behind a row of blue police barriers, and I saw a group of what looked like very concerned parents and a few nanny or housekeeper types waiting closer in toward the main gate. Some students were crying.

There wouldn't be any official statements for several hours, if at all, but that wasn't going to stop people from figuring out what had happened. The whole scene was barely contained chaos. Something terrible had obviously gone down here and none of us knew the full extent of it yet.

'Catch me up,' I said to one of the uniforms lined across the sidewalk. 'What's going on? Anything in the last hour?'

'All I know is what you can see right here,' he told me. 'MPD's on street security. But FBI's got the whole school locked down tight.'

'Who's the lead agent on campus?' I said, but

the cop just shook his head.

'Nobody's going in, Detective, and the only ones coming out are kids and parents. They're literally clearing them one by one. They're even detaining the teachers. I wouldn't hold my breath for intel.'

I left the officer alone to do his job, and I got on the phone instead. For several months now, I'd been the police department's liaison to the FBI's Field Intelligence Group. I figured that had to be worth some kind of ticket inside.

But I figured wrong. Every line I tried at the Directorate of Intelligence went straight to voice mail.

Same deal with Ned Mahoney, who was a good friend at the Bureau. They were all probably on the other side of that damn school fence right now. Maybe even Ned was there. It was crazy-making.

The worst of it was worrying about Ethan and Zoe Coyle and what they might be going through while I was out here spinning my wheels. The first twenty-four hours after a kidnapping are absolutely crucial and I didn't think the Secret Service would make all the right decisions.

So I did what I could. I started walking. Maybe I wouldn't get onto campus, but I could get a feel for the school perimeter, including any possible exit points the kidnapper — or kidnappers — might have used.

I also kept working the phones while I walked. I put in a call to MPD's Command Information Center. I finally got through to somebody. 'CIC,

31

this is Sergeant O'Mara.'

'Bud, it's Alex Cross. I need to get a couple of disks burned, ASAP. I'm looking for everything we've got in a two-block radius around the Branaff School. From five to eleven this morning.'

Washington's metro surveillance isn't state of the art, like London's, but we are ahead of the curve, nationally speaking. We've got cameras at intersections all over the city; maybe one of them had picked something up.

'You want me to have someone drop these off at headquarters when they're ready?' O'Mara asked.

'No, I'll swing by and get them myself,' I said. 'Thanks, Bud.'

I turned off my phone when I hung up. I didn't want anyone calling and telling me where to be today. If I played it right, I could pick up the disks, spend some time going over them at home, and not show my face at the office until the next morning. I'd learned a long time ago that it's better to ask forgiveness than permission.

Maybe I was just flattering myself — or even lying to myself. Maybe there was nothing I could do on this that the Bureau or Secret Service wasn't already covering. But I'd worry about that after the first twenty-four hours.

Finally though, around six, I gave up and went on home. Obviously nobody needed my help here. I didn't like it, but what I thought didn't matter. The president's kids were missing.

11

If I'd had any idea about the string of horrifying things that were about to happen in Washington, I wouldn't have gone to help out Sampson that night.

My best friend, John Sampson, and his wife, Billie, were on the steering committee for a much-needed charter school they were trying to get going in our neighborhood in Southeast DC. Tonight's event was supposed to be an informational meeting, but people around the neighborhood had already started lining up on either side of the issue.

So I brought reinforcements with me — my 'ninety-something' grandmother, Nana Mama; and my wife, Bree, who works as a detective with the MPD's Violent Crimes Branch and was also just crazy enough to marry me a few months earlier.

The three of us showed up early at the community center to help set up. I was trying to keep Ethan and Zoe Coyle off my mind.

'Thanks for doing this, sugar. I owe you,' Sampson said. He was running sound cable while I pulled folding chairs off a big rack. 'It's probably going to get a little ugly in here tonight.'

'Can't be helped, John. You were just born that way,' I said, and he started for me. Sampson and I bring out the smart-ass kid in each other

— ever since we were smart-ass kids growing up in this same neighborhood.

'And we're *focusing*.' Billie came whizzing by with a handful of flyers for us to give out at the door. She was excited, but also nervous, I could tell. A lot of misinformation had been spread around the neighborhood, and the opposition to the charter school was mounting.

I thought the rain might keep people away, but by seven o'clock the room was completely full. John and Billie got things started, talking about a small-community approach, double periods of math and reading, parental involvement — everything that had them jazzed. Just listening to them, I was getting excited myself. My youngest, Ali, might go to this school one day.

But this is Washington, where nobody lets a good idea stand in the way of the status quo, and things started to go downhill in a hurry.

'We've heard all this before,' a woman in a housedress and sneakers without laces said from the mike in the aisle. I recognized her from church. 'The last thing we need is another charter around here drawing down our public school budget.'

There was a mix of half applause, half boos, and some unpleasant shouting around the room.

'That's right!'

'Come on, get real!'

'What's the point?'

'*The point*,' Billie cut in, 'is that not nearly enough kids from our neighborhood go on to college. If we can get them started on the right foot from day one — '

34

'Yeah, that and a dollar won't even get you a cup of coffee anymore,' Housedress Lady said. 'We should be getting some of our closed schools reopened, not trying to start up new ones.'

'I hear that!'

'Sit down!'

'*You* sit down.'

The whole thing was kind of depressing, really. Made my head hurt. I'd already taken two turns at the mike and gotten nowhere in a hurry. Sampson looked like he wanted to hit somebody. Billie looked like she wanted to cry.

Then I got a hard nudge in the ribs. It was from Nana. 'Help me up, Alex. I've got something to say.'

12

'Well, doesn't this feel familiar?' Nana stood at her seat and launched in. 'Or is it just me?' She already had everyone's attention, and apparently she didn't even need a microphone. Just about everybody here knew her.

'Last I checked, this wasn't the House of Representatives, and it wasn't the floor of the Senate,' she said. 'This was a neighborhood meeting, where we can speak with more than two voices, have different ideas, listen occasionally, and who knows, maybe even get something accomplished every once in a while.'

The woman had a forty-year teaching career in the day, and it wasn't hard for me to imagine her lecturing a roomful of disobedient students. A few people around me were nodding their heads. A few looked like they didn't know what to think about this fierce old lady yet.

'I suppose some of this is understandable,' she went on, tapping her cane as she spoke. 'We all know how cheap a promise can be in Washington, and as you said, ma'am, you've heard it all before. So if some of you are feeling a little frustrated, or burned out, or what have you, let me be the first to say I understand. I feel the same way most days.'

'But,' I whispered in Bree's ear.

'*But*,' Nana said, poking a finger in the air,

'with all due respect, we're not here to talk about you.'

Bree squeezed my arm like the Wizards had just sunk a winning bucket.

'We're here to talk about the eighty-eight percent of eighth graders in this city who aren't proficient in math, much less the ninety-three percent in reading. *Ninety-three percent!* I call that an emergency worth doing something about. I call that a disgrace.'

'That's right, Regina,' someone said, and 'Mmm-hmm,' from another corner. I love when Nana 'goes to church,' as we call it at home, and she wasn't done yet.

'So if you're here for an actual conversation, I say let's have one,' Nana went on. 'And if not — if you came for politics, and side-taking, and business as usual, I say we've got a whole big city out there for you to play in.' She paused just long enough that I could tell she was secretly loving this. 'And there's the door!'

About half the room broke into laughter and applause and cheering. Maybe even a little more than half. In DC, that's what you call progress.

After the meeting, Sampson came over and gave Nana a big hug, then a kiss on the cheek. He even picked Nana up for a few seconds.

'I'm not sure I changed any minds,' she said, taking me by the arm to leave. 'But I spoke my own, anyway.'

'Well, I'm glad you did,' Sampson said. 'And just for the record, Nana? You haven't lost a step.'

'*Lost* a step?' She reached up and swatted him on his huge shoulder. 'Who said anything about that? I've *gained* a step on you, big man.'

And of course, she got no argument from any of us on that point, either.

13

The husband-and-wife team of Hala and Tariq Al Dossari hid inside their dingy room at the Wayfarer Hotel, waiting for instructions and watching the insipid, repetitious news coverage about the kidnapping of the president's children while they did. They wondered whether the abduction had something to do with The Family, and thought that it might. Whatever was happening now, it was meant to have historic implications.

'There's a good likelihood our people took those two spoiled brats,' Hala said. An image of the Coyle children's smiling faces from some happier time played across the television screen, but all she felt was contempt. No one in this country was innocent. No one was exempt from retribution for America's so-called foreign policy.

'I'm sure The Family's plan is the correct one,' said Tariq, who was a good man, but not a complicated one.

'President Coyle's thinking will be clouded. That's good for us,' Hala said. 'We should eat something. It wouldn't hurt to get some air, so our thinking doesn't get clouded.'

When she rose from the bed, Tariq stood up to follow. Hala was in charge in America.

Back home, marriages were still arranged in some families — including their own — and Tariq knew exactly how well he'd done for himself. Hala was a medical doctor, while he was merely an accountant. She was beautiful, especially by Western standards. He was plain and fat, by just about any standard one used. His wife had even come to love him, in time, and had given him two beautiful children, Fahd and Aamina.

Will we ever see our children again? Tariq wondered. It wasn't a question he allowed himself too often, but all this waiting around was driving him crazy. It felt good to get up and leave their stuffy hotel room for a little while.

Outside, the streets were almost empty. On Twelfth Street they had trouble finding anything acceptable to eat. They passed McDonald's, Pizza Hut, Dunkin' Donuts, and then Taco Bell, whatever it was they sold there. What would bells taste like?

'Junk food and nothing else,' Hala said with derision. 'Welcome to America.'

They were standing beneath an overhang to an office building, when a man suddenly stepped out from the shadows. He had a pistol in his hand and waved it at them. 'Give me the pocketbook. Wallet. Loose change, watches,' he growled.

Hala put her arms across her chest and spoke in a high-pitched voice. 'Please, don't hurt us. We'll give you our money — of course. No problem there. Just don't hurt us!'

'Shoot you both dead, motherfuckers!' said the thief.

In their country, there were few men as

desperate as this, Hala thought. A criminal like him would have his hand cut off if he were caught.

'No problem, no problem,' she answered, nodding. She offered up her knockoff Coach handbag with one hand, and then with the other — pepper spray! She doused the young fiend's eyes with it.

He screeched and raised both hands to his face, trying to scrub away the burning poison. But his pain was only just starting. Hala dropped the spray and easily grabbed his gun.

She was so angry now. She sent a sharp kick to the boy's kneecap, buckling it in the wrong direction. He went down screaming, and she kicked at his chest, fracturing a few ribs while she was at it.

Hala's movements were fast and instinctual and athletic. She never seemed to be more than a foot or two away from the boy. He moaned on the ground — until her foot snapped into his throat. She kicked him in the forehead. The jaw. She broke bone there, too.

'Don't kill him!' Tariq said, placing a hand on her arm.

'I'm not going to,' she said, and she stepped back. 'A dead body would raise too many questions. We mustn't draw attention. Not yet.' She leaned down to speak directly to the boy on the ground. 'But I could have killed you — easily! Remember that the next time you put a gun in somebody's face.'

They left the moaning boy in the shadows and crossed the street, then hurried back to the

Wayfarer. There was nothing decent to eat out there anyway. This country was like the desert — just an arid wasteland that ought to be destroyed.

Without a doubt, it would be soon.

14

The FBI's Strategic Information and Operations Center was overflowing with somber, stressed-out police personnel that Sunday afternoon. This was a full-court press if there ever was one. The main briefing theater on the fifth floor of the Hoover Building was standing room only.

Ned Mahoney rocked back on the heels of his black boots and tried to take the situation in. He could feel exhaustion taking over his body, but his mind was running full tilt. Odds were good that everyone in the room felt the same way. Ethan and Zoe Coyle had been missing for *fifty-two hours and twenty-nine minutes*, according to the red-digit count clock on the wall.

The Bureau director himself, Ron Burns, had insisted it go up and stay up, front and center, until they got the kids back. *One way or the other*.

There were live camera feeds from the Branaff School playing on several of the big screens, and area maps of a fifty-mile radius of Washington. Some of those had blinking red flags on them, though Mahoney wasn't sure what they meant. The Bureau was operating like the well-oiled octopus it could be, with everyone on a strictly need-to-know basis.

The briefing came to order as soon as Director Burns arrived, trailing half a dozen harried-looking ADs and addressing the room even as he came in the side door at the front of the theater.

'Okay, I want a rundown from section heads right now,' he said. 'Have we got Counterterrorism here yet? Ops Two?'

'Over here, sir.' Terry Marshall, the deputy section chief from that branch, held up her hand and hurried to the front. When she pointed a small remote at the wall of screens, Mahoney was surprised to see two grisly morgue photos come up. They were from the double suicide at Dulles.

'Farouk and Rahma Al Zahrani,' Marshall said. 'Both Saudi citizens, educated at UCLA. He taught in the physics department at King Saud University; she worked for a small import-export house in Riyadh. No criminal records, no known criminal or terrorist associations, no known aliases.

'We've double-checked all threat lists, repeat, *all*, and they're not on any of them. Same goes for every other passenger on their flight.'

'Yes, and?' Burns said. Thirty seconds in the room, and already he was impatient and demanding of his staff. Burns was infamous around the Bureau for the line 'If you don't come in on Saturday, don't bother to come in on Sunday.'

'On paper, these are still separate incidents,' Marshall reported. 'But the timing is suspect, to say the least. The Al Zahranis flew in Thursday afternoon, approximately eighteen hours before Zoe and Ethan disappeared. Given that nobody's claimed responsibility for the abduction, or for the Al Zahranis, for that matter, we can't afford

44

to rule out a connection between the two.'

The room went quiet for several seconds. This was exactly the problem — since the twenty-four-hour mark had come and gone, the silence was killing them.

'Okay, what else?' Burns demanded. 'Where are we with the driver of that van?'

Matt Salvorsen from the DC field office took Marshall's place at the front of the room.

'So far, his story checks out,' Salvorsen said. He brought up an image of a Maryland driver's license. The name on it was Ray Pinkney. The picture was of the driver.

'We've been over his home computer, and he did in fact receive a private IM from this 'NE1NE1' character. Contact was made four days before the abduction.'

'Which my ten-year-old granddaughter could have faked,' Burns said.

'Yes, sir,' Salvorsen answered. 'Even so, we don't believe that Pinkney had the means to pull off the larger operation. He's kind of . . . '

'Thick?'

'Something like that, sir. In any case, we're sitting on him twenty-four/seven at the hospital. He knows he's up a creek now, and we're fairly confident he's giving us everything he's got.'

'Who else talked to him?' Burns said. 'Besides EMTs and hospital staff.'

'Secret Service Agent Findlay,' Salvorsen said. 'He's been temporarily decommissioned. And then Detective Cross, from MPD's Major Case Squad. He managed to interview Pinkney before the Bureau took jurisdiction.'

Mahoney looked up from his notes when he heard Cross's name. He was surprised to find Director Burns looking right back at him.

'Ned, you know Alex Cross pretty well?'

'Sure,' Mahoney said.

'Get him in on this, but light duty. We don't need any more chiefs. Just close enough to keep an eye on him. Don't tell him anything you don't need to. *I don't want MPD in our way.* Understood?'

Mahoney nodded several times, trying not to say what he was thinking — that Alex deserved better than this. 'Sir, Cross was instrumental in the Soneji case — '

'Not looking for your opinion right now. I respect Cross. Just get it done, please. We don't want MPD involved in this, and Cross is MPD!' Burns said briskly.

Mahoney gave the only answer there was to give at that point. 'Yes, sir. Will do.'

Freeze out Alex.

15

Already, the high-energy director was onto something else on his busy agenda. A crew-cut assistant, female, had just come into the briefing theater, and she whispered in Burns's ear. Didn't seem like good news. What was happening now?

At the same time, two Secret Service agents entered from the back, strode up the center aisle, and took a position at the front.

Two more agents appeared in each of the rear corners. Something was definitely up. What?

'On your feet!' Burns said, and everyone rose — just as the president and First Lady entered the room.

President Coyle looked exhausted but somehow had pulled himself together in a dark blue suit and gray tie. Mrs. Coyle, likewise, was camera ready, but anyone could see the stress and pain in her red, puffy eyes, and the sharp lines on her face.

Good God, Mahoney thought, *to live this unfolding tragedy in front of the whole world. Your kids missing. No word from whoever took them.*

'Sit, please,' the president said, and waited for everyone to settle down. Finally, he spoke again. 'Regina and I just wanted to come and thank you all for everything you're doing,' he went on. 'Obviously, we're not speaking with the press, but if there are any questions while we're here, we can answer them. Feel free to ask anything. Please. You can be candid, and you can be honest.'

'Mr. President,' Burns cut in from the side. 'We can meet privately with section heads, and then get you both out of here as fast as possible. They'll have questions.'

'Fine,' the president said. 'Then just one other thing.'

He walked over to one of the freestanding whiteboards in the room, picked up a green dry-erase marker, and wrote down ten digits. Then he reached into his pocket and held up a small blue phone.

Mahoney felt a ripple of surprise, even shock, run through the room. The two agents at the front exchanged a look as well. This was clearly news to them, alarming news. A breach of not only protocol, but security.

'My detail probably won't let me keep this phone now, but at a minimum, the nearest active-duty agent to me will have it at all times,' Coyle said. 'If anyone on this team has a time-sensitive question that Regina or I could answer, or any exigent reason at all for reaching us with information about our children, that's the number to use.'

It was an extraordinary gesture, unlike anything Mahoney had ever seen a president do before. Of course, it was also *wildly* off protocol. He wondered if — or when — his security brass would put the kibosh on it, and whether they'd actually tell the president when they did.

For the meantime, Director Burns seemed to

48

take it at face value. 'Memorize it,' he told the room. 'This is the first and last time that number appears in print.'

Then he gestured to the president and First Lady, and everyone was back on their feet as the entourage left through a glass door at the front, headed for the smaller conference center in the rear.

The Coyles' drop-by had lasted a couple of minutes, if that. Already Mahoney was turning the appearance over in his head, looking at it from different angles.

There was always another angle, wasn't there? The pretense of rallying the troops played out pretty well, but it seemed thin under the circumstances. This was a man who brought the world to his doorstep, literally, every day. And to say the least, this was no ordinary day. Security had to be at an all-time high. So why bring the president over here unnecessarily? Why now?

Part of the explanation — the easy half, anyway — was obvious. Someone at the top wasn't reporting everything they knew to the larger group. That was a given. But what was it? What had changed? What did they know? Did they already know who was behind the kidnapping?

Agent Mahoney had never aspired to be at the pinnacle of any FBI organizational charts, but that didn't stop his mind from running all the time, or curiosity from burning a hole in his brain whenever he was on the outside looking in.

So what the hell was the director telling the president and First Lady in that conference room right now?

16

'Sir. Ma'am. please. If you could have a seat,' Director burns said as he motioned the president and First Lady to the long conference table in the center of the room. Executive AD Peter Lindley was closing all the vertical blinds on the windows and doors. A single Secret Service agent took his post inside, while the rest of the traveling entourage waited in the corridor.

'What's going on, Ron?' Edward Coyle asked. At the same time, he laid his hand over his wife's shaking fingers. 'Obviously something's happened. You'd better tell us right now. I'm serious. No politics, no games. Not this time.'

Burns stayed on his feet. 'First, let me emphasize that we can't fully trust anything we receive from an unknown source. For all we know, this could be a deliberate attempt to distract or mislead our investigators.'

'All right, all right. Enough with the prelude,' the president ordered. 'Let's hear it. Please.'

The director nodded to Lindley, who set a briefcase on the table. He opened it and took out two sealed plastic evidence bags.

As soon as Mrs. Coyle saw the little black lacquered case in the first envelope, her hand flew up to take it from Lindley.

'*That's Zoe's!*' she said. 'She bought it in Beijing this summer.'

In the other bag was an eight-and-a-half-by-eleven-inch sheet of paper. It was laid out flat now, but several creases showed where it had been folded.

'These came into a suburban Washington field office by regular mail this morning,' Burns said. 'I can tell you that Zoe's fingerprints are the only ones on that black case.'

Mrs. Coyle stared at the little box, running her finger slowly across its contours through the plastic. It was heartbreaking to watch.

'This note was folded up inside,' Burns pressed on. 'It's totally clean of prints as well. We've already taken a sample of the ink. We could get something there. I want to assure you we're putting every resource onto this.'

'*What do they want, Ron?*'

Unlike his wife, the president was stone-faced. During the campaign, he'd been equally praised and criticized for his stoicism — or robotic quality, depending on whose story you were reading. He had been a law professor at one time and it showed. Burns admired the man's strength, in any case. He knew he couldn't have held up nearly as well under similar circumstances. His two daughters, and his wife, were his life, at least his life away from work.

'This is going to come as a shock,' he told the First Couple. 'But again, let me stress that we can't assume anything about this, true or false.'

Even now, Burns realized, he was stalling the president of the United States. Finally, there was nothing left to do but lay the note flat on the table in front of them. It was only a few sentences, and they were brutally succinct.

'There is no ransom. There will be no demands. The price, Mr. President, is knowing that you will never see your children again.'

17

Hala Al Dossari popped open her eyes and looked with alarm around the room. For the fourth straight morning, it took a moment, maybe five seconds, to remember exactly where she was.

Wayfarer Hotel.

Washington.

America.

It was strange, waking to silence, in such an uncomfortable, foreign environment. At home, they woke to the *adhan* every morning, ringing out from two dozen mosques in the neighborhood. Back in their coral house. With their two beloved children.

That all seemed like somebody else's life now — finishing up her residency, worrying about what to make for dinner, eating alone with Fahd and Aamina most nights while Tariq worked late at his accounting firm.

That was before he started coming home from the mosque talking about American devils, and the inevitable war — any number of things Hala knew in her heart to be true. He rambled nightly about how the United States was a cancer, one that would spread and infect the entire globe if it was left unchecked.

And now here they were. The Wayfarer Hotel. Washington. The previous night she had nearly killed a man on the street. A petty thief.

The clock on the nightstand said four fifty. Hala slipped out from under the cheap hotel comforter and took the television remote to the foot of the bed. She sat there in her nightgown, flipping channels with the sound off so as not to wake Tariq.

It was the same story everywhere — CNN, Fox News, MSNBC. The Coyle kidnapping had become a national obsession, while the suicides at Dulles had already disappeared into the background. It seemed so incredibly apt to her. Systematic. What were two dead Arabs worth here, as compared to two white, wealthy American children? Everything had a price in this country. *Everything*. And these self-obsessed fools wondered why the rest of the world hated them?

As to whether any of these recent events had something to do with the lack of communication from The Family since they'd arrived, Hala could only guess. It had been four days of convenience store food and lying low in this dank hotel room, this cave, waiting for word that she'd begun to suspect might not be coming.

'Hala?' Behind her on the bed, Tariq stirred. '*Ha-laa*. Turn it off. It only upsets you.'

'It's always the same,' she said. 'Every single channel. The same babble, the same video.'

'I know,' he said. 'That's why you should turn it off. Leave it off, my darling.'

She reached up to do it, but then stopped short when the light from the screen caught something on the floor. It was a glossy piece of paper, or a brochure of some kind.

Someone had slipped a note under the door in the night.

Even before she knew what it was, Hala's pulse began to race faster.

'What is it?' Tariq asked. 'When did it come? Who delivered it?'

'It's from the Smithsonian,' she said, bringing it for a better look under the bedside lamp. 'The Museum of Natural History. I'm sure it wasn't there before.'

They unfolded it on the bed.

Inside, the brochure showed a map of the museum's galleries and current exhibits, but it was nothing more than any ordinary tourist might pick up. There were no instructions or additional markings of any kind. And yet, wasn't that exactly what she and Tariq were meant to be here — just any tourists?

'It says they open at ten,' she read off the page.

For Hala, the implication was clear. *First contact had finally been made.*

18

This was it, then. Their mission had begun. *Something involving* the president's missing children? That could very well be.

It was odd that they would be as much in the dark as everyone else in Washington. Odd, but also brilliant, wasn't it? The Family gave them only as much information as they would need to fulfill their obligations — no more, no less.

At nine thirty, the Al Dossaris left their hotel and walked the glass and concrete canyon of Twelfth Street all the way down to the National Mall. They passed through the high-columned entrance of the Museum of Natural History just minutes after it opened, blending easily into the crowd of international tourists and school groups already clogging the galleries.

This was it.

But it wasn't.

For the next two hours, they wandered in a perpetual state of anxiety and frustration. Hala passed by glass cases of preserved sea creatures, and fossilized remains, and African artifacts, never quite seeing any of it. She focused on the faces of the people instead, scanning for anything that might tell them why they were here. The waiting, the suspense, was becoming excruciating, almost impossible to bear.

It wasn't until their fifth or sixth pass through

the museum's central rotunda that something finally happened.

A dark-eyed young woman with an ornate neck tattoo caught Hala's gaze from across the room. She held it for several seconds and then looked away, ostensibly taking in the enormous bull elephant that dominated the space between them.

Hala stopped to regard the display, then looked back. Again, the girl was staring. Was she from The Family? Or was this just Hala's imagination working too hard?

'Tariq?' she said.

'I see her,' he said. 'Go. I think she wants to talk.'

He kept his position while his wife worked her way slowly around the room, never losing sight of the stranger. She was Saudi, presumably, but dressed like an American college student. Ripped jeans, a peasant blouse, scuffed clogs. On her shoulder she carried a brightly colored Guatemalan bag. It appeared to be full. With books? Or maybe a bomb? For here? For now?

As Hala reached the back of the gallery, the girl came over and spoke to her.

'Excuse me,' she said. 'Do you know where the reptile hall is?'

Her perfect American accent was a surprise. Had this one been recruited stateside? Or, Hala suddenly wondered, was this maybe not what she'd thought? *Was this girl with the police?*

'I'm sorry,' she answered. 'I don't know. I'm not from here.'

'Maybe I could take a look at your map?'

When the girl pointed at the brochure Hala had carried from the hotel, any last doubts left her. 'Of course,' she said, and handed it over.

The girl unfolded it on top of her bag and studied it for several seconds while a stream of waist-high children in school uniforms ran past, squealing out ridiculous laughter having something to do with the elephant's tusks.

'Here it is,' she said finally. 'Reptiles. This is what I want to know more about.'

When she refolded the map and handed it back, something flat and hard was inside that hadn't been there before. Hala looked down to see the silver edge of a disk tucked into the folds of laminated paper. It sent a quickening sensation up her spine.

'Thanksalot,' the girl said in a familiar American singsong style. She smiled vacantly, then turned and walked away without once looking back.

'No,' Hala said, too quietly to be heard by anyone but herself. 'Thank *you*. And thank Allah.'

19

Police work isn't usually about surprises. It's more about routines. This was completely different. Something incredibly strange was going on, not all bad, necessarily, but strange. It was like no case I had ever worked before, or come across.

One of the special agents in Ned Mahoney's unit at the Bureau called me on Monday morning and said he wanted to send over some files.

'Files?' I said. 'Like, just *any* files?'

'Some reinterviews from the Coyle investigation we'd like to get your take on,' he said.

After days of being totally shut out, this request felt random, even disorganized on the part of the Bureau.

I tried calling Ned Mahoney several more times that morning, but all I got was his voice mail. It didn't make sense. Why would he pull me in and avoid me at the same time? Or was I just being paranoid?

When the courier came, I expected at least one of those files to be about Ray Pinkney, the van driver I'd already interviewed. Instead, what I got was a thick stack of second- and third-tier leads, which I guess made me the Bureau's newest second- or third-tier gofer. *What the hell was that all about?*

'They just want to keep an eye on you, sugar,'

Sampson said in the car on the way to the first interview. 'This is the Bureau's version of a short leash. You're officially on it now. I guess I am too.'

He was probably right. John's always good for a dose of perspective, and common sense, which is why I wanted him along. I hadn't asked anyone's permission to bring a partner, but as we say in the business, Fuck that.

'I've seen this woman on TV,' Sampson said. He was looking over the files on his lap while I drove. 'Don't think it was BET.'

'Probably not,' I said. 'More likely MSNBC, or maybe *Meet the Press*.'

Isabelle Morris had been the scheduled speaker at the Branaff School on the morning of the kidnapping. Her field was U.S.-Middle East policy, and she was a regular fixture on the Sunday-morning talk circuit. Obviously, some part of that equation was enough for the Bureau to keep her on their radar. And now she was on mine.

When we pulled up to her red stone town house on Calvert Street, a Grand Marquis was parked out front with a suit behind the wheel and a big Starbucks cup on the dash.

I didn't recognize the agent, but he gave us a nod as we started up the front steps. 'Good luck,' he called out.

'Why? Am I going to need it?' I asked, but he just grinned, shook his head, and went back to slurping his coffee.

20

'Do you believe that *fricking* guy drinking *fricking lattes* down there? I mean, twenty-four hours a day he's parked in front of my house — him or one of his moron cronies. Really? *Really?* All the criminal possibilities in the world. This is how you people want to spend your resources. Is that supposed to impress me somehow? Or maybe just keep me from slipping out of the country?'

Those were Isabelle Morris's first words to us, delivered rapid-fire, starting more or less the second she'd opened the door. She was shorter than I expected, maybe five one, or less. On TV, she was always just a talking head — which I guess was still the case here.

'Ms. Morris, I'm Detective Cross. We spoke briefly on the phone,' I said. 'This is Detective Sampson. Can we talk inside? Out of the glare of the FBI? I think that might be better. Please?'

She stared at me a little but then stepped back to let us in. We followed her through the house to a kitchen and family room at the back, with a glass-walled breakfast nook looking out to a brambly garden. A teenaged boy on the couch was playing Mortal something or other with headphones on, and he never even looked over at us.

Ms. Morris went straight to the stove, turned down the flame under a steaming double boiler, and then started chopping a pile of red peppers on the butcher-block counter. When I realized she was playing ball's-in-your-court with me, I jumped in.

'Ms. Morris — '

'Isabelle,' she said.

'I know you don't want us here right now, can't blame you, but you can at least understand why the Bureau and the police might be interested in you?'

She stopped chopping and looked up at the ceiling.

'Hmm, let's see here. Because I'm on MSNBC more than Fox? Because I worked for the Fulani campaign in the nineties? Or maybe because I dared to criticize the Coyle administration for egregious mistakes they themselves have admitted making in Afghanistan and Pakistan? Is that the kind of thing you mean?'

'Yes, actually,' I said. 'All of which is irrelevant to why I'm here. I need to get a statement from you about the night before, morning of, and afternoon following Zoe and Ethan's disappearance.'

'So you can look for inconsistencies,' she said.

'Not me,' I said. 'But someone, yes. That's the general idea.'

'*Unbelievable*,' she said. 'The FBI and the DC police have no clue where those poor kids are, so they keep up the witch-hunt with people like me, just to be able to say they're doing something. And you're comfortable with this?'

'I didn't say that,' I told her. 'I think you satisfy certain criteria as a person of interest, and

I think that's as far as anybody's gone in an analysis of you. The Bureau has an amazing machine over there, but emphasis is definitely on the 'machine.' Sometimes, anyway. Meanwhile, *two kids are missing.* Can we please focus on that?'

She was squinting at me now, almost like I'd gone out of focus. I don't think she expected any of that to come out of a cop's mouth.

'Haven't I seen you on the news before?' she said then. 'I think I have.'

'Probably,' Sampson told her. 'He's about half famous.'

Isabelle Morris smiled, sort of. 'Just like me,' she said, then went back to chopping vegetables.

'So where should I start? You want to hear about what I had for dinner Thursday night? What book I'm reading? *A Life of Montaigne*, okay? Because I'm sure that'll bring those kids home faster.'

21

There wasn't a single note about Isabelle Morris's earlier interviews in the thin unclassified file I had gotten from the Bureau, so I couldn't compare her stories with what I was hearing now. She told us she'd been home the evening before the kidnapping, left the house around seven thirty the next morning for the Branaff campus, and then went right back home again after she'd been released. None of it ruled out a connection to the case, but I thought we were probably wasting our time with her as much as she did.

On the way back in, Sampson and I stopped at an empanada place he likes on Sixteenth. We ate our turnovers in the car with a couple of Yoo-hoos. God save our digestive systems. Mine anyway. Sampson eats like he's part goat. It's been that way since we were ten years old.

'So what are you thinking?' Sampson said. 'Those kids still alive? Any chance at all?'

I stared over at him. 'If no one's made any demands yet, that's a terrible sign. On the other hand, the FBI or Secret Service could be sitting on something. Let's face it, Ethan and Zoe Coyle are two of the highest-value targets in the world.'

John demolished half an empanada in a single bite. 'You thinking this could be international?' Sampson said. 'Terrorism?'

I shrugged. 'For the moment, I'm throwing

darts, John. But I'll tell you one thing. I keep coming back to the Gary Soneji case.' Prior to this, the Soneji mess had been the biggest kidnap investigation — and in some ways, the biggest debacle — I'd ever been attached to.

'Soneji worked at the school he took those kids from,' Sampson said. 'I remember they had to drag you kicking and screaming onto that case. And now here you are, kicking and screaming to get onto this one.'

'Yeah.' I looked down at the pile of busywork files on the seat between us. 'I just hope those kids are alive. John, I still remember the day we found Michael Goldberg in that grave. I don't want to relive it. I don't want to find another dead child.'

22

'*Be ready to die at any time. Be ready to sacrifice everything.* Your life, your family.' That had never been more true than right now.

At eight o'clock Monday night, the Al Dossaris arrived at the Harmony Suites Business Hotel on Twenty-second Street. Neither of them carried anything with them — no weapons, no ID.

They took the rear stairs to the third floor where they knocked twice at the door of Room 345. It was all exactly as specified on the disk they'd received at the Natural History Museum.

A smiling, round-bellied Saudi promptly answered the door. He was clean shaven, with a Washington Nationals ball cap perched on his head. *A Family member. Finally.*

'Come in, come in,' he said, smiling as he closed the door. 'Everything is ready for you. Welcome, brother. Sister.'

He nodded deferentially as he shook Hala's hand, even as his small eyes lingered over her breasts.

'Please take off that silly hat,' she said to him. He immediately did as he was told.

The man's much younger wife was inside, spreading clear plastic sheets over both of the queen-size beds. She smiled, too, but didn't speak, not even to offer any sort of refreshment. Hala noticed that she had very large breasts.

Augmented? she wondered. Disgraceful if that was the case. A ridiculous Western custom, dangerous as well.

In the corner, several unmarked cardboard boxes were stacked against the wall. This was the poison, wasn't it? A great deal of it. Two large empty canvas duffels and a plain black briefcase sat on the dresser. Once the perfunctory greetings had been made, they got to work on the death hit. Tariq and the other man began unpacking cartons while the young woman went to the briefcase and flipped it open for Hala to inspect.

'Weapons,' the young wife said shyly, nervously.

'Yes, weapons. We're at war with America. Oh, hadn't you heard?'

Nested in the case's foam liner were a bowie knife in a leather sheath, a tightly coiled garrote with small wooden handles, a Taser, a Sig Sauer combat model pistol. The kit also included six fifteen-round magazines and a suppressor.

Hala picked up the Sig, keeping her eyes raised, as she'd been trained to do. Her hand found one of the magazines, slapped it into place, then twisted the suppressor onto the threaded muzzle.

Tariq caught her eye and smiled. He liked her with a gun. Liked the ease with which she fondled the weapons. She was the soldier, not him. She was the trained assassin as well.

'This will do,' Hala said, mostly for his benefit, and set the Sig back down.

'Here.' Tariq handed each of the women a pair

of latex gloves and a blue filtration mask. 'We should get started on the rest of our task.'

'Be careful. Very careful,' Hala warned the other couple. 'Do not touch your skin or eyes once we begin. I'm serious about that.'

For the next several hours, they were all extremely careful. The two women cut dozens of squares from a roll of fine-mesh cloth and laid them out in rows on the bed. Tariq instructed the male, as the two of them painstakingly measured out white crystalline powder from large plastic canisters, mounding the substance in the center of each cloth square. The cloth was then tied at the corners into tight bundles and secured to one of several lengths of clear nylon line.

Every string of ten bundles was placed into its own plastic bag.

The bags were then tucked into duffels.

They finished their task at just past midnight. Tariq opened a window and lifted his mask to indicate it was safe for the others.

Their host was grinning as he took off his own mask. He clapped a hand onto Tariq's shoulder.

'Brother, I know I'm not supposed to ask where you're taking these, but I can't wait to find out. We're all very excited about this.'

Tariq only stared at the man's hand until he took it away.

Hala answered for them. She picked up the loaded Sig from the dresser and pointed it at their hosts.

'Sit down, both of you,' she said. 'We're not quite done here. I said, *Sit down.*'

23

'I said, sit.'

'What do you think you're doing?' the fat man asked, even as he sat obediently on the bed. Hala kept her gun trained between his eyes, the same ones that had been undressing her all night.

'We watched two of our own die at the airport last week,' she said. 'I thought they had done something stupid to get themselves pulled out of line, but apparently not. Someone's talking to the Americans. There's been a leak. The Family is sure of it.'

'And they think it's *us?*' the man asked incredulously. 'That isn't possible. It's ridiculous.'

'It's all been spelled out,' Hala told them, referring to the disk they'd been given. 'Not just our instructions, but everything you two have been doing since you came here.'

'Sister, I swear — we're with you!' the wife blurted. 'We are Family, too.'

'No,' Hala said, waving her pistol at the woman's ridiculous chest. 'You're whores to the American cause. *Traitors.*'

'It's not true,' the man insisted. 'No . . . no.'

The two were so intent on their denials, they didn't even seem to notice what else was happening in the room.

Tariq had taken a plastic canister to the sink and begun mixing a small amount of the white powder into two glasses of water. Now he was using someone's pink toothbrush to stir each one into a cloudy mixture.

He carried the glasses over to the couple on the bed.

'Don't make a fuss,' he said. 'Just drink this down. Have some dignity.'

There was fear, but also anger in the fat man's eyes. 'Or what? You'll shoot us?'

Hala said, 'It's preferable that you do this quietly, but if you need encouragement, I'm supposed to remind you of your family back home.'

'*But this is a horrible mistake!*' the wife babbled on. 'We haven't done what you said. We are loyal to the cause.'

'That's very touching,' Hala said. 'But it doesn't matter to me or to The Family. Not anymore. Now I'm going to count to five.'

'Please — '

'One.'

'I'm begging you! Sister?'

'Two.'

The man snatched both glasses from Tariq. He pressed one into his wife's hand. 'We have no choice, Sanaa. Think of Gabir. Think of Siti.'

'Think of *three*,' Hala said as she continued the countdown. She had no pity for these people. They were disloyal, and they were weak. This mission was too important to risk a mistake. '*Four.*'

The man tilted his head back and shot the mixture down like whiskey. Then his hands were on his wife's, helping her to do the same.

70

The woman gagged, sobbing as she drank the milky liquid, but it went down. Enough of it, anyway. Right away, her lips went pink. Her breath started coming in sharp rasps. 'I'm dying,' she whispered. '*Why? Why must I die?*'

The husband looked up at Hala with hatred in his eyes. '*Assassin,*' he said.

'Don't flatter yourself,' Hala told him, and gestured at the empty glass in his hand. 'You're no murder victim, you fool. You're a suicide statistic.'

Tariq took the two duffels and carried them to the door. Hala stayed where she was. There was pleasure in watching these people die, but it was also her job to see it through.

The wife was the first to spasm, violently, bucking and kicking until she collapsed to the floor. The husband, maybe twice her size, hung in longer. He watched Hala with huge bug eyes — as she calmly watched him. His sense of taste and smell would be gone by now, no doubt. The eyesight would fade next. Then the hearing, just at the very end —

'Hala!' Tariq raised his voice. 'It's done. Let's go. Please, let's go!'

She picked up the weapons case and slowly backed toward the door, observing all the way. With one last spasm, the fat man lurched forward. He landed facedown on the carpet and was still beside his wife.

'*Now* it's done,' Hala said, and turned to leave. 'I thought that went rather well. We're getting better at this, don't you think?'

71

24

I woke up in a bad mood that morning. Grumpy, cranky, in need of caffeine. Unusual for me, but there it was.

Most days, Nana and I spend breakfast talking about the day ahead, or debating some foolishness from the headlines. But it was the headlines that were making me angry now.

I hid behind my *Post* and steamed, reading about how the 'authorities' weren't getting anywhere with the four-day-old Coyle kidnapping.

Somewhere around my second cup of coffee, I heard a little tap on the other side of the paper.

'You learning anything new in there?' Nana said. 'Or just stewing?'

'I'm stewing. I don't want to talk about it,' I said.

'Talk about what?' said Jannie, coming in from the hall. I could hear her brother Ali bringing up the rear, thunk-thunking that backpack of his down the stairs. The kid had barely started elementary school. How much stuff did he need? Sounded like about fifty pounds of books.

'Ali, pick that thing up! Don't scratch up my stairs!' I called out. 'Please and thank you.'

'You're welcome,' he called back and kept thunk-thunking anyway.

My oldest, Damon, was away at boarding school — and I still hadn't gotten used to having him gone. These mornings always felt just a little bit empty without all of our family.

'Talk about *what*?' Jannie asked again. She gave me a kiss good morning and pointed at a news photo of Ethan and Zoe. 'That kidnapping?'

'Excuse me, but which part of 'I don't want to talk about it' didn't you understand?' I said. 'And by the way, let's make this a quick breakfast. The Alex bus leaves in fifteen minutes — sharp.'

Jannie made a face she probably thought I didn't catch, then went to pour some juice for herself. I retreated back into my paper while Nana dished up cheddar eggs with whole wheat toast and cocoa for the kids.

For a minute or two, it was conspicuously quiet in the kitchen. I could feel them all staring at me through the paper, though.

Then Jannie piped up again. 'Hey, Dad?'

'Yes?' I said, trying my best to be calm.

'The Seven Dwarfs called. They want their Grumpy back.'

What could I say? Ali roared with laughter and high-fived his sister across the table. I heard Nana snickering over by the sink. The FBI obviously had no respect for me, and now neither did my family. Damn it, though, I had a right to be out of sorts.

'Lord, let this man catch a bad guy today,' Nana said. 'We could all use it.'

'No comment,' I said, and gave a little growl for good measure.

Then just as the mood was lightening up a

little, Bree came charging down the stairs. Mussed hair, rumpled T, bare feet. Something was wrong.

'Alex! Turn on the news! Turn on the news right now!'

She never moves that fast before her first cup of coffee, so I knew this couldn't be good. I hustled out to the living room, where she was standing in front of the TV. Channel 4 had a live report going.

'What is it?' I said.

'I don't know,' Bree said. 'Something bad happened at the McMillan Reservoir. There's some kind of problem with the water supply.'

25

District officials closed the DC schools. Bree stayed home with Ali and Jannie while I rushed to work. All the info I got from making a few phone calls on the way was that hospitals were overwhelmed with emergency admissions. Hundreds of people had been showing up with bouts of vomiting, blurred vision, trouble breathing, loss of consciousness, even a few heart attacks.

It wasn't hard to go right to the worst-case scenario. Washington was under attack. But who was behind it?

Did it have anything to do with the Coyle kidnapping? Was that nightmare a real possibility?

It sure looked like it at MPD headquarters, the Daly Building. Police trucks and buses were double-parked out front, ready to go; cruisers were leaving the garage in a solid stream. I felt like I was going the wrong way down a one-way street.

Inside, officers and detectives were literally running up and down the halls. It was as close to an all-out mobilization as I'd ever seen.

I went straight to the Joint Operations Conference Center. More chaos on a very large scale. Phones ringing everywhere, briefings happening on a rolling basis. I found two guys from my squad, Jerry Winthrop and Aaron

Goetz, standing off to the side, waiting for orders.

'Fatalities?' I said to Jerry. 'You heard?'

He shook his head. 'Don't know, Alex. Everything's nuts. As you can see. We're waiting to hear where to go. Fucking water supply.'

At the front of the large room, Ramon Davies, the superintendent of detectives, was on his phone. Standing next to him were Jocelyn Kilbourn from MPD's internal Homeland Security branch and Hector Nunez from Special Operations, plus a few other unfamiliar faces.

'Who are the suits up front?' I said.

'EPA on the left,' Jerry said. 'Interior by the door. And don't ask who's in charge, because I don't think anybody knows yet.'

As soon as Davies was off the phone, he waved his arms to get the room's attention. 'Listen up. We just got word from the Bryant Street Pumping Station over by McMillan Reservoir. They've found signs of tampering on one of their lines. Whatever happened over there, it was no accident!'

'What kind of tampering?' someone called out. It was the question I had.

Davies took a breath, then answered. 'This does not leave this room. Handmade dispersal devices, presumably to leech whatever poison this was into the system. It seems to be contained in the second high-water district. That's between Eastern Avenue and Rock Creek. The other districts are clear so far. We've got emergency testing going everywhere. Expanded security at all processing facilities.'

Davies handed it over to Assistant Chief Kilbourn. She pulled up a quick PowerPoint and ran everybody through a list of contingencies. Some were immediate and practical. Others were theoretical — from citywide water shutdowns to looting and riot control, even municipal evacuation plans and declarations of martial law. This sure looked like the 'big one' that everybody was always worried about.

'No one's saying any of these emergency protocols are going to become necessary,' Kilbourn told us. 'We don't even know if this is terror-related. But it's essential that everyone knows what to do if, or when, things go south.'

In other words, we were on the verge of uncharted territory. On paper, we were ready for anything. All kinds of emergency preparedness systems had been put into place in the years since 9/11, with every work group, simulation, and special training the department could throw at it. But the thing no one ever wanted to talk about was that there were some emergency situations you couldn't possibly prepare for.

Because you just couldn't imagine them happening.

26

I left the room feeling like I was still basically unassigned — and also at a real crossroads on the Coyle case. I needed to know if I could accomplish *something* — and also, whether the kidnapping of the president's kids could possibly be connected to the water supply emergency. The possibility had been raised by the FBI *and* the CIA. It was one of the first things I'd thought of when I heard about the reservoir problem.

I walked out to a stairwell for some quiet. Then I dialed Ned Mahoney's number. When he didn't pick up, I kept going down to the parking garage.

I got in my car and drove to Ned's little Cape house in Falls Church, Virginia. If he was going to play hard to get, I was going to have to become more irresistible.

I'd been out to Ned's for the occasional barbeque, but when Amy Mahoney saw me standing on her front porch, her eyes opened wide.

'Alex? What's going on?'

'Nothing's wrong,' I said right away, which wasn't exactly the truth. 'I'm just trying to track Ned down. I need to talk with him, Amy.'

She looked relieved. Ned heads up the Hostage Rescue Team out of Quantico, and it's not just him who lives with the stress of that job.

'Come on in,' Amy said. She pecked me on the

cheek as I stepped past the screen door. 'I'll call him right now.'

I stood in their foyer, feeling a little awkward, a little embarrassed. This wasn't exactly an aboveboard maneuver, but it had to be done. A minute later, Amy had Ned on the phone.

'Hey, hon, it's me. I've got Alex Cross here. He's looking for you. You have a second?'

I'm not sure what Ned said next, but I could hear the tone of it. It was Amy who looked embarrassed now. I held out my hand for the phone, and Ned was still railing when I took it.

' — kicking my ass, and I don't need to tell you — '

'Ned,' I said. 'It's me.'

'Alex?'

'Sorry about this.'

'Jesus, you're killing me here.'

'Then it's mutual,' I said. 'Just tell me I'm in the dark on the Coyle case for a good reason. I'll trust your word. But I'm lost here, and there are plenty of other places I could be today.'

'Yeah, like someone else's house,' he said.

'Ned, Washington is in the middle of an emergency. My kids are home from school. It's scary as hell. They got to the water supply. Maybe to the president's kids.'

At first he didn't answer. Then it was just 'I don't know what to tell you.'

'Not exactly what I was looking for,' I said. 'I need you to tell me *something*, Ned.'

'Alex, what do you want me to say? They're compartmentalizing the shit out of this thing,' he said. 'I doubt I've got much more intel than you do at this point.'

Ned and I have known each other a long time. We've been through some impossible situations, and done some off-the-record favors for each other, too. So it was strange, and kind of hurtful, trying to gain his trust now. I told him as much.

There was a pause. I heard Ned take a deep breath on the other end. This whole thing was making me feel bad. Talking to him this way. Coming out to his house. Using Amy.

'Listen, I've got to go,' he said. 'I have a conference call waiting.'

'Ned!'

'Just hang in there.'

'Don't hang up!' I said, but he already had. If it had been my own phone in my hand, it probably would have gone sailing.

When I turned around, Amy was staring, looking like she might start to cry. 'You looked like you wanted to reach right through the phone and strangle him,' she said.

'No,' I said. 'Don't mind me. I just . . . ' Why was I ready to punch a hole in my friend's wall? What was it that I wanted to do here?

'I just want those kids to be found,' I said. 'That's all I care about, Amy.'

27

He was definitely going to write a big, fat book on this someday, when it was all far, far behind him. And not the way everyone and his brother-in-law says they're going to write a book 'someday.' He was really going to do it.

Record.

'It wasn't that Zoe and Ethan did anything wrong, themselves. They just happened to be born into the wrong family, at the wrong time. None of this was their fault, any more than it's your fault, or mine. Maybe it goes without saying, but someone has to play the sacrificial lamb. History tells us that much. Every tragedy has repercussions.'

Stop.

That actually sounded half-decent to him. Important. Had a ring of truth. He was getting the hang of this now. Maybe there was even a title in there. *Sacrificial Lambs?* Possibly, although he still kind of liked *Suffer the Little Children*, as in, 'those who come unto me.'

But that wasn't a decision he had to make today. The book wasn't even written yet. Hell, the story wasn't even told yet, wasn't finished. There was still plenty of time for the peripheral details to work themselves out. So far, he had the beginning — and he had the end.

Record.

'The juice boxes come in a three-pack for a

dollar ninety-nine at the Safeway, two blocks from my house. The Rohypnol's a little harder to come by, of course, but not impossible if you know where to look. Two milligrams every twelve hours seems to do the trick beautifully. They're so out of it, I'm not even sure they know what's going on.'

Stop.

Maybe nobody would care about the Safeway part, but whatever. Tape was cheap as dirt. He'd just keep throwing everything down and sift through it later. The blank cassettes could live in the glove compartment of his vehicle. The used ones, he kept where no one would ever find them. Just like Ethan and Zoe.

Meanwhile, the light was getting long outside. He needed to start moving — if he wanted to be back to the car by dark, which he definitely did.

From the seat next to him, he pocketed two of the juice boxes, the ones with Scotch tape covering the tiny hole the syringe had left. The third box he'd drink on the way. It was an hour through the woods, and an hour back to his house, if he kept up a good strong pace, which he would. He was in excellent physical shape.

He got out and took the recurve bow from the trunk, along with a leather quiver of arrows. Deer season was still six weeks off, but rabbits and squirrels were always fair game. More than that, the hunting thing was a good excuse for being all the way out here in the first place. Not that anyone came around these woods much, but it didn't cost anything extra to be careful.

Record.

'That's another thing. The FBI hasn't said one word about my little note. So just in case it's not already clear, none of this has ever been about money. Not taking the kids, and not the book, either. I mean, it's not like I'm going to be able to collect royalties when this thing is done. I'll just have to buy it at the Barnes and Noble or Walmart like everybody else.'

Stop.

Record.

'It's going to be one hell of a story. It really is. Just you wait and see.'

Stop.

Book Two

ALPHABET SOUP

28

'At five hundred and fifty-five feet, the Washington monument towers majestically over the National Mall. Completed in December of 1884, it was formally dedicated on . . . '

Hala tried to tune out the tremendously irritating, prerecorded propaganda and other drivel as their tour bus rolled down Independence Avenue. It sounded like the tires of the bus were sticking to the littered street. Everything seemed dirty. What a disgusting city! And yet everywhere you looked, there was another hulking monument to American arrogance and power.

It was ironic, really. She hadn't learned to truly hate this country until she'd come here for her education. Four years at Penn, and what had it taught her? Only that the United States was just about the biggest failed experiment in human history.

'As we cross the bridge toward Arlington, you can look back and see the Tidal Basin and the Jefferson Memorial . . . '

She looked down instead at the Tourmobile brochure on her lap. It had been slipped under their hotel room door with a few instructions. When the tour bus reached Arlington National Cemetery, they were to get off. And guess what? Here they were.

Tariq stood in the aisle, shifting from foot to

foot. He looked odd, but oddly handsome this morning, with a Baltimore Ravens cap shading his freshly clean-shaven face. Hala's own hair was now in a blunt cut around the nape of her neck and dyed as close to auburn as she'd been able to get it. She was still pretty, though, and she did like that about herself. Absolutely no ball cap for her.

'Please watch your step, and enjoy your visit to Arlington National Cemetery!'

They milled off the bus with the other tourists, onto a plaza in front of the white stucco and limestone Visitors Center. Hala looked around, unsure about what to expect next. Almost right away, a familiar face emerged from out of the crowd. It was the hippie girl from the museum. She was carrying the same brightly colored woven bag. Probably so that Hala would recognize her right away.

There was no dance this time, no slow approach. As soon as they'd seen each other, the girl came over and stood next to them, as if they were all waiting for the same bus.

'Hey, could I borrow your map for a sec?' she asked.

'Of course. No bother.'

This girl was good, actually. Very natural and fearless. Hala watched closely and still barely saw the disk as it came out of her bag.

What would it be this time? A high-rise in the heart of Washington? A government building? Another utility? More important eliminations? Kidnapping?

'Thanksalot,' said the girl.

'No problem. Have a nice day.'

The whole exchange was as quick as it was seamless. If anything, there was just the hint of a knowing smile on the girl's face before she turned away. The mission was gaining momentum. The excitement was palpable between them, though only for a moment of shared expectations.

'Come on,' Hala said. Another red, white, and blue Tourmobile was pulling into the plaza. She took Tariq's hand and started walking in the opposite direction.

'Where are we going?' he said. 'The tour buses are over there.'

'To find a cab. If I have to get back on that bus for one more minute, I'm going to kill someone right here.'

29

My car was quickly becoming my office these days, and there was no way around it. I was shuttling between some ongoing casework I wasn't ready to drop and the Coyle interviews that the Bureau kept sending my way in a steady trickle. Most days, I worked with Sampson, but now and then I was on my own. The Dragon Slayer.

I kept myself updated on the fly, usually with a phone pressed against my ear — since my Bluetooth was on the fritz and who had time to go to Best Buy these days?

'So what's the lab saying? They must have something?' I asked. I had my old buddy Jerry Winthrop on the line. He'd been my inside source on the water scare. The rest I got like everybody else — from CNN and the Internet. So far two people had died and the city was close to a panic state. Sampson was off checking other water sources today.

'Looks like the second district line was tainted with high-grade potassium cyanide,' he said.

'Isn't that — '

'Yeah, it is. Same thing that killed the two suicides out at Dulles. What a coincidence.'

'And no one's taken responsibility?' I asked.

'Beats the shizz out of me,' Jerry said. 'FBI's not exactly knocking down our door with useful information.'

That was typical. The 'open' line of communication between MPD and the Bureau tended to be a one-way street. Jerry told me the official story to the press was that we'd had a chemical overspill and that the problem had been contained. Of course, that depended on what we meant by 'problem.'

After I got off the phone, I stopped at a 7-Eleven for some much-needed caffeine. Inside, there was a hastily scrawled NO COFFEE sign taped to one of the pots. I grabbed a Coke instead — and couldn't help noticing the empty coolers where all the bottled water had sold out.

When I went to pay, the cashier, who had multiple piercings, chinned down at the badge on my belt. 'So what's going on out there, man? How screwed are we?' she asked.

'I wouldn't close the store just yet,' I said with what I hoped was a disarming smile. 'Problem's been contained.'

The whole idea was to keep the peace — maximum public confidence, minimum panic. But I think that clerk's real question was the same one we all had. *What next?*

About ninety seconds later, I found out.

30

I was just pulling away from the curb when I picked up a call from Sampson. 'Psych ward, hold please?' I answered with a bad joke.

'Alex, you heard the latest?'

'Yeah,' I said. 'I was just talking to Jerry Winthrop.'

'He say anything about when they're going to start the autopsies?' John asked next.

The word *autopsies* stopped me cold. 'What are you talking about? What autopsies?'

'Two more bodies found. At the Harmony Suites on Twenty-second. I'm on my way there now. Appear to be Saudis. What are *you* talking about?'

'Not that. Keep going. Who was found, exactly?'

'It's another couple. Middle Eastern. Two empty glasses on the floor. Nobody's saying suicide yet, but I'll bet money there's going to be cyanide in the coroner's report.'

I pulled back up against the curb. I needed to try and absorb everything for a half second. Coincidences like these are usually a leg up in an investigation, but the more this thing folded in on itself, the scarier it got, the more bizarre and unpredictable. And definitely unprecedented.

'It's getting too weird around here, Alex,' Sampson said. 'I keep thinking what they always say about the next big attack, you know? Not if but when?'

'I know,' I said. 'I know.' It was starting to feel a whole lot like *when*. 'I'll meet you at the bodies.'

31

It was hot and humid for one thirty in the morning, too hot for a jacket, but Hala needed something to cover the Sig holstered under her arm. She pulled at the front of the coat, to let in some air, for what it was worth. What she really wanted was to shoot somebody — anybody. She hadn't known she had this much anger against the Americans, but clearly she did. It wasn't just the wars they had waged in the Middle East, or the puppet leaders they had supported. It was the insults she had received as a student here.

'Who builds a city on a swamp?' she said. 'At least the desert cools down at night.'

'Do you think something's wrong?' Tariq hadn't really been listening to her. He was pacing the sidewalk while Hala tried to keep as still as possible.

'They'll be here,' she said. 'Don't worry the details. You're the one who always says The Family knows what they're doing.'

'The instructions clearly said one o'clock.'

'They'll be here. You're like an old woman.'

It wasn't the hour that was bothering him, she knew. *It was the sarin gas.* They'd never worked with it before, but pointing that out now wasn't going to do anything to calm his nerves.

Fortunately, the light blue Toyota minivan pulled up to the curb just a few minutes later. The side door flashed open, and a tall, gangly woman motioned for them to get in. They climbed into the backseat beside her as the door closed again, and the van took off. The whole thing took about fifteen seconds.

The feeling inside the vehicle was immediately tense. Besides the woman, Hala, and Tariq, there were three other men on the team. Actually, one man and two boys, Hala realized, each one as tall and thin as the other, with the same sharp, angular features as the adults. Two parents and their children.

Interesting group. *To do what, exactly?*

They all sat face front, not speaking, until Tariq broke the silence.

'We were waiting quite a while back there,' he said.

'Good for you,' the mother answered. 'Here. Put these on.'

She handed back two tactical headsets with transmitters small enough to fit invisibly in their pockets. 'Channel twelve. Stay on that station throughout the action.'

'Where's my case?' Tariq asked. He turned around on the seat to look for it.

'Leave it alone,' the mother said. 'It's fine where it is.'

'I need to check it,' he said.

'I'm not going to have you opening that in here. You can check it when we arrive. Don't be so nervous.'

Tariq ignored the woman's suggestion as well as her insulting manner. He pulled a reinforced aluminum alloy briefcase from the back and set it on his lap.

Her hand flew across the space between them in a way that showed some training. In a moment, her fingers were locked around Tariq's throat, pressing him back into the seat.

But Hala was having none of it. Her Sig was out and against the self-appointed queen's temple almost as quickly.

'Get your hand off of him,' she said.

'I told you to leave it alone,' the woman said, speaking to Tariq, not Hala.

'*Everyone calm down!*' The father shouted at them from the front, while the two boys looked on with wide eyes and closed mouths. Tariq stayed where he was, both hands still on the case's spring clasps.

'Now,' Hala said evenly. 'If he says he needs to check the case, he's going to check it. We're all here for the same reason. Isn't that right, sister?'

She kept the Sig where it was, waiting for her answer. Finally, the mother bitch sat back, though not without a last, searing look at Hala.

'That's much better,' Hala said. 'Use that murder in your eyes for the benefit of The Family. Our enemies are outside the minivan, not in it.'

'Go to hell' was the answer she got.

It was a shame, Hala thought. Here was a woman she could respect on any other night. She was exactly the kind of soldier the movement needed. In any case, this argument meant nothing to the larger picture. It was time to focus, time to kill as many Americans as they could, time to send an unforgettable message.

Tariq worked slowly. He eased open the clasps

on the case and gingerly lifted the lid. Nobody spoke as he began taking stock of the small metal canisters inside.

When the van bounced over a pothole on First Street, Hala saw the woman reach across for her younger son's hand in the dark.

She's just afraid for her children, thought Hala. *She's a good mother. Better than me.*

32

They came to a very sudden, jolting stop on a gravel utility road. Nerves on the part of the driver. To the right, a thick stand of hawthorn shielded them from traffic passing on New York Avenue.

To the left, Hala could see the rail yard through a chain-link fence. Dozens of dark-windowed subway cars slumped in rows on the tracks. Their deadly target for tonight.

Tariq kept charge of the aluminum alloy case. The mother, father, and younger boy each took a different piece of mismatched luggage from the back of the van, and then the older son drove off to circle the neighborhood.

Hala took up a position just to the west, on a pedestrian bridge that spanned the yard. She backtracked maybe thirty yards and climbed the winding metal stairs to the walkway above. Once she was up there, she found that the area was fully enclosed with more chain link. But the bridge still offered a perfect view.

From the center of the bridge, she checked once in each direction. 'Clear,' she radioed softly.

It took a few minutes for the others to appear.

They looked like animated silhouettes as they moved out onto the tracks, laterally at first, and then up between the rows of train cars, where they disappeared. *Sarin gas*, Hala was thinking.

This was impressive. It would resonate power-fully around the world.

Several minutes ticked by. Slowly, very slowly. There had been no word about how long it would take to install the material. Hala could actually hear them breathing as they worked, but conversation was held to a minimum.

She kept her eyes moving constantly. They swept the yard, over to Brentwood Road and T Street on the far side, then back again to the utility road nearer by, and New York Avenue beyond. It wasn't difficult to stay alert. There was plenty of adrenaline for that.

So when a police cruiser appeared on the scene, Hala saw it right away. It eased down the utility road and came to a stop not far from their original drop-off location.

'Up near the bridge,' she said softly. 'We may have a serious problem.'

33

'Police at the south fence. One car so far,' Hala whispered. 'Hold your positions. I'm watching them. I can take them out if I have to. I hope not to do that.'

The cruiser's passenger door opened, and the shadow of a cop flowed out.

Hala leveled her Sig through the chain link, siting the man's chest. He was as good as dead, if that was what she needed to do. Yet she felt nothing. As he stepped up to the fence, another surge of adrenaline ran through her. It felt as though her blood was running a race. *She wanted to kill him.*

The policeman stopped and looked around. As casual as a tourist. Then he leaned back slightly. When Hala saw the stream arcing away from his body, she almost laughed out loud.

'Stand by. He's just urinating,' she said. 'I'm watching the idiot relieve himself.'

As the cop finished up and turned to go, his partner called out something from the car. Whatever it was, the first officer stopped and turned back toward the rail yard. A flashlight came up in his hand.

He shone it through the fence and onto the tracks — where it caught a glimpse of a moving body. Hala saw it too — the younger boy. Just before he darted back out of sight. *Imbecile! Amateur!*

She didn't hesitate, squeezing off three fast shots. The flashlight dropped first, then the cop himself. She was pleased with her shooting, the accuracy under duress. This was excellent practice.

'Everyone out of there,' Hala radioed. 'Bring the van to the opposite side. Brentwood and T. Do it now!'

Another light, even brighter, came right up in her face!

She realized it was the search beam on the side of the cruiser. Hala fired into it, two more rounds. There was a popping sound — and the night went dark again.

For a brief moment, she couldn't see anything, but she could hear the second cop. He was radioing for backup even as he ran toward the bridge and his fallen partner. His *dead* partner, Hala knew.

'Shots fired! Officer down! Request immediate assistance at the Brentwood rail yard! Repeat: officer down!'

That was followed by heavy footsteps pounding up the metal stairs.

Time to run. Time to get everybody out.

The rest of the team was scrambling and directing one another to the pickup point in breathy, frantic voices. Hala ignored all of it as she made for the far side of the bridge.

Then the cop's voice came again, directly behind her. '*Freeze!*'

She didn't.

A bullet ricocheted off the metal cage just over her shoulder. There was nowhere to go but straight ahead. Unless — Hala stopped short.

She turned and dropped in one fluid motion, firing blindly down the alley of the walkway. Everything else disappeared for two very long seconds. Then the second cop dropped to the ground.

Dead? Almost definitely. She never missed. That was why she had the gun, not Tariq. Then Hala was up and running again.

She hit the stairs on the far side at full speed and almost barreled over the railing. Even now, she felt proud of herself. She was good at this, very skillful.

'We have to wait!' Tariq's voice sounded over the radio as he scanned the area for Hala.

Then the mother bitch's answer. '*You* wait,' she said. 'We're leaving right now.'

As Hala hit the sidewalk, she saw the van pulling away from the curb, its side door still open. A taxi swerved to avoid being hit. The van didn't slow down. It ran a fast left turn through a red light and was gone into the night.

Tariq was still there, looking around frantically. The poor man seemed lost.

'I'm here,' Hala said. 'To your left, Tariq.' *Come to mother.*

He ran toward her and they met in the middle of the sidewalk.

'What should we do?' he said. 'They drove away. They left us, Hala!'

The sound of police sirens was already closing in around the neighborhood. They had no money for a cab, or even the subway, once it started running. If the van was apprehended, it could even be unsafe to go back to their hotel room.

Still, there was one place. Hala wasn't supposed to know about it, but she did. The question was, *Which way from here?* She was completely turned around in an unfamiliar part of this large American city, this enemy outpost, their capital. It was impossible to know which way to run.

But staying put was no option. 'This way,' she said, picking a direction. They'd figure it out. 'Just run. Run as fast as you can, Tariq. Follow me.' *I will take care of you, as I always do, my love.*

34

It's not like my phone rings in the middle of the night all the time — but I'm sure it does more than most. 'Alex Cross,' I answered. There was a click, then two short beeps. That meant a secure line of some kind. Whose line?

'Detective Cross, this is Betty Chow with the CIA Directorate of Intelligence. I'm very sorry for the hour, but I'm calling to ask you to come to a meeting out here at the counterterrorism center in Langley.'

That woke me right up. What had happened now? And what was the CIA suddenly doing in the mix? For that matter, what was *I* doing in it?

'Can you tell me what this is regarding?' I asked while wiping the sleep from my eyes. 'That would help.'

'I'm not at liberty to discuss any details, but you'll be fully briefed at the center,' she said.

I looked at the clock. It was just after four a.m. 'When's the meeting?' I asked.

'We're set to convene at five thirty, Detective. Can I tell them you'll be here?'

I didn't even know who Betty Chow meant by 'them.'

'I'm on my way,' I said.

'And, Detective? I'm to stress that this is a classified matter and that you're not to tell anyone where you're going this morning, under penalty of federal law.'

'Of course,' I told her, and hung up.

I thought about calling Bree anyway. She was still on duty, working the graveyard shift these days, and might even have some idea about what had happened to initiate all this. But then I thought the situation through again. If I was getting secure calls from the CIA on classified matters, there was a good chance — a very good chance — they were already listening in on my line.

I got dressed quickly and left the house in the dark.

Figuratively and literally in the dark.

35

The usually long drive to CIA headquarters in Langley took no time at all without traffic.

What I got off the car radio was that two police officers had been killed sometime overnight at the Brentwood rail yard. Was that why I had been summoned to the CIA? Doubtful. I figured it must be something even worse. But what did they know that I didn't? I didn't like being on the wrong side of this mystery again.

Bree, after so many nights on duty, would be exhausted when she got home and would wonder where I was. I missed her like crazy. That's a good thing, but sometimes it feels so bad.

An escort met me inside the main entrance to the agency's complex. He took me up to one of the nicer conference rooms on the sixth floor, where most of the two dozen high-backed leather chairs were already taken.

I recognized only a few people around the table. Ned Mahoney was one of them.

He came right over and shook my hand. A little formal for Ned. 'Alex. It's good to see you,' he said. 'I mean it. This's been about the craziest week of my life.'

I hadn't laid eyes on him since this roller-coaster ride had started. Part of me still wanted to be pissed at him, but what was the point? Ned was a friend.

'Any idea what we're doing here?' I asked him in a quiet voice.

'I'm not sure. But listen,' he said. He turned me around so we were both facing a glass wall that looked out to guest parking and the rolling, deep green woods beyond. The sun was just coming up over the hills.

'I need to apologize for how this mess has gone down so far,' Ned said. He spoke quietly but still in that rapid-fire way of his. 'It wasn't my call, but I know that doesn't mean anything when you're at the shit end of the stick.'

'Don't worry about it,' I said.

'I *do* worry about it. I think you're a hell of a resource, Alex. And a friend, too. I don't want to lose either one. We okay?'

'Just write me a nice check or something. Buy me a Philly cheesesteak and a beer.'

He smiled at that and I guessed we were already over the hump. 'Anyway, I'm glad you're here. I wasn't sure they'd listen to me,' he said.

'About what?' I asked.

'About bringing you into the loop.'

Before I could respond, a voice behind us was calling the meeting to order.

'Good morning, everyone. For those who don't know me, I'm Evan Stroud, head of the Directorate here at the agency.'

Ned and I sat down at the far end of the table. I knew Stroud's face, but only from the news. He'd made a blip in the media when he started this job, all of four weeks ago.

'If you're here, you've already been cleared by

107

the heads of your respective organizations,' he went on. 'Beyond that, everything we cover is for the eyes and ears of this group only. You'll find clearance credentials in the folders in front of you. You have to fill them out before you leave.'

Stroud made all the introductions himself. He impressed me by knowing everyone's name and title without notes. It was a complete alphabet soup in that room — CIA, FBI, NSA, MPD. There were counterterrorism analysts, as well as reps from Secret Service and Homeland Security, and one exhausted-looking agent from the National Clandestine Service who had just arrived from Riyadh.

When he was done, Stroud sat down and nodded to the analyst on his right. 'Let's begin,' he said. 'We have a hell of a lot of material to cover this morning.'

I raised my eyebrows at Mahoney. This was a big meeting. Ned made a little circling gesture with his finger, mouthed the words 'in the loop,' and then pointed at me.

Yeah, I guess so.

36

'At approximately three o'clock this morning, two DC Metro police officers were shot and killed at the Brentwood rail yard in Northeast Washington,' the analyst started in. It wasn't any easier to hear about the murders a second time. Both officers had families. I didn't know them, but that didn't matter. When another officer goes down, we all feel it.

'An indeterminate number of suspects were on-site, all of whom escaped. What we did find, however, was twenty pounds of Semtex explosives. And six canisters of aerosolized sarin. The sarin had already been deposited in the air-conditioning ducts of several Metro subway cars.'

My head was starting to buzz. That was a staggering amount of deadly material. A couple pounds of Semtex can take down a high-rise, and sarin gas is a nightmare at any dosage.

The professional decorum in the room began to break apart at that point. Several side conversations started up around the table, and the questions were flying all at once.

'Are we any closer to knowing who's running this . . . this attack?' one of the NSA guys asked. He was bigger and louder than the rest of us.

'Actually, yes,' the analyst said. He looked across the table at his colleague from Riyadh. 'You want to take that?'

The man from Riyadh's name was Andrew Fatany. He was clearly running on fumes and needed a shave. His voice was disturbingly hoarse when he got up to speak.

'Here's what I can tell you,' Fatany said. 'We now have credible intelligence on the existence of a fledgling, independent terror organization based out of Saudi Arabia. Beyond that, we have several unconfirmed reports regarding the establishment of a multifunctional cell here in Washington, a very serious and deadly one, I'm afraid. They're well financed and organized.'

It felt like half the oxygen had been sucked out of the room. Nobody said a word now, just listened.

Fatany went on. 'Our liaison with the Istikhbarat tells us they're aware of the group but not of any criminal activity inside the Kingdom itself. That said, we've been moving as many operatives as possible out of the embassy in Riyadh and into the southern part of the country, where we believe Al Ayla is training its people before sending them abroad — meaning here, the United States. That includes Washington for sure, possibly New York and Los Angeles as well.'

'Al Ayla,' Stroud repeated for him.

'Right. Sorry.' He got a few grim, sympathetic smiles as he took a long swig of coffee. 'Al Ayla is the purported name of this organization. It translates as 'The Family.''

'Which may or may not have something to do with the use of married couples at the operational level,' the first analyst said. 'It could

110

also just be a coincidence.'

'But I sincerely doubt it,' Fatany said, half to himself.

'Excuse me.' Ned raised his hand. 'Not to get too far ahead of ourselves here, but do we know anything about Al Ayla's larger objectives? Current targets, future targets, ideology, anything like that? Anything useful to us on the ground.'

Both analysts automatically looked to the head of the table.

'No,' Stroud answered for them. 'Nothing at this time.' It was less than subtle code for the fact that we'd reached a wall in terms of what they were prepared to tell us. At least on the topic of Al Ayla, The Family.

'But we do have one other important piece of intel to throw into the mix. This could be useful,' Stroud added. 'It's about Ethan and Zoe Coyle.'

37

One of the assistant directors from the Bureau, Peter Lindley, took over now.

'We've received a second package from Ethan and Zoe's presumed kidnapper,' he said. 'At a minimum, this is someone who has or has had access to the children since they were taken from the school grounds.'

Everything about this was news to me. *Two packages? What packages?* I could tell I wasn't the only one playing catch-up at the table. Lots of frowns and head shaking around the room.

'The first came to us several days ago,' Lindley said.

He pulled a pair of eight-by-ten photos out of his briefcase and started them around the table. 'The little black case you'll see is known to belong to Zoe. And the note in the other photo was folded up inside.'

A respectful silence followed the pictures as they were passed around. When I saw what was in that note, I understood why.

'*There is no ransom. There will be no demands. The price, Mr. President, is knowing that you will never see your children again.*'

You can't read something like that and not feel compassion for the victims — the kids *and* their parents. I have an unfortunate tendency to take these things personally, as if my own family had been harmed. That's my strength, and my weakness.

'And yesterday, we received these,' Lindley said, passing around two more photos. 'They've already been DNA-tested and matched to Ethan and Zoe, respectively.'

The new images were of a boy's white oxford shirt and a pair of thick-soled red boots, the kind a girl like Zoe might wear to school.

'Any formal theories?' someone asked.

'Actually, I was going to ask Detective Cross for his take on all this,' Lindley said. Everyone turned to look at me, probably in time to catch the surprise on my face. 'I know you've only been working around the edges so far,' Lindley said. 'I don't mean to put you on the spot here.'

'It's fine,' I said. At least I knew why I'd been brought in now. I've done as much profiling for the FBI as anyone in Washington. The pictures were all passed back my way, and I looked at them as a set.

'First thoughts?' I said. 'The note's unequivocal — no ransom, no demands, period. So then the next question, *Why send the second package?*'

'Maybe just to string us along?' one of the Bureau wonks contributed the obvious. 'Flaunt an advantage. Hang it over our heads. Show off.'

'I think that's probably true,' I said. 'But there's a personal element here that's directed at the president. He's the one named in the note. If someone wanted to make him suffer, the best way to do that would be to draw this search out for as long as possible.'

'Go back a second,' Stroud said. 'When you

say this is personal, are you suggesting it's also an individual act? Is this one man's vendetta against the president?'

I thought about it before I answered, but my first impulse didn't change.

'If you want my best guess,' I said, 'yes. That's what this feels like to me. But for the sake of argument, terrorism can be very personal, too, even in the name of a larger cause.'

'*Especially* in the name of a larger cause,' Fatany said. 'Most of these shits take what they're doing very personally. They're willing, even eager, to die — as we've already seen.'

Lindley started to move on, but I jumped back in when one other thing occurred to me.

'This is above my pay grade — but I'd also recommend keeping President Coyle out of the public eye, if that's not already in the plan,' I said.

'Why is that?' Stroud asked, although I think he already knew the answer.

'If I'm right, it deprives the kidnapper, or kidnappers, of a primary motivation. Don't let them see the president dealing with this. That's probably exactly what they want. To humble the United States president in front of a world audience.'

One of the Secret Service reps cleared his throat. 'The president and First Lady are in a secure location,' he said. 'We'll keep Detective Cross's recommendation under advisement, but any decisions about that kind of thing — '

Just then, a familiar voice came into the room from an unseen speaker.

'Excuse me. I'd like to say something.'

It was coming from the wall, or the ceiling, or maybe even the table itself. I couldn't tell. But there was no mistaking who it belonged to.

President Coyle was there with us, and apparently he was ready to make a statement.

38

Two wide screens flicked on, one at either end of the room. Suddenly President Edward Coyle was there, sitting at a generic-looking desk, with a set of plain blue drapes drawn behind him.

For all I know, it was a set piece, a bit of theater meant to hide any clues about where he actually was at this time. Still, it gave me a chill. Probably did the same for everybody in the room.

'We have you, sir,' Stroud said. 'Go ahead. We're here and we're listening.'

Coyle looked bone-tired, and his face was drawn. There was a kind of sadness in his eyes I'd never seen before. I also got the impression he hadn't been planning on doing this, speaking to our group right now.

'Let me state the obvious first,' he said. 'I have two separate and distinct obligations here. One is to Ethan and Zoe, and the other is to this country.

'Right now, we don't seem to know how enmeshed those obligations might be. But I do know that by all indications, and according to the best advice I can get, our capital city is under attack.'

The president was incredibly focused. I thought of the eye of a hurricane as I watched him. He was obviously a strong man and it was no fluke that he had risen to this position.

'I'm not saying that we've reached some critical point at which a decision has to be made between my children and our nation's security — '

'No sir, not at all,' Stroud cut in.

The president immediately put up the flat of his hand to quash any discussion. 'I need to make one point very clearly,' he went on. 'With all due respect to the opinions in the room, if I have to show my face to lead the country through this crisis, then that's exactly what I'm going to do.'

'Sir — '

'That's all for right now. Carry on,' he said. 'Evan, I'll expect my next briefing by ten o'clock. I should be back in the residence by then.'

'Yes, sir,' Stroud said.

There were a few more mumbled 'thank you, sir's around the table before the screens went blank again, and the president was gone. He'd said all he needed to say.

I looked down at my watch. It seemed impossible, but it was only a few minutes past six a.m. Bree would be getting off work about now. The kids would be waking up and starting to get ready for school after their day off. It sounded like President and Mrs. Coyle would be headed back to the White House. And two murdered policemen's families were going to have to start piecing their lives back together this morning.

It was another day in Washington, DC, and none of us — the ones who were supposed to protect the city — had any idea what it would bring.

117

39

Hala woke up first, as she almost always did. But something was different, she sensed. No, she *knew* something had changed. For the better?

It was the sound of the *adhan*. The sound of *home*, ringing out from somewhere nearby. She raised her head to see where she was.

Tariq was still asleep on the metal cot across from hers. Shelves of paper towels and toilet paper, the most pedestrian materials imaginable, lined the corner space above his bed. *Where were they?*

Her clothes were the same as the night before, except for a slight stiffness where they'd been sweated through and dried again.

How many miles had they run? It had seemed as if the night would never be over. But now they were here. Safe for the moment, in a new hiding place.

'Tariq?' She swung her legs out of bed. It was stuffy in the room, and the cool cement felt good underfoot. 'Wake up. Tariq. *Tariq.*'

His eyes fluttered open just before he sat up fast. 'What's wrong?' he asked. 'What's happened? Are the police here?'

'No. Nothing like that,' she said. 'I don't think so.'

This wasn't a place they were supposed to know about. A dear friend at the camp outside of Najran had given her the name of the mosque.

Just in case, he'd said. *And use the back door in the alleyway.* Hala hadn't even told Tariq about the location until last night.

It had been pitch-dark when they came in, and lights were prohibited. Now a single high window was letting in just enough gray dawn to show her details she hadn't seen before. This was a storage room, wasn't it? There were boxes of paper and other office supplies. Some canned goods. An enormous wooden lectern, listing a bit to the side, like an old person who needed to use a cane.

And what was this? She saw that their things had been brought from the hotel. Both suitcases, Tariq's laptop, and the black weapons case were stacked neatly by the room's only door.

'Is it safe to move around?' Tariq asked.

'I suppose it is. Let's see.'

Hala stood up. They could at least change their clothes. She was halfway across the room when the door suddenly opened from the outside. Had someone been watching them all night?

A portly woman, somewhere between middle-aged and old, walked in on them.

'You're awake,' the woman said in Arabic. 'Good. We brought your suitcases here.'

She had a basin of water in both hands, still steaming hot. There were two hand towels on her shoulder and what looked like a blue silk *hijab* for Hala. Clothes from back home.

'As soon as you're ready, you can come have breakfast with him,' she said. She set the basin

119

and towels on a chair, then turned to go. 'I'll just be outside.'

'Excuse me. Breakfast with who?' Hala asked.

The woman stopped, but only to look them over again, assessing them in some way. 'Don't be too long,' she said. 'He's waiting.'

40

They were brought around through the darkened back of the mosque. Hala could hear the Fajr prayer coming through the walls as they moved quickly along, carrying their shoes.

The housekeeper, or whatever she was, stopped at a tall carved door and let them inside, but she didn't follow. The breakfast was already set.

'Brother. Sister,' the man at the table greeted them, also in Arabic. 'Come and sit. The coffee's getting cold.'

He was squat, like a man crossed with a toad, but his face was open and seemed friendly. He watched them come into the room with the kind of amused curiosity one usually reserved for a visit by children.

It was only when they came closer that Hala noticed the wheelchair. The heavy table and his long shirt had obscured it until now.

'Thank you for having us, Sheikh,' Tariq said. 'We're very sorry for the imposition. We apologize.'

He waved their concern away. 'You were right to come here,' he said. 'And I'm not the imam of this mosque. Just a Family member like yourselves. You can call me Uncle. Now, please, don't be so polite. I know you must be hungry.'

She was, but Hala still paused to take stock. The man — Uncle — had scrambled eggs, pita, and jam on his plate. There were several other untouched dishes on the table.

He picked up on it right way. 'Smart,' he said. 'But completely unnecessary. What would you like me to try?'

'The *labneh*,' she said. 'And the date spread.'

She didn't back down, and it seemed to please rather than antagonize Uncle. His grin only broadened as he took large bites of both, then poured coffee for all three of them from the same pot.

'Very good. I'm impressed. Now, enough antics. You can relax,' he told them in a quiet voice that was also firm and reassuring.

As they loaded their plates, Hala's mind came back to the night before. 'What about the others?' she asked. 'Is everyone — '

'Perfectly safe, thanks to you,' Uncle said.

It seemed imprudent to complain about the mother bitch right now. 'The assignment didn't come off,' she said instead.

'Yes, but not without some impact all the same,' he answered. 'Two of their police officers are dead. That's a powerful symbol to the Americans. They both hate and love their police. The authorities are terrified, mostly because they don't know what to make of us. The kidnapping of the children has them baffled as well.' He paused for a moment, then went on. 'Of course, we are responsible for that.'

Tariq passed her a piece of bread, smiling with his eyes. He was obviously proud that The Family had already accomplished so much.

Hala sipped her coffee. It was Arabic, and not

122

entirely hot, but delicious. She wanted to ask more about the president's children but thought it would be wise to let Uncle take the lead on that subject.

'There will be other important assignments,' Uncle went on casually. 'In fact, we'd like to reposition you. We're prepared to do this now, the sooner the better. As you know so well, we are at war!'

The words hung there in the air.

'I'm sorry? Reposition?' Tariq asked.

'Take charge of the next phase we have planned for the Americans. Part of it, anyway.' He took a large manila envelope from the pocket on the back of his chair and slid it across the table.

'Go ahead,' he said, smiling as though it were a personal gift. 'Take a look.'

Tariq tilted the envelope to empty its contents — a disk in a thin jewel case, two American passports, a car key, and an engraved hotel folio with a room entry card inside.

'There's a list of our targets there,' Uncle said, indicating the disk. 'We will assemble a team for you. Whatever you like, whatever you need.'

Hala took it all in, searching her mind for an appropriate response. 'Thank you, Uncle,' she said finally. 'We're honored.'

'Don't be.' For the first time, there was a scowl on the man's face. 'This is about The Family, not some American version of self-glorification.'

Hala felt embarrassed. 'Of course. I understand,' she said.

Then the man's face turned again. He grinned that grin of his, and winked as he took another bite of breakfast.

'But I do think you'll like the Four Seasons,' he said. 'It is a very good hotel.'

Book Three

WAR!

41

The kidnapper understood everything there was to understand about the case, and definitely more than the Washington police, the plodding Secret Service, and the painstakingly ineffective FBI. He watched them as they continued to search for any hint of a clue or evidence misplaced on the campus of the Branaff School. They weren't going to find anything, though. He was certain of that.

Record.

'I have been thinking, obsessing over these desperate measures for over two years, and actually planning it for fourteen months. I believe that I've covered my tracks, and the more I go over the details, the more confident I am that this will go down as one of the great unsolved cases in history.'

A school bell rang just then — lunch!

He slid the tape recorder into a trouser pocket and decided to stroll out onto the school campus, to parade among the still-nervous students and teachers, but also the cops who were there performing their tireless yet pointless interviews. *Talk to me, just me,* he couldn't help thinking.

As he strolled along, he noticed a tall MPD detective, a striking figure, an obviously confident man. He knew this one, had read about his becoming part of the investigation. This detective had a success record that was some cause for concern.

The kidnapper didn't turn the tape recorder back on now, though his finger played over its shape. Still, he was recording inside his head.

Record.

'One of the MPD detectives on the case solved a major kidnapping years ago. If I am as thorough as I believe I am, I have to admit that he's a danger to everything I've done, to all that I have accomplished, to the entire plan and its rewards. I feel this everywhere in my body. He's different from the others, just as I am different from my fellow man and woman. I think I know what I should do now, but can I do it? *Can I kill Alex Cross?* It's the right thing to do.'

42

Just off the northwest corner of Sixth and P streets, A plain white van sat stationed at the curb. The aluminum ladder and PVC pipe on the roof rack masked an air vent, which in turn masked a six-millimeter lens taking live footage of the mosque across the street.

FBI Agent Cheryl Kravetz was on periscope. She shifted the joystick control in her right hand, bringing the double front doors of Masjid Al-Qasim into focus, just as the early morning service began to let out.

The sidewalk filled up quickly. There were more men than women by far, in everything from *thobes* and skullcaps to Abercrombie T-shirts and patent leather high-tops. But there were families, too, and a good number of couples. Kravetz was particularly interested in the couples.

'Is it just me,' she asked, 'or does this whole thing seem kind of — '

'Open-ended?'

Her partner, Howard Green, kept his eyes on the console in front of him, where a bank of five small screens and two large ones showed various surveillance images. One of the big screens had a shot of the intersection, patched in from a Department of Transportation camera on the stoplight just outside the van. The other showed what Kravetz was seeing.

'I was going to say 'racist,'' she went on.

'Here we go again.'

'I mean, seriously. We have no idea what we're looking for here. 'Suspicious Muslims?'' Kravetz took her hand off the controls to air-quote the last part. 'I don't even know which of these people are Saudi, or if that even matters.'

'Nobody said 'suspicious Muslims,'' Green countered.

'They didn't have to,' Kravetz said. 'We all know what they want us to do. Scan the brown faces for a while, see what we see. Make sure everyone feels like we're on the job.'

'We *are* on the job,' Green said. 'How do you think this works? You prefer to sit around and wait for more Americans to die? 'Cause you can bet your ass these bad guys aren't going to sit on their heels.'

'All right. Cool your jets. I'm just saying — '

'Yeah, I got it the first couple times.'

' — ACLU's going to have their hands full before this thing is over. That's all.'

Agent Green reached down and took the last bacon, egg, and cheese biscuit from the greasy McDonald's bag at his feet. He knew he was better off not going there with Kravetz, especially this early in the day. The Bureau was spread thin, and their relief wouldn't be coming for another ten hours. Maybe more.

Then, as Green looked up again, something caught his attention. It was a well-dressed couple, coming out of the mosque at the back of the crowd. Nothing strange there — except they were both loaded down with luggage.

'What's with the suitcases?' he said. Kravetz took her eye off the periscope to see what Green meant. He put a finger up to the screen. 'That couple, right there.'

The woman had stopped to lower her *hijab*. The man, clean shaven with a Ravens cap on his head, took up the larger bag she'd just set down and handed her a briefcase to carry instead.

'Maybe they came in on a red-eye,' Kravetz offered. 'Went straight to services from the airport.'

'Maybe,' Green said. 'Stay with them.'

He watched as Kravetz put the couple in the center of her frame. She pressed a thumb control on the joystick and zoomed in close enough to snap a still image of their faces just before they continued up the sidewalk.

'Nice work,' Green said.

Kravetz was still watching the young Middle Eastern couple walk away.

'Nice ass,' Green went on. 'She's kind of smoking hot, isn't she?'

'I'm sending this in,' Kravetz said dryly. But yes, the woman was definitely hot.

With a few keystrokes, the image was on its way to IDENT. Both faces would be electronically logged and then scanned against an international database of known terrorists and persons of interest. Secret Service's facial recognition system would pick it up, too.

'See, this is exactly what I'm talking about,' Kravetz said. 'Do you know how many random, innocent people are pouring into the system right now?'

'There must be some kind of compelling intel on that mosque,' Green said. 'They've got us on this corner for a reason.'

'Yeah, us and a hundred other JTTF teams on a hundred other corners. This is a needle in a haystack. On a good day.'

Agent Green took a bite of his sandwich and tried not to think about it. They had a long shift ahead, and they were already talking in circles. Even if Kravetz was right — and she probably was — there was no sense in admitting it now. He'd never hear the end of it.

43

After our early morning meeting at CIA headquarters, Ned Mahoney and I were both detailed straight over to the FBI's Counterterrorism Division, also in Langley. It's housed in a secure building called Liberty Crossing, or LX1 for short.

The command center was a cavernous space with the soft lighting of a movie theater. But the volume was more like the floor of the New York Stock Exchange, and the tension was sky high.

Thousands of personnel had been dispatched to locations all over the city, and reps from every major agency had been assigned to this room, like me. Each area was marked with quickly made signs taped to the front of the desks — HOSTAGE AND RESCUE, MPD, CIA, MOBILE CTOC COMMUNICATIONS, and on it went.

Beyond the rail yard incident itself, we had a whole new element to deal with this morning. As of five a.m., Homeland Security had raised the terror threat level for Washington's mass transit system from orange to red. All subway service, bus routes, and commuter trains were suspended until further notice.

This was only the second time any sector had gone red since they established the alert system after 9/11. There was no soft-selling it to the locals anymore.

Reports were steadily coming in that people

were starting to flee the city in noticeable numbers.

The story had gone fully national, too. CNN was up on several screens around the room, covering the shootings and transit shutdown to the exclusion of everything else. They had a live helicopter shot of the rail yard, crawling with TV crews.

You could see officers from the Explosive Ordnance Division in their bulky suits, climbing in and out of the subway cars, like something right out of *The Hurt Locker*. It was the kind of imagery news directors love, and law enforcement hates.

I took my seat next to Javier Crist, an MPD sergeant who worked at LX1 full-time. He had the computer-assisted 911 dispatch up on one of the screens in front of him, monitoring the distress and emergency calls that were pouring in from everywhere. Our job was to gather information from the field, report it to the room, and send back a constant stream of leads for MPD to run down.

'Welcome to Camp Hell' was all Crist got out before he had to take another call.

That was the extent of my orientation. My own phone was already ringing.

I slapped on a headset and got straight to work. This wasn't what I had been hoping for, but at least it was something. I was on the inside now.

44

Bree Cross was reading in bed at two o'clock that afternoon when the doorbell started ringing. Not just once, but over and over and over.

Something was wrong.

And if it wasn't, someone was going to get a piece of her mind once she got to the front door.

She jumped up and dropped her book on the bed. The title was *You and Your Stepkids*. She was supposed to be getting some sleep before the night shift, but this was a chance to sneak in a few chapters while no one was looking, especially Alex, who would be sweet enough about the book but would be unable to stop at least one snorting laugh.

'I'm coming!' Bree yelled from the stairs. The bell was still going. She could see two shadows on the other side of the front door's frosted glass, one of them a good head taller than the other. Now what?

When she flipped the dead bolt and threw open the door, Nana was standing there. Next to her was a man Bree had never seen before. The man had his arm around Nana's middle, and she was holding a red-stained handkerchief up to her forehead. Her left knee was dripping with blood as well.

'Oh my God! What happened?'

'My key was in my purse,' Nana said — and her purse was nowhere in sight.

'Some punk knocked her down,' the man said. He had bloodstains on the sleeve of his khaki jacket. 'I didn't get there in time to see anything. I'm sorry.'

'Thank you *so* much,' Nana said as he handed her off to Bree's care. 'A real gentleman. And you will absolutely be sending the cleaning bill to this address!'

As soon as the man had gone, though, her face fell into a grimace. Bree eased her down onto the old caned chair in the hall for a better look. The cut on her forehead wasn't deep, but the knee was badly abraded.

'Goddamnit! Who would do something like this?' Bree said.

'There's no need for language. I'll be fine,' Nana told her. 'I'll live.'

'Sorry. Just . . . stay right there.'

Bree raced to the bathroom for a first-aid kit and a couple of washcloths. She was silently fuming the whole time. Her head felt like it was burning up, and her chest, too.

I'm going to kill someone. I swear to God, I'm going to commit murder today.

Back out in the hall again, she put on a calm face. Then she knelt down and gently pushed Nana's hair away to clean the wound.

'What happened, Regina? Tell me.'

'Well . . . ' Nana took a deep breath. 'I was walking back from the pharmacy up on Pennsylvania. It was across from United Methodist, right there in the middle of Seward Square. Maybe I should have gone around the long way, I don't know — '

136

Bree stopped with the washcloth in midair. 'Don't you dare blame yourself for this! Since when is Seward Square dangerous in the middle of the day?'

'Since about fifteen minutes ago,' Nana said, half joking, but also on the verge of tears. She looked down at the blood-stained handkerchief in her hand. 'Seventy years in this city, and I've never been mugged. Good Lord, I'm getting old.'

It made Bree want to cry herself. This damn neighborhood, this city, what was it doing to people? She quietly finished up the first aid and walked Nana over to the living room couch to rest.

Then just as quietly, she slipped back upstairs and took the Glock 19 out of the lockbox in her closet.

When she came down, Nana was sitting and staring out the front window toward Fifth Street. An issue of *O, the Oprah Magazine* sat unopened on her lap.

'I'm going to run out for a minute,' Bree told her. 'You need anything right now?'

Nana eyed her suspiciously. 'Why? Where are you going?'

'Just up the street. Now tell me what this asshole — excuse me, this mugger — looked like.'

45

The temperature was high for September. In more ways than one. Sweat started dripping down Bree's back before she'd gone a block. It was shades of running the 440 at UVA all over again — not quite a run, not quite a sprint. She wasn't sure how much ground she'd have to cover.

Or whose butt she was going to have to kick.

At the south side of Seward Square, she stopped to catch a breath and look around. This was most likely a wild goose chase, but she was too pissed to just sit home and file a police report like somebody else might do. Somebody sane.

And then —

'Well, I'll be damned.'

There was the mugger, squatting in the shade of an old cherry tree in the middle of the square. Didn't even have the sense to make herself scarce.

This had to be her. Nana had been pretty specific — red Hollister hoodie, brown denim shorts to the knees, dirty white ball cap, and a pair of ridiculous-looking white plastic shades that were too big to be anything but stolen.

Way to blend in, girlie.

She looked all kinds of stupid, but the girl did know enough to leap up and bolt as soon as she saw Bree, who was clearly on a mission. She sprang away on a pair of long skinny legs, going straight up Pennsylvania in the direction of the Hill.

She was quick, too. But she had probably never ran NCAA track, had she?

Once Bree had her on a straightaway, it took less than half a block to close the gap to an arm's reach. She nabbed the girl by the hood and practically yanked her off her feet as they came to a stop and near collision.

The little thief didn't weigh anything inside those baggy clothes. And her height was deceptive. Up close, she looked even younger than Jannie. She was maybe twelve years old, could be thirteen.

'Get off me!' she screamed, scrambling to get away. 'Help! Somebody call the damn po-lice!'

Bree's badge was already out and in the girl's face. The Glock, she left in its holster.

'I am the damn police, little girl. Now turn around! You knocked down the wrong grand-mother.'

She put the girl up against the wall of a corner Exxon and gave her the full treatment. There was nothing down her sides, nothing in the hoodie's pouch when she squeezed it. But then she felt something in the front right pocket of the shorts.

'Is that a credit card?'

'Yeah,' the girl said over her shoulder. 'My mama's card, okay? We done here?'

Bree stepped back, but not more than arm's length. 'Show me,' she said.

'Bite me,' the girl snapped. 'I don't gotta.'

'You know what? Screw it.'

She grabbed the young suspect by the arm and reached into the pocket herself. So much for the Fourth Amendment. It was too hot for this nonsense.

Sure enough, she pulled out a sweaty wad of three twenties and a familiar-looking Visa card. The name embossed across the front was Regina Cross.

'Your mama's, huh?'

'All right, all right!' The girl didn't miss a beat. 'Some kid down the street gave it to me. I swear to Jesus Our Lord and Saviour! Right over there!' She pointed back toward the square.

Bree didn't take the bait. 'Let's go,' she said, and started walking.

The mouthy little con artist didn't have any choice but to move her feet and keep up. 'What're you doing? Where we going?' she said. 'You can't arrest me, I'm just a damn kid!'

'I'm not arresting you,' Bree said. 'You're going to show me where you dropped that purse. Then you're coming down the street to apologize for what you did. And I suggest you watch your mouth when you do.'

46

Nana got up off the couch as Bree came in with their mugger in tow. She seemed to want to make a point of meeting them in the front hall on her own two feet.

'Oh now, see that?' she said, looking the girl up and down. 'I'm a little embarrassed. I told my granddaughter-in-law here that you were something scary.' She pointed a crooked finger at the dusty ball cap on the girl's head. 'And you need to take that off inside the house. It's only polite.'

The girl squinted back. 'You joking, right?' she said, but Bree snatched the hat off for her.

The hair underneath looked like baby dreds at first, but it wasn't quite that. It was regular braids that had been chopped off at some point. Maybe to look more like a boy out on the streets, Bree thought. In the close quarters of the front hall, it was obvious this one hadn't known a shower in a long time cither.

'What's your name?' Nana asked.

The girl thrust the tan leather purse out at her. 'I'm sorry, okay?' she said, not sounding very sorry at all.

Nana let the bag hang there between them. 'I didn't ask if you were sorry. I asked what your name was.'

'Ava,' she grunted out. Then she set the purse on the newel post and looked at Bree. 'I said I was sorry, didn't I? Can I go now?'

But Nana wasn't done. She still had the floor. 'Tell me something, Ava, and that's a beautiful name, by the way. What was the first thing you were going to buy with my money?'

'Huh?'

'*Huh* is not a word. What I want you to tell me is why you needed to take my purse. I got knocked down for it. I think I deserve to know why.'

Bree was almost starting to feel sorry for the girl now. Ava's face was like a stone mask, but one tear had escaped down each cheek. She scrubbed them off with her sleeve right away.

'I dunno,' she finally said.

'Well, if you don't know, then you can't go,' Nana told her.

The girl's jaw dropped open. 'Say what?'

'That's what I used to tell my students,' Nana said. 'I was a teacher, see, about a hundred years ago, maybe more than that. It seems to me you need some time to come up with a better answer.'

The tears were coming faster now. 'I never done anything like this before!' Ava blurted. 'I swear!'

'That much I can believe. She was just hanging out in the square when I found her,' Bree said.

Nana turned away from both of them and headed toward the kitchen.

'Come on, Ava. I'm going to make some tea with milk. And from the look of you, I don't suppose you'd mind a sandwich.'

Ava didn't move, but Bree noticed she wasn't

angling for the front door anymore, either.

'I don't drink tea,' she said sullenly.

'You do if I make it!' Nana said, and she disappeared on the other side of the swinging kitchen door.

47

If Bree hadn't called to give me the lowdown, I would have been caught completely off guard. Apparently, Nana had taken in a stray that afternoon, and the girl was still there when I got home after a long day of bureaucratic nonsense.

I could hear everyone talking — and laughing — as I came onto the back porch, but they all went still when I stepped into the kitchen. It was like something out of an old Wild West movie.

Jannie and Ali were at the table with the other girl, whose name was Ava. The kids all had plates of lasagna in front of them, but Ava was the only one eating right now. In the silence, I could hear the dryer running downstairs, and I recognized the old Bob Marley T-shirt she was wearing. It was something Damon had left behind when he went away to boarding school.

'Alex, this is Ava,' Nana told me. Despite the bandages, my grandmother didn't look too much the worse for wear and tear. In fact, she looked a little smug.

'Hi, Ava,' I said.

'Hello.'

Ava didn't look up and kept eating with her elbows jutted out on either side, like she expected someone to take her plate away at any second.

Jannie and Ali both sat up tall like a couple of meerkats, watching to see what I'd do next. I wasn't quite sure myself.

'Nana, could I speak with you in the living room?' I finally said.

'I'm an old woman, Alex.'

'Now, please?'

I held the door for her and we walked to the far end of the house before either of us spoke. Then she jumped in first.

'The girl's got nowhere to go,' she said. 'She just needs a place to sleep where she doesn't have to keep one eye open all the time.'

I ran my hand over my head, trying to gather some patience at the end of this very long day. 'That's what Child and Family Services is for,' I said.

'Why? So they can put her in *the warehouse?*' Nana said, and pointed up at me. 'That's right, I know what they call it down at the police department, so don't even try that on me, mister.'

I couldn't argue that point. The temporary holding facility where Ava would probably land was, in fact, pretty bleak, and it *was* called 'the warehouse.'

'The poor thing's been on the street for a month,' Nana added.

'So she says.'

'Look at her! She's no bigger than my little finger. I don't need a polygraph to tell me no one's been looking after that child. Do you?'

Bree had wandered out behind us. She'd been playing Switzerland so far, but she spoke up now.

'For what it's worth, Alex, her story checks out. The mother's name she gave us is Olivia

Williams. There was an Olivia Williams who died of a heroin overdose, DOA, at Washington Hospital on August tenth. Also, Kramer Middle School had an Ava Williams enrolled last year, but she hasn't shown up for seventh grade.'

Nana gave me a told-you-so kind of glare. I could feel myself losing ground already.

'What about the father?' I said. 'Other family? You check any of that?'

'Nothing on the school records. I think she really is alone,' Bree said.

'Damon's room is just sitting empty up there. Besides, I already put clean sheets on the bed,' Nana said. Like that settled everything. The fact that I owned this house didn't seem to count for much right now. Not enough, anyway.

'All right,' I said. 'One night. But first thing tomorrow, Bree's taking her over to CFS.'

'We'll see,' Nana said.

'And I'm putting a lock on Damon's door.'

'You most certainly are not!' she told me. 'You can sleep out in the hall if you like. Now if you'll excuse me, we've got a guest in the kitchen.'

I looked at Bree again, but her expression said it all: *If you can't budge Nana, how do you expect me to?*

'One night,' I said again.

'We'll see,' Nana said.

146

48

Bree took a little nap after dinner before she went to her shift at work. I snuggled with her until she was asleep, then I went up in the attic to work some myself.

I must have fallen asleep at my desk and when I woke up Bree was gone and everyone else was sleeping. I checked on Ava and she was out for the count. Then I went to bed — alone.

I hated leaving everything so undone the next morning, but it wasn't exactly a call-in-sick kind of day. I got up at four thirty and made it out to Langley by six.

The morning was a beauty, a burst of burnt orange on the horizon, but I wasn't going to see much more of it, was I?

The truth was, I didn't want to be anchored at LX1. Cops are creatures of the field. It's where we do our best work. I wanted to be out there chasing leads and working the case at street level. That's where I might actually do some good.

Then about halfway through the day, I got my wish. Kind of.

It was just after one o'clock. Peter Lindley came out of his makeshift office at the command center and waved to get my attention. Half a dozen agents and supervisors were coming out behind him, and he motioned me over. I was next.

Mahoney caught my eye as I crossed the floor.

I shrugged back. I had no idea what this was about. He gave me the old pinkie and thumb to his ear — *call me later* — and I nodded that I would. Ned will never admit it, but he hates to be left out of anything. He's also a lot more ambitious than people might think.

'Come in,' Lindley told me. 'And close the door behind you, please.'

The space was normally a conference room, but most of the chairs had been taken out. Lindley's desk was just an eight-foot folding table in the middle of the room. He had a triple monitor set up, just like everyone else, and half a dozen phones. One of those was in his hand right now. He was also holding a small yellow Post-it note.

'As soon as I have you, I'm supposed to call Nina Friedman at the White House,' he said, wagging the Post-it. 'Do you know who that is?'

'No idea,' I said. 'Should I?'

'Regina Coyle's deputy chief of staff,' Lindley said. 'What's going on, Alex? Why is the First Lady's office looking for you? Is there something I need to know about?'

I couldn't tell if Lindley was pissed off, overcaffeinated, or just trying to be thorough. Maybe he didn't like feeling left out, the same as Ned Mahoney.

'Peter, I don't know what to tell you,' I said. 'I'm guessing this must have something to do with the kidnapping. Why don't you give that number a call and we'll both find out?'

He glared at me over the top of his half-frames like I was being coy or something. But he went

148

ahead and dialed the number.

As soon as I took the phone from him, a woman's voice was there.

'Detective Cross?'

'Speaking,' I said. 'How can I help, Ms. Friedman?'

'I'm calling from the Office of the First Lady, here in the East Wing,' she said, unnecessarily. There was a rote kind of formality to her voice. 'Are you available for a meeting with Mrs. Coyle?'

Even the question was a formality. Was I available for a meeting with the First Lady of the United States?

'Of course,' I said. 'I could be there in about forty-five minutes.'

'Very good. I'll have your name at the East Appointment Gate,' she said crisply. 'I can meet you at the top of the drive, under the porte cochere.'

And out of sight of the press, if I was reading her correctly. This meeting wasn't a secret, but discretion seemed to be the m.o.

When I hung up, Lindley was still staring at me. Two of his other phones were ringing, but he ignored them, waiting for an explanation.

'Well?' he said.

I shrugged. 'I'm going to need some coverage on the desk.'

I didn't really care if he thought I was tap-dancing or not. I had a meeting to get to.

49

At the white house, there was all the expected, overt security — ID check and magnetometer at the East Gate; stepped-up Secret Service presence; Capitol Police everywhere. And then there was everything I couldn't see. I wondered how many surveillance cameras and maybe even rifle sites were on me as I walked up the curved drive to the East Wing's main entrance.

My only regret was that Sampson wasn't here with me to see this. And Bree. And maybe Nana and the kids. A quick photo op with everybody?

Nina Friedman was waiting on the front steps as promised. She was just as efficient in person, juggling her BlackBerry to shake my hand even as we turned to head inside.

'Thank you for coming. Won't you please follow me?' she said. That was it. There was no briefing, no explanation.

Once I cleared the security desk and another magnetometer in the entry hall, I expected to be taken to a conference room, or maybe up to the First Lady's offices on the second floor.

But it quickly became clear that wasn't going to happen. Ms. Friedman walked me straight through the East Wing lobby and out the other side.

I kept my mouth shut as we passed from one building to the next, down the long East Colonnade with its view of the Kennedy Garden, and into the ground floor of the White House itself.

It made sense, now that I thought about it. Secret Service was probably restricting Mrs. Coyle's movement as much as possible. Her office time would have been kept to a minimum, at best.

They stopped us for another ID check at the base of the main stairs. Then again on the first-floor landing before we could continue up to the residence. By the time we got to the stair landing on the second floor, the agents seemed to be expecting us. They only nodded at Ms. Friedman as we passed.

The museum quality of the lower levels had given way to something more like a home up here. There was plush blue and gold carpeting, a baby grand piano, several built-in bookcases, with hardbacks that looked like someone had actually read them.

I'm not so jaded that I wasn't tripping out a little on where I was, either. It was impossible to be there and not think about all the presidents and First Ladies who had walked through these very rooms for the last two hundred years — all the way back to John Adams.

I guess the word for what I felt is *humbled*.

The hall narrowed and then narrowed again through a deep arch that opened to a sunny sitting room on the other side.

Mrs. Coyle was there with two female aides. To my right was the Lincoln Bedroom. This was just shy of surreal. I was definitely in the loop now.

The First Lady's deputy chief of staff started the introductions.

'Mrs. Coyle, this is — '

'Detective Cross. Yes, of course.'

As Regina Coyle came over to shake my hand, I could see her eyes were still red from whenever she'd last cried. Probably not long ago.

'Thank you so much for being here,' she said. 'I'm hoping you can be of some help to me.'

50

'Mrs. Coyle, I'm so sorry about everything that's happened,' I said. 'I'll do whatever I can.'

She gestured me inside while the others quietly left the way I'd just come. A few seconds later, the First Lady and I were as alone as we were going to get in that building, even upstairs in the private quarters.

She sat on a long couch with a view of the Treasury Department building behind her. I took one of the yellow upholstered chairs, the same color as the walls and curtains, while she poured coffee from a service of White House china.

'You have some relevant experience with kidnap investigations, isn't that right?' she started in. 'The Gary Soneji case and others?'

'Yes, ma'am,' I said. 'Three major cases since Soneji. It's not my primary expertise — '

'But you're good at it,' she said. It wasn't a question, but she waited for an answer anyway.

'Experience is probably the best teacher,' I said. 'So yes, I'm pretty good.'

Mrs. Coyle nodded, then looked down. She seemed to be building up to something.

She was a quiet First Lady, as they went. More Laura Bush than Hillary Clinton. Both she and her husband were originally from Minnesota farm stock, and I don't think she ever relished the high-profile aspects of this job.

153

When she looked up again, her gaze was steady. More focused than before. I realized she was as strong as her husband.

'I know that most of the people looking for Ethan and Zoe right now probably don't expect to find them alive,' she said all at once. There was no outward emotion to it. Just a fact. 'I'm not blind to the statistics on this kind of thing.'

'No, ma'am,' I said. 'But I hope you also know that you've got some of the best people in the world on this. You have since day one.'

'Of course,' she said, and fell back into another silence. There was obviously something else. I did what comes naturally to me and waited quietly for her to go on.

Then she said, 'Your son was held hostage for several months, wasn't he? Around the time he was born?'

That one, I didn't see coming at all. Mrs. Coyle had done her homework and then some. It was true. Ali's mother, Christine, had been kidnapped while she was still pregnant with him. The memory of it cut right through me. Christine and I had never recovered from the incident and its trauma.

I nodded. 'It was the worst year of my life,' I said. 'Ali's mother's as well.'

'And how is your son today?' she asked.

'He's great, actually,' I said. 'A little bigger every day. I'm very proud of him.'

'So you understand,' she said. The look on her face was as close to a smile as anything I'd seen. Just a softening around her eyes, really.

And of course, I did understand now. If it was

154

possible for me to get my beautiful son back, then it was possible for her, too. For Ethan and Zoe to be returned to her somehow.

As Mrs. Coyle went on, she seemed to choose her words very carefully. 'Detective Cross, I would never presume to tell you how to do your job,' she said. 'But if you were to call your supervisor after this meeting and express an interest in getting more involved with Ethan and Zoe's case, I can guarantee you that the answer would be yes. Whatever assignment you wanted, however you wanted to do your work. With a pretty free rein.'

This was the Regina Coyle I didn't know — the politician's wife. I don't mean that in a bad way. What I really saw was a mother living through her own worst nightmare and doing whatever she could to save her children.

I set down my cup and took out a pen and a small pad from my jacket pocket.

'May I?' I asked.

'Of course,' she told me.

It was time to start from square one with the president's wife.

'Tell me about Ethan and Zoe. What are your children like?'

51

Their hands were on the neck of the devil. Now it was time to tighten their grip.

Hala sat cross-legged with the laptop on the bed. She dragged several of the files she'd been compiling to an encrypted disk image on her desktop and reviewed its contents one more time.

Once the disk was finished, only the intended recipient would be able to open it. Every Family member assigned to Washington had his or her own unique sixteen-digit alpha-numeric string. Hala's code had been what allowed her to access the disks she and Tariq had received up to this point.

While she worked, she kept the local news playing on the television. There was a constant stream these days: frightened faces, traffic warnings, and of course endless speculation about what might be coming next.

It was electrifying, for Hala, to be the one with the answer to that question. Uncle had entrusted her and Tariq with several key targets. Now it was up to them to decide where to strike first; pair the operatives with their assignments; and send out the orders.

Any single one of those targets could change history — much less a fast, violent run through them all. That was exactly what Hala hoped to pull off. Every American life they could take was one more step in the proper direction. There was no such thing as too much punishment for the people of America.

Or as they liked to say in this country of excess and greed: *more is more.*

'Hala!'

Tariq appeared suddenly in the bathroom door, dripping wet. His chubby body was drifted with mounds of soap bubbles and nothing else.

'You look ridiculous,' she said, but with a laugh. It was good to see him so at ease. He was obviously drunk on their good fortune.

'*Ha-laa!*' he sang out, and began a little dance for her while he was at it. 'Come join me! The hot water is endless.'

'Not while I'm working, darling. And it's Julia, remember?' she said.

'Ah, yes.' He grinned broadly. 'I forgot that I'm in love with another woman.'

They were Julia and Daniel Aziz from Philadelphia now, and they had American passports to prove it. They'd arrived at the Four Seasons just the day before. Uncle called it hiding in plain sight.

The pace of all these changes was absolutely breathtaking. Only two days earlier, they'd been waiting in the dark to find out what would happen next — and now this.

After Tariq had sloshed back into the tub, Hala returned to her work. Let him enjoy this ridiculous American palace a while longer, she thought. The less he worried, the better it was for everyone. As far as Tariq was concerned, everything had changed for them.

But it hadn't, of course. The elders were still watching. It was more important than ever that she and Tariq make a good impression, and soon. If they weren't careful, they could become expendable to the Family just as quickly as they had risen to this position.

Be prepared to die at any time.

That, above all, remained true. Because it wasn't just an opportunity they'd been given, Hala knew. It was also a test.

This war was now in their hands.

52

I can't say I was surprised to find out that Nana Mama had forbidden Bree from bringing Ava over to Child and Family Services the next day. Never mind that I'd insisted on the trip to Family Services. Bree told me on the phone that afternoon than Nana was digging in her heels.

So I came home determined to get the situation taken care of myself.

Nana was waiting for me when I got there. I found her alone, reading *Little Bee* at the kitchen table, like a security guard.

'I need to talk to you,' she said.

'I'm not going to fight about this, Nana. We can't help every kid on the streets of DC,' I said, and kept moving.

'Who said anything about *that*?' she called after me, but I was already halfway to the stairs.

I hated being cast as the bad guy. It wasn't like I thought Nana was crazy for feeling the way she did, but I truly believed I was doing the right thing here. For everyone involved, even the girl.

At least up until what happened next.

When I got upstairs to Damon's room, Ava was sitting on the bed reading one of his old X-Men comics.

'Ava, it's time to go,' I said. 'I'm going to bring you down to the intake center and get you settled over there, okay? Just like we talked about last night.'

She wouldn't even look at me. She lifted and lowered one very cold shoulder and swung her feet onto the floor. Maybe she'd been getting pointers from Nana.

Then, as she got up to shuffle over to the door, I noticed something on the floor behind her. Something under the bed.

'What's that?' I said, pointing.

'Nothin'.'

She didn't even glance back. The girl was a terrible liar.

'Hang on a second.'

I walked over and knelt down on the rug to have a look. There, between the bed and the nightstand, was a small pile of food. I saw half a loaf of bread, some bananas, a sleeve of crackers, and a jar of peanut butter.

Honestly, I wasn't so surprised. It's not unusual for a kid from the streets to hoard food, given the chance. And I wasn't even remotely mad about it, either. Ava had done this by instinct, as likely as anything. Survival instinct.

Maybe that's why it broke my heart. Why should a thirteen-year-old kid have to think about where her next meal might be coming from?

Why should Ava? Or anyone?

Just like that, something shifted inside me. It happened the way these things do sometimes, when you least expect it — or even want it.

But that was also the moment that Ava made a break for the stairs. When I turned around, she was gone.

'Ava, wait!'

By the time I got out to the hall, she was already down by the front door, trying to get out. Our dead bolt's a little complicated, a little tricky, and it was slowing her down.

'Ava!' I called out again.

As I came closer, she gave up and ran for the back of the house instead. She crashed right through the kitchen door and just kept going. I heard the sound of breaking glass.

Then Nana's voice. 'What in heaven's name — ?'

When I rushed into the room, Ava was still there. One of the panes in the back door was shattered, and her hand was bleeding. She stood staring at it, frozen in her tracks like a trapped animal.

I put my hands out in front of me. 'It's okay,' I said. '*Really*. Everything's okay.'

Nana grabbed a dish towel to wrap the cut. She put her arm around Ava and made her sit down.

'Nothing to worry about,' she said in a soothing voice. 'Just a little cut, but you go ahead and cry if you need to, sweetheart.'

'I'm sorry,' Ava said, more to Nana than to me. 'I didn't mean to . . . '

'Don't worry about it,' I told her. 'It doesn't matter about the food. The window, either. None of it matters. We'll work it all out.'

Still, Ava tried to squirm away toward the door. She stood up again, and Nana pulled her back down with that surprising strength of hers.

'You sit down, right now!' she commanded. 'You're not going anywhere, young lady.'

I stayed where I was, giving her a little space. 'You know what, Ava?' I said. 'Nana's right. We don't have to make any decisions about this tonight.'

But in fact, that wasn't entirely true. I'd already decided something.

Nana *was* right. Maybe we couldn't save every kid on the streets of DC, but there was no reason — no *good enough* reason — why we couldn't help this one. Right here, right now. Even if it was only for a little while.

I'd call whoever I needed to in the morning. Get an expedited home check. Pull a few strings, if I had to. Make things right for this young girl.

'Just . . . stay,' I said. 'Please.'

53

The next morning, Bree took over at home, and I was back at work. Whatever influence the First Lady had exerted on my behalf, I had no trouble getting onto the Branaff School campus — *inside* the gates this time.

I got there early so I could get a better feel for the place before the school day started. I wanted to retrace, as much as I possibly could, Ethan and Zoe's footsteps on the morning they had disappeared.

As I came up the front drive toward Branaff House, the school's Georgian-style mansion of a main building, I couldn't help thinking about the modest charter John and Billie Sampson were trying to start up just a few miles from here. It was a world apart, that's for sure. Branaff House was the crown jewel of an eighty-acre campus, with the kind of restored beauty that persuaded parents to part with forty-five thousand dollars a year for middle school.

It was also where the Coyle kids had last been seen. What had happened to them?

I started in the main foyer. According to the reports I'd read, this was where a fight had broken out that morning, between Zoe and Ryan Townsend.

It hadn't lasted long, and Secret Service Agent Findlay immediately pulled both of the Coyles away from the scene and into an adjacent lecture hall.

At 8:22 a.m., Findlay had radioed his team that he was giving the kids two minutes alone to speak privately.

At 8:24, he opened the door again and found the lecture hall empty.

About ninety seconds after that, the van driven by Ray Pinkney had gone tearing off campus through the east gate — *without* Ethan and Zoe on board, as it turned out.

What that left was a three-and-a-half-minute window, from the last time Findlay saw the kids, until that van left the school grounds.

Somewhere in there, a kidnapping had taken place.

So what happened in those three and a half minutes?

I let myself into the lecture hall and closed the door behind me.

The room was high-ceilinged, with several austere portraits looking down from the walls. It was a little creepy, actually, but definitely imposing. It made even a big man like me feel small.

Whatever had gone down in that room, Zoe and Ethan couldn't have been there for long. The clock was ticking on those three and a half minutes, whether they knew it or not.

There were two doors at the front, both covered by the same security camera in the hall outside. The only other possible exits were the five windows at the back.

Agent Findlay had reportedly found the center

164

one unlatched, and I went to it now.

I hopped up on the heat register, slid open the window, and ducked outside.

It was an easy drop to the ground, landing me behind a thick tangle of lilac bushes.

Footprints found in the dirt that day confirmed that two people Ethan and Zoe's size had come this way.

But where did they go from here? Were they still alone at this point? *When exactly did things turn horribly wrong?*

We had just a few facts. The rest of the scenario was mostly supposition.

But there was one other known piece of the puzzle, and I needed someone here at the school to show it to me.

54

George O'Shea was the head of maintenance at Branaff. He was a big, redheaded fireplug of a guy, with arms that bulged against the sleeves of his uniform the same way his gut strained at the buttons in front. I found him in his basement office under the main building.

'Nice to meet'cha,' he said, half crushing my hand. 'I'm guessing you came down to see the tunnel? Headmaster's office called ahead.'

'If you have a minute,' I said.

'Come on with me. I'll give you the nickel tour, five cents off today.'

'Much obliged. Thank you.'

There had been a lot of speculation in the press about the underground passage at Branaff, and a lot of assumptions that it figured into the kidnapping somehow. What wasn't public knowledge was that Ethan and Zoe's electronic locators had both been found down here, smashed to pieces at the far end of the tunnel. Whether someone had deliberately put them there to throw us off the scent or dropped them on their way through was still a question mark.

I followed O'Shea through the basement, to an old black steel door at the back. It looked original to the building, except for the brand-new hasp and padlock that had been bolted on.

The custodian used a key from his retractable

ring to open it for me and then flipped a light switch just inside.

'Whole thing's like a T,' he said, leading the way. 'Straight on, it's just a sealed-up hatch where the old coal barn used to be. But if we take a right turn up there, it comes out in the groundskeeping shed down by the playing fields.'

It was supposedly true that Noah Branaff had used this tunnel as part of the Underground Railroad, back in the nineteenth century. It had clearly been refitted since then, with riveted I-beams, a poured concrete floor, and tile on the domed ceiling. Mostly it was used for storage now.

There were mesh lockers with cleaning supplies near the entrance and gardening tools and sports equipment as we got closer to the far end. Very orderly, surprisingly clean.

O'Shea did most of the talking as we walked. He'd been with the school 'since Clinton,' he told me, and had seen a lot of 'big' families come through, although none bigger and more important than the Coyles.

'What's your impression of Ethan and Zoe?' I asked. 'What kind of kids are they?'

'Ethan's a good enough egg,' he said. 'Scary-smart, too. A lot of the other kids think he's kind of weird. He got picked on some. Make that *a lot*.'

'What about Zoe?'

At first, he didn't answer. He raked his fingers through his hair and seemed a little nervous about the question. 'I suppose you want the truth, huh?'

'Don't worry, Mr. O'Shea. I'm not writing any of this down,' I told him.

'All right, well . . . truthfully? Zoe Coyle's a little trouble-maker. Anyone who tells you she didn't try to take advantage twenty-four/seven is either lying or kissing up. And believe me, this school is full of kiss-ups.'

'I can believe that,' I said honestly.

'Don't get me wrong,' he said. 'I've been praying for those kids every night. But that girl's all about seeing what she can get away with. I chased her and her little smoking friends out of here more than once. And she would give me lip.' He stopped as we came to the end of the passage. 'Anyway, here we are.'

In front of us, there was a half flight of concrete steps up to another door. This was where the locators had been found, although the crime scene had been cleared days ago. There wasn't much to see now, but I needed to walk through here at least once.

We kept going and emerged through the groundskeeping 'shed,' which was about the size of my house. That put us on the school lawn next to a couple of practice fields and the south gate.

Up the hill, past a line of old bur oaks, I could see the main building we'd just left behind. Very pretty landscaping. Not the kind of scenery you associated with tragedies.

'That's where the kids came out, supposedly,' O'Shea said, pointing up at the lecture hall windows. 'I suppose that they did come out there.'

I turned in a full circle, taking it all in. Did

168

they come this way? Were they conscious?
Drugged?

'Kind of a straight line from up there, isn't it?'
the custodian said. 'Right through this spot and
out that gate. You suppose that's where they took
them?'

'Maybe,' I said. 'Maybe not. People don't
always travel in straight lines. In fact, the ones
who have something to hide usually don't.'

He nodded, a little like he was playing cop
with me.

'Well,' he said, 'you ought to know.'

55

I spent the rest of the day talking to as many people at the Branaff School as I could. The students were strictly off-limits until I could get parental consent, so I focused on the faculty and staff for the time being.

Dale Skillings was the headmaster. He seemed pretty tightly wound to begin with, but he'd also been through the wringer in the press, and no doubt with the parents as well. Everyone wanted to know how this could possibly happen at Branaff. Inevitably, some of the blame had already landed on the headmaster's desk. If he was terse, or defensive with me, I could understand why.

'Enemies?' he said when I asked. 'They're two of the most famous children in the world. It's not possible to avoid some amount of animosity. But if what you're really asking about is Zoe's fight with Ryan Townsend, I can't discuss that with you. You'll have to take it up with Congressman and Mrs. Townsend.'

In fact, I already had a few calls in on that one. Skillings wasn't going to budge on the rules where the kids were concerned, but he did make his staff fully available to me, which I appreciated.

One of the sixth-grade math teachers, Eleanor Ruff, told me about how Zoe had barely scraped by in her class and about how Ethan was testing off the charts, no surprise. She was a twenty-year veteran at the school, but her feelings were as close to the surface as anyone's I interviewed.

'You don't even like to imagine something like this happening,' she said. She fluttered around her classroom, watering the plants while we talked. Meanwhile, I sat uncomfortably in a student chair that was much too small for me, or even half of me. 'Then one day, everything changes. I'm just glad they were taken together. At least they have each other — '

The second she said it, her hand flew up to her mouth and she burst into tears. 'Oh, my God! That's not at all what I meant. I'm so sorry!'

I handed her a tissue from the box on her desk and told her not to be too hard on herself. Every adult at the school had been questioned extensively, multiple times by MPD, the FBI, and Secret Service. The strain was starting to show. That's also when people tend to say things they might not the first several times around.

The school nurse, a guy named Rodney Glass, held it together better. He'd been in the Peace Corps in Uganda before this, he told me, and it seemed like he'd seen a lot of suffering in Africa. I'd been there and understood what he was talking about.

'Ethan? Yeah, he's my little lunch buddy,' he said. 'I think he's just more comfortable with adults, you know?'

'Did he come here very often?' I asked, looking around the small, very organized infirmary.

171

'Sometimes. Pretty much anywhere he could find a quiet corner. I call kids like him free agents. You go into any school at lunchtime, and I guarantee you'll find a few in the nurse's office, or hanging around the librarian's desk, or in guidance. Actually, you should talk to Pam Fitzhugh over there. If you haven't already. She knows both the Coyles as well as anyone.'

I was lucky to get a few minutes with Ms. Fitzhugh, as it turned out. She and the other guidance staff had been seeing kids for crisis counseling nonstop since the first day.

'Were Ethan or Zoe under any particular stress that you know about?' I asked her. 'In the days before, weeks before?'

'No more than usual,' she said. 'But that's all relative, isn't it? It's not easy being the president's children, or any celebrity's, really, and they both put a lot of pressure on themselves. In different ways.'

'Different, how?' I asked.

'Well, let's just say Zoe spends a lot of energy trying *not* to be the perfect First Daughter everyone expects her to be. And Ethan's kind of the opposite. He gets an A-minus, and all he sees is that minus.'

She laughed softly, but in a melancholy way, as if she were remembering something one of them had done at some point. Maybe also wondering, like everyone else, if she was ever going to see Ethan and Zoe again.

'Those poor kids,' she said. 'God, those poor, poor kids. I wish somebody could help them.'

Yes, so did I.

172

56

Secretary of State Martin Cho's motorcade was running behind schedule, as usual. He'd kept the House and Senate Intelligence Committee chairs waiting most of the morning, and now he was almost an hour late for the Saudi ambassador.

'Call the office, tell them we're on our way,' Cho said to the aide sitting across from him in the short Mercedes limo. Her name was Melissa Brandt. She was a recent Harvard grad and young for the job, but promising. Also maybe a little naïve.

'Mr. Secretary, they've been notified by the scheduling office already. I called them — '

'Just do it again, please, Melissa,' he said. 'Make sure the ambassador knows we're thinking of him. That's important to them. They're sensitive people. The ambassador has been pampered all his life.'

'Yes, sir,' the aide answered.

Crisis talks had been quietly taking place between the two countries for several days now. With the president indisposed, as he was, it was up to the secretary to put in the face time on this one. So far, it had been a dour affair. The pre-9/11 days of arm-in-arm policy making with the Kingdom seemed like a quaint bit of history now.

As Melissa Brandt pulled up the State Department on her phone, she craned her neck to see outside and check their progress up Constitution Avenue.

'Hi, Don, it's Missy with the secretary's office,' she said, still looking out the window. 'We should be there any minute. We're just passing by the, um — '

All at once, the young woman's pale blue eyes flew open wide.

'*Oh my God!*' she said. 'They're going to hit us! Secretary Cho, look out!'

Secretary Cho turned just in time to glimpse the grill of a white pickup before it slammed full-speed into the side of their car. A black Lincoln Navigator from the motorcade raced up to ram the intruder, a fraction of a second too late. All three vehicles came to a sudden and violent stop.

The space inside the limo's backseat seemed to fold in half. Cho felt himself thrown sideways. A searing pain tore through his chest as one of several broken ribs punctured his right lung.

'Mr. Secretary?' The head of Cho's security detail, bleeding from the forehead, scrambled to turn around from the front seat. 'Sir? Can you hear me?'

Cho could hear, but he couldn't move. The slightest shift sent a shock wave of agony through him, as the panic rose.

Even now, his eyes were on the truck outside the car. The driver was getting out of the cab. He was young — just a boy. In his hand, there was a cylinder of some kind. Silver and red. What was that?

'Sir?' the agent tried again. 'Sir, can you hear me?'

Cho's mouth flapped open and then closed immediately. Air was supposed to fill his lungs, but it didn't. Words were supposed to come out, but there were none. There was only the thought, screaming through his brain.

Bomb! He's got a bomb! That boy —

Because the secretary knew enough to have recognized the thing in the boy's hand just before he turned to run away. It was a detonator.

The blast ripped through all three vehicles when it went off. Drivers in the nearest cars saw a white-hot flash, then a much larger orange fireball, before the whole thing coalesced into a rolling cloud of charcoal gray smoke. Glass gravel peppered the area. Chunks of metal rained down onto the pavement, some of them still in flames.

It was all followed by a much softer shower, of leaves and small branches from the trees lining the avenue, before everything went oddly, eerily still once again.

57

'Tariq, come and look! hurry in here. You have to see this.'

Hala was glued to the television. It was a ridiculous business, this nonstop diarrhea of news, but it had its advantages. Within minutes of the deadly car bombing on Constitution Avenue, she had a front-row seat at the spectacle.

There was no word on victims yet. Still, the sight of the burned-out limousine was all she needed to know that the assignment had come off flawlessly. Secretary of State Martin Cho, one of the primary architects of American foreign policy, had been taken out — right here on American soil, here in the capital city.

It was a stunning blow for justice and retribution. Tonight there would be dancing in the streets of Riyadh. And there could be much more to celebrate soon.

Tariq came in from the bedroom and stood behind the couch, watching.

'*We are coming to you live from Washington, DC, where a possible terrorist attack has just taken place moments ago . . .* '

'Where is that?' Tariq asked. 'Is it close to our hotel?'

'Not far,' she said. It was tempting to walk over and have a look for herself, but that was an unnecessary risk. Police would surely be filming the crowds.

She scrubbed her hair dry with a towel as they watched. The color hadn't changed much — a little more toward brown — but it was much shorter now. For better or worse, she was starting to look like an American.

Tariq put his hands gently on her shoulders. 'You did it, Hala. You are the one responsible.'

'Not me,' she said. 'The Family did this.'

She knew that it was vanity to focus on her own role. It was wrong to be seen taking too much pleasure in the accomplishment. But even so, the images on the television filled her with an indescribable sense of pride. One of the worst devils in America was dead because she alone had decided that he should go first. When Hala reached up and pulled Tariq closer, he stiffened at first. She'd forbidden any intimacy since they'd come to the States. It was a distraction, she'd told him. One they couldn't afford.

But as they both knew, Hala was in charge in America.

'Kiss me,' she said then. 'Right now. Here.'

Tariq needed no second invitation. He leaned down and kissed her neck softly — but not too softly. His hands were moving on their own now, across her face, her soft breasts. One might not have guessed it to look at him, but Hala's husband knew exactly how to pleasure a woman.

Her heartbeat quickened as he came around the couch to face her.

'I love you, Hala,' he said. 'So much. I'm so proud of you.'

'I love you, too,' she said. And she did.

He knelt down on the carpet and parted the

fabric of her white hotel robe. He kissed her thigh. Hala breathed deeply, allowing the pleasure to rise up inside her.

'... what we can tell you is that this attack was on an official government motorcade, but as to who was inside those vehicles ...'

When Tariq reached for the television remote, she put out her hand to stop him.

'No,' she said. 'Leave it. Let it play.'

She kept her fingers in his hair and her eyes on the screen, while Tariq's hands and mouth found somewhere else to be. And for just a little while, Hala felt more at peace than she'd ever known it was possible for a woman to feel.

58

The minute that word of the bombing came in, a special team of Secret Service agents left their command post, officially known as W-16. From the long rectangular room, they ascended a single flight of stairs and, without knocking, entered the Oval Office directly above.

'What is it now?' the president asked, standing up as they came in.

'Sir, please come with us,' the shift supervisor said. He and a second agent crossed behind the office's famous Resolute desk and did something neither had ever done before. They laid their hands on the commander in chief to move him forcibly from the room.

The president's secretary rose to her feet as they passed through reception. 'What's going on? What's happened now?'

'Stay where you are,' a third agent told her, then ran ahead to clear the way. Word had already begun to circulate through the West Wing. The building was going into lockdown. Nobody was allowed in or out. Except, of course, for the president and First Lady.

'Command, Torchwood is on the move,' the agent radioed ahead.

'Tucson as well,' a voice came back. A separate protective detail was simultaneously escorting Mrs. Coyle down from the residence. 'We're proceeding to the South Lawn.'

'Would somebody please tell me what's happening!' the president ordered anyone who would listen.

'There's been an incident, sir. I don't know the details. You'll be briefed on *Marine One*' was all the lead agent would — or maybe could — tell him.

The tight scrum moved without stopping, back down to ground level, where they crossed into the White House and then out again, through the door obscured under the South Portico stairs.

Outside, it was obvious that the entire White House Complex had been shut down. Armed Capitol Police officers were lined up along Executive Avenue on either side, and there was no dress blue marine to meet them as the Sea King white-top helicopter descended onto the lawn.

As soon as it touched down, the chopper's front hatchway opened. The stairs were lowered to the ground.

Only then was the president escorted the rest of the way across the grass, at the center of a fast-moving ten-man human shield.

Two passengers were already waiting on board — another breach of protocol. FBI Director Burns and the president's counterterrorism adviser, Norma Tiefel, stood up as Coyle came into the main cabin.

Mrs. Coyle boarded with her escort just a few seconds behind the president, and they all took their seats.

Four of the Secret Service detail stayed with

them. Once the hatch had closed and *Marine One* was on its way, they continued to the rear cabin, leaving the president with his advisers.

'Tell me what's happened, Ron,' the president commanded Director Burns. 'Tell me everything, right now.' Regina sat next to him, clutching his hand. How much were they capable of taking at this point?

'Sir, I'm sorry to tell you that Secretary Cho and three of his staff were just killed in an explosion.'

'Oh my God. Martin Cho.'

'An attack on his motorcade, to be precise,' Burns went on. 'Presumably Al Ayla, but we can't say for sure. However, it is consistent with one particular stream of intelligence we've received.'

'What do you mean? What kind of intelligence?' the president asked.

'An inside informant, sir. We don't know if she's an operative with the organization, or somewhere on the sidelines, but her intel is good, as it turns out.'

'Her?' the president asked.

Burns nodded. 'Up until now, it's been one of a thousand possibilities. We've had claims from Al Qaeda, Hezbollah, and everything on down.'

'What about the children?' Mrs. Coyle asked. 'Did this woman — this informant — say anything about Ethan and Zoe?'

'I'm sorry, ma'am, but no,' Burns told her. 'What we received was a list of targets. Something that, quite honestly, sounded improbable until about fifteen minutes ago.'

'Go on,' Coyle told him. 'What kind of targets are we talking about here?'

'All human, sir,' Burns said. 'It's a list of eighteen names. Vice President Flynn is at the top, with Secretary Ribillini from Homeland Security at number eighteen.'

'Oh, Jesus.' Coyle had heard everything he needed to know. 'Tell me Martin Cho wasn't on that list.'

'I'm afraid so. Right below the Speaker of the House and the president pro tempore of the Senate.'

'So in other words . . . ,' the president said slowly.

'That's right, sir,' Burns affirmed. 'We're talking about the entire line of succession to the presidency.'

59

Norma Tiefel, the counterterrorism adviser, spoke next. 'Everyone on that list will be receiving a full protective detail in addition to whatever security service they already have. That means dedicated intelligence agents, CAT teams on standby, also advance and transportation. Although we're hoping to keep travel to a minimum.'

'They can't shut down our goddamn government!' the president shouted at Tiefel. 'That's exactly what they want! And exactly why I came back to Washington. Do you know what kind of flak they gave Bush for being in the air on Nine/Eleven?'

'That wasn't his call, sir. I'm aware it wasn't his fault,' Tiefel said as diplomatically as she could.

'Yes, exactly. I'm sure it wasn't his fault,' Coyle said. It was all this programmed movement he hated. The sense of traveling through the world not as one person, but as five, six, ten, and twenty at a time. *That* was the real weight of the presidency.

'For the time being, sir,' Tiefel said, 'it is best for you to keep out of sight.'

'*Again*,' the president grumbled, and turned in his seat, away from all the unwanted advice. 'Archie, where are we going?' he called back.

Agent Walsh, the head of the president's

protective detail, stood up in the small passageway between them and the pilot.

'Andrews, sir. *Air Force One* is on standby.'

'And then?'

Walsh stayed where he was but was mute, awkwardly not answering the question. It wasn't for Burns's or Tiefel's ears at this point.

'*Never mind, goddamnit*,' the president barked. He could feel Regina's hand on his own, gentle and firm at the same time. When he looked at her, she seemed to be holding it all together by a sheer act of will. He owed her the same self-control. Actually he owed it to his advisers as well. They were in danger now, too.

'What about Cho's family?' he asked.

'We've got agents on the ground in Bethesda and Oakland,' Burns told him. 'They'll have a full security detail within the hour — Mrs. Cho, both of their sons, and Secretary Cho's mother.'

'I'll want to speak with Lottie directly.'

'Of course, sir. We'll also have the Joint Chiefs in a video conference once we're away,' Tiefel said. 'And after that, the same CIA work group as before, if you care to sit in. It might be a good idea.'

'Of course it's a good idea,' said the president.

'That's the group with Alex Cross, isn't it?' Mrs. Coyle asked.

'Yes, ma'am.' Burns anticipated her next question. 'He won't be asked to change focus.'

'Good,' she said. 'Thank you.' It was no secret by now that the First Lady had handpicked the well-known police detective for the kidnap

184

investigation. Nobody was going to tell her *no* on that one.

'The world's watching us, Ron,' the president said. 'Especially our country's enemies. We need to get this in hand, once and for all. I want hourly reports, and I want a briefing on a full range of options. Do you understand?'

'Yes, Mr. President. Completely. We all do.'

'I *mean* a full range.'

'Of course, sir.'

'I'm not going to fuck around with this anymore.'

'Ed — ' The First Lady slid a hand up her husband's arm.

'Sorry,' he said. '*Sorry*. But this ends here. *Now*. Whatever it takes.'

The president sat back. Out the window, he could see one of four other identical choppers flying alongside, a standard protocol to reduce the risks from a possible ground attack. *Anything* seemed possible right now. Their departure from the White House had gone smoothly enough. Now the convoy headed southeast, toward Andrews, eleven miles away.

After that, Edward O. Coyle, the most powerful man in the world, had no idea what to expect. Hell, he could be dead in the next few minutes. The unthinkable was no longer unthinkable.

60

CIA headquarters was lit up like a fluorescent box when I got there late that night. The powers that be had decided to share what they knew with our de facto advisory board. What they told us was a mindblower. An unnamed informant was claiming the entire line of succession to the presidency as Al Ayla's new target list.

Secretary of State Cho's murder was a testimony to how seriously we needed to take this new threat.

The symbolism of the day's attack was devastating to all of us. Not only did Cho represent the United States to the world, but Al Ayla was clearly using this incident as their foray onto the international stage. Statements claiming responsibility had come in through Al Jazeera, indicating the organization by name for the first time. Every news outlet from Jakarta to Madison, Wisconsin, had picked up the story.

Al Ayla, it seemed, was ready for its close-up. What was worse — so far they were winning.

'Today, they got us by surprise,' Evan Stroud told the assembled two dozen people at headquarters. 'That's not going to happen again. Not to anyone on that wish list of theirs.'

'Is there any thought about leaking back that we've got this informant?' one of the Bureau ADs asked. 'Maybe to put a wedge inside the organization? Do a little dividing and conquering?'

'I'm afraid they're already dividing.' Andrew Fatany, the analyst based in Saudi Arabia, stood up to speak. It was Fatany who had done most of the talking so far that night, breaking down what they knew about Al Ayla from the Riyadh office.

'These newer organizations are more adaptable and flexible than anything we've seen before,' he told us. 'It's entirely possible — I'd say probable — that Al Ayla's already handed off some measure of control to their Washington operatives. The faster they can create these self-directed cells, the harder it is to penetrate the larger organization. In fact, it may already be too late.'

'Too late for what?' I asked Fatany.

'To ever know who Al Ayla really is. Our best recommendation is to focus on finding the local leadership, and of course whoever they're talking to. But we have to move carefully. If we take out an individual cell, it's like tearing the limb off a starfish. The organization simply moves on and grows another limb.'

'Hang on a second,' Peter Lindley interjected. 'Are you saying we shouldn't bring down these people — because if they stay on the loose they *might* lead us up the ladder? I don't think I can live with that. And I don't think the president can, either.'

Fatany blinked back his frustration. He was sick and tired, just like everyone else. 'I'm saying, and excuse me for stating the obvious, that you need to be aware of what you're losing when you *do* bring them down.'

One of the flat-topped NSA guys grunted out his own annoyance. 'I say we find the sons of bitches and interrogate the shit out of them,' he said. 'Use the Patriot Act, send their asses to Egypt if we have to. Our priority should be saving American lives. It's that simple. At least it should be.'

Fatany put his hands up. He'd made Riyadh's opinion clear on the matter. The decision about what to do with it wasn't up to him.

'We'll take all of this under advisement with the president,' Stroud said, trying to cut through the tension. Not that anyone could right now. This crisis was a fire that had to be put out. Period. Anything short of that was no option at all.

Meanwhile, the fire raged on, and it almost seemed out of control.

61

Ned Mahoney and I trudged out of CIA headquarters around two o'clock that morning. I felt like we were leaving a cocoon, which we kind of were, but not a warm and cozy one. The president had come on the line at midnight, ten hours after the bombing of Cho's motorcade. In the morning, he'd make an emotional national address, condemning the attack and calling on America to remember the victims for everything they'd stood for against murderers exactly like these.

'I think I liked it better when I was out of the loop,' I said. It was hard not to feel overwhelmed. My intention was to be back at Branaff as soon as possible, but there were a lot of other places I felt like I could and probably should be.

Surveillance was about to make a quantum leap in DC. Government affidavits were being written through the night, and several new Title III warrants were expected to go through as early as the following afternoon. That meant listening teams in all kinds of places they hadn't been before — more mosques, more online networks, more phone lines, all of it. The personnel demands alone were going to be unprecedented.

'Where are you going to be?' I asked Ned.

'Quantico. *Unless* Hostage and Rescue has to move,' he said. 'But I'll be putting in some

189

surveillance time, too. Your phone going to be on?'

'Only at lunch and study hall,' I deadpanned.

'I'll call you if there's anything to tell,' he said.

'Okay. I'll do the same.'

We hadn't talked about it specifically, but Ned and I seemed to have fallen into an agreement. I'd have his back on this, and he'd have mine. Before we got to the parking lot, he stopped and put a hand on my shoulder.

'It's good to be on the same side,' he said. 'I know I pissed you off for a while there, but it won't happen again. That's a promise.'

'Is this where we cut open our thumbs and shake?' I said. 'Triple-dog swear, or whatever?'

Ned didn't miss a beat. 'I'll pass,' he said. 'I don't know where that thumb's been.' He grinned at me before he turned and started across the lawn toward his car. 'But I will return your calls from now on.'

62

The kidnapper always carried the little tape recorder with him on these pleasant hikes through the woods. You never knew when inspiration was going to strike, and it was good to capture the details when they were fresh.

Record.

'The first mile or so is just a little hilly. I can cover that stretch fast enough. Eventually, it starts to get pretty steep, up toward the ridge. That's where I lose a little time, but I'm getting better at the climb.

'Theoretically, I could drive in from the other side, but that's only going to happen once. By the time you're done reading this, you'll understand why.

'Meanwhile, I hike in the long way. Hell, maybe I'll even lose some weight in the bargain. You can appreciate the efficiency in that, can't you?'

Stop.

The book was coming along well. It was practically writing itself these days. Anyone with a pulse could tell you this was a huge story. Even bigger than he'd thought it was going to be at first. Interesting times, these.

He pocketed the recorder again and traded it for the recurve bow on his shoulder. The ground was getting scrubbier. It didn't usually take long to spook something around here. He loaded an arrow while he walked and started kicking at the bushes, watching for prey, any movement at all.

Sure enough, just past the crest of the first hill, an eastern cottontail darted out.

It came right at him, God bless its tiny little brain, but then turned and bolted off in the other direction.

He let it get a good head start. Anything less than twenty yards was just fish in a barrel.

But then he raised the bow, drew back to the corner of his mouth, and let it fly.

The cottontail stumbled hard, ass over whiskers. It came to a stop in some tall grass and was still quivering when he got there. A quick snap of the neck finished it off. It took only a minute after that to truss it up with some twine, and he was moving again.

Going faster now, he jogged down the next slope and across a small ravine.

It took another twenty minutes to climb back up to the other side, where he stopped just before a line of giant spruce growing along the ridge.

Record.

'You'd never know it to look at these trees now, but they probably marked a property line at some point. Back when this was dairy country and not woods. Now it's just our own little home away from home. It can't compete with the White House, of course, but lucky for me, it doesn't have to.'

Stop.

He stood among the trees for several minutes, scanning the area down below.

After he'd satisfied himself that it was safe to move out into the open, he broke through the line of evergreens and started down into the hollow, where the old farmstead sat moldering away to nothing.

63

The fencing was long gone. The whole back half of the old house was sagging right into itself, almost like it was taking a final bow. And the driveway — what used to be the driveway — was just a long patch of goldenrod and buckthorn, with two ruts in the ground you couldn't even see from a distance.

The barn was still standing, though. More or less. Thick brush and vines had made the back of the place nearly impenetrable. In front, someone had torn off the big double doors a long time ago, and the flap to the hayloft above that. With a few pieces of missing siding near the peak, the whole thing looked like a face with black gaps for orifices. He always thought of the entrance as the mouth.

Just inside, he untrussed the fat little rabbit and let it roll out onto the floor, right next to the last one. From his pack, he took a plastic travel container of granular lye and a small Poland Spring bottle he'd filled from the tap at home. He sprinkled both over the animal. The lye sped up the breakdown of tissue, and the water sped up the lye. It was an old farm trick, and a half-decent little insurance policy, too. Nothing said *keep walking* like a goopy carcass in your path.

Not that anyone ever came back this far anymore — but just in case.

At the back of the barn, in the last stall, he moved aside the stack of rotting wooden pallets and lifted the layers of moldy cardboard away.

There was no handle on the trapdoor anymore, but just enough gap in the floorboards to get a grip. He raised the flap and let it rest against the stall wall. Then he climbed down the ladder inside.

The root cellar — if that's what it had been — was no more than six by six in the antechamber, and then maybe twice that on the other side of the door.

There was just enough light from above to show him the sliding panel he'd installed a long time ago. He opened it now and dropped in the granola bars and the juice boxes.

Neither of the two inside spoke to him. They'd stopped trying after the first few days. But he heard one of them stir, and a soft scrabble across the floor.

Then, 'Ethan? Ethan, here.'

There was the crinkle of plastic wrappers, and the sound of them gobbling down the food. If they'd figured out what was in the juice by now, they didn't much care.

He sat crouched with his back against the door, listening. It never took too long once the juice was gone. Their breathing slowed and became regular. Within a few minutes, they were both out cold.

Record.

'Everyone's going to want to know what I was thinking. They're going to wonder what kind of monster could do something like this, and they're going to make a lot of assumptions.

'But maybe — just maybe — this is all for a reason that you can't see right now. Did that ever cross your mind?

'I know that Ethan and Zoe don't deserve their fate, but then again, neither did I. You think I wouldn't rather be somewhere else right now, with nothing to say? I only *wish* I was that lucky.

'So, here it is. If you want to know what I'm thinking while I'm doing this, I'll tell you. The answer's simple. I'm thinking about my son. My love.

'What are *you* thinking about?'

Stop.

64

Ryan Townsend was a fidgety kid. Not that I could really blame him. He had a police detective staring him down from one side, and his parents from the other. His feet never stopped swinging, back and forth, the whole time we talked.

It had taken half a dozen phone calls, but Congressman and Mrs. Townsend had finally given me some time to speak with their son. All on their terms, of course. We met on Saturday, eight thirty a.m., at their sprawling mansard-roofed house on Thirtieth Street in Georgetown.

'This shouldn't take too long,' I told Ryan up front. 'I've read everything you told the FBI agents already. Most of it's about the fight between you and Zoe on the morning of the kidnapping — '

'It wasn't a fight,' the congressman cut me off. He and his wife were both perched on a clawfoot settee across from me. 'With all due respect, Zoe hit Ryan with a book and bloodied his nose. Let's just be clear about that.'

Ryan sank lower in his chair. His bare feet scuffed the walnut floorboards a little faster.

'Fair enough,' I said. 'Ryan, what I'd really like to know is how things got so bad between you and Zoe to begin with.'

'Is that even relevant?' Mrs. Townsend asked.

'Surely you're not suggesting Ryan had anything to do with this.'

'Nothing like that,' I said. 'I'm just trying to learn as much about Ethan and Zoe as I can. I think your son might have a unique perspective.'

This was why I wanted to meet with Ryan alone, but that issue had been a nonstarter with his parents. They had every right to sit in, and every intention of doing so.

'Go ahead, Ryan,' his father told him. 'We've got nothing to hide here. You can answer the question.'

Ryan took a deep breath and puffed out his cheeks. 'Zoe started it,' he said. 'We were on this field trip to the Air and Space Museum last year, and I left my phone on the bus. Then she gets this stupid text from me — I mean, not from me. From my phone. And she just freaked.'

'Sweetie, don't say 'freaked.'' Mrs. Townsend gave me a quick self-conscious smile. Ryan rolled his eyes. The congressman checked his Black-Berry.

'Anyway, she got all in my face about it and didn't believe me when I said I didn't do it. So I said fine. Let her believe it. Ever since then, she's just kind of had it in for me.'

I wasn't convinced I was getting the whole story, but more than that, I just wanted to hear Ryan tell it. His words, his memory of the details.

'Do you know what was in that text?' I asked.

'I didn't send it,' he said right away. 'I swear!'

'That's fine. I just need to hear what happened,' I said. 'From you.'

'Ryan, answer the detective's question. Do you know what was in the text or not?' the congressman asked.

For the first time, Ryan was looking me right in the eye. He wound the drawstring of a crimson Branaff School hoodie around one finger, then unwound it. Then he wound it up again.

Finally, he said, 'Do you think they're dead?'

'Ryan!' His mother looked horrified. 'That's a terrible thing to say.'

I think he was just trying to change the subject, but I answered him anyway. 'I hope not,' I said. Then I tore a page out of my notebook and slid it across the table. 'How about if you write down what was in that text, and we'll call it a morning?'

Ryan twisted around in his chair to look at his father again. The congressman nodded, and I set my pen down for him. He cupped his hand around the page while he wrote something, then turned it over and weighted it under an antique snow globe on the coffee table. For a few seconds, some glittery snow flew around the miniature Victorian house inside.

'Can I go now?' he asked.

'You can go. Thank you, Ryan. That was helpful.'

I waited for him to leave the room. Then I turned the paper over where his parents and I could see it. In a ragged, kid's handwriting, it said, 'Zoe C — I want 2 cum on yr tits.'

'Oh my God.' Mrs. Townsend looked away. 'That is absolutely disgusting.'

The congressman took the paper off the table and pocketed it before there could be any question of my keeping it. 'We're going to speak with Headmaster Skillings about this — independent of anything else,' he said.

I could understand their embarrassment, but the profanity seemed like typical middle school bravado to me. Sad, but true. It was just the kind of thing a boy might write to impress his friends, sometime after the hormones started kicking in and before he really understood what it all meant. In any case, I thanked the Townsends for their time and quietly let myself out of the house.

When I got back to the car, I scribbled a single note to myself for later:

'*Where is Zoe's phone?*'

65

I spent most of that day crisscrossing the city, interviewing other Branaff students who knew either Zoe or Ethan and socialized with them. Then late in the afternoon, I drove up to Riverdale, Maryland, for one last stop. This one was unannounced.

George O'Shea lived on a corner lot in a gridded, middleclass neighborhood just off the East-West Highway.

I parked under the basketball hoop on his freshly black-topped driveway and went up to ring the bell.

He was smoking a cigar when he answered the door. At Branaff, O'Shea's custodial uniform was always clean and pressed, but here he was wearing an old flannel shirt, open halfway down his chest. I could hear a game on the TV somewhere behind him.

'It's Detective Cross, right?' he said, squinting at me through the fly-specked screen.

'Sorry to come by on a Saturday,' I said. 'We're working around the clock on this. Just a few follow-up questions if you don't mind.'

For a brief second, he looked like he *did* mind, like he wasn't entirely sure I was giving him the whole story. And I wasn't.

Ever since I'd met O'Shea, my mind kept coming back to him. It wasn't anything I could put my finger on. Just a vague sense that behind all the smiles and the interest in police work, there was something he wasn't saying. It was only a hunch at this point, but I've taken action on less than that before.

'How's it going, anyway?' he asked. 'Any good leads, or whatever you call it?'

'Nothing I can really talk about,' I said.

He nodded and rocked back on his heels. 'Right. I understand. Still, it must be interesting work, huh?'

I watched him through the door. *What was he thinking about right now?*

'Do you mind if I come in?' I asked.

'Oh — yeah. Of course,' he said, like it hadn't occurred to him. 'I was just ruining a pot of coffee. You want some?'

'No thanks. I'll try to be quick here.'

He thumbed over his shoulder as I came in. 'Let me just switch off the machine. Make yourself comfortable.'

I hung back and looked around as he headed toward the kitchen.

'Must be a real drag working on the weekend,' he called back. 'That's the one thing about my job. At least I've got a nice regular schedule.'

'Uh-huh,' I said, fingering through his mail. It was out on an end table, mostly bills, mostly unopened. A dusty collection of salt and pepper shakers sat in a curio cabinet on the wall. 'Speaking of schedules, do you keep records of the custodial staff's time at the school?' I asked.

O'Shea didn't answer. An announcer on the TV hooted out his approval for a double play that had just gone down. And I knew right then that something was wrong.

'*George?*'

When I got to the kitchen, it was empty. No George anywhere. The back door was wide open, and I could see O'Shea out on the lawn, scrambling over his chain-link fence toward the street.

The son of a bitch was making a run for it.

66

There is nothing that pisses me off like a footrace I don't want. When I ran out of George O'Shea's house a half second later, I think I bent his screen door right off the frame.

O'Shea was a big guy. The kids at Branaff called him Hagrid behind his back. But he was a lot faster than he looked. By the time I was out on the street sprinting after him, he was halfway up the block. Clearly he had a good reason to run.

'Don't do this, George!'

A guy raking his leaves had already taken out his phone when I passed. 'Call the police!' I yelled at him. I noticed he took my picture first.

Two kids on the sidewalk screamed at me and pedaled their Big Wheels like crazy, trying to keep up.

The top of the block ended in a cul-de-sac. O'Shea cut between two of the houses and kept going.

When I caught sight of him again, he was trying to scale a tall cedar fence in somebody's backyard. He had to jump a couple times before he got a grip on the top of it and started pulling himself up.

Then the plank in his hand cracked. He slipped back down a few feet — and that's when I caught up with him.

I got hold of his ankle before he could muscle

all the way over, and I pulled him right off the top of the fence.

That brought him down fast — but he took me down with him, too.

And he wasn't done yet.

My cuffs were out, just as O'Shea popped up onto one knee and elbowed me hard under the chin. My head snapped back. I tasted blood. In fact, it was probably the blood that helped me add a little speed and leverage to the right hook I gave him in return. That was enough to knock him back on his ass again.

This time I took out my Glock.

'Roll over, facedown! Hands on your head!' I told him.

He seemed half out of his mind. Even now, he started up at me again, but only until he saw the gun a few inches from his face.

'Don't, George. Please — *don't*,' I said.

It was like all the fight drained out of him at once. Even his face dropped, and he just melted back down to the ground.

When I put the cuffs on him, he started to cry.

'What have I done?' he kept saying over and over. 'Oh God, what have I done?'

That was my question exactly.

67

The backtracking and denials started in my car and continued over the next several hours.

O'Shea was taken directly into FBI custody. I drove him in myself, right through the sally port at the side entrance to the Washington field office.

From there, it's a straight shot back to the interview rooms on the ground floor. Word was kept tight. There would be no announcement of the arrest yet. Not until we knew more from O'Shea.

A forensic unit was dispatched to his house in Riverdale. Another one went to his office at Branaff, to see what they could turn up. There was no question that O'Shea was hiding something. It was only a matter of finding out what it was.

Around seven o'clock, we got word back from the team out in Riverdale. A Dell laptop had been found in O'Shea's master bedroom closet. It was loaded with pornographic images, most of them involving children. George O'Shea seemed to have a thing going for little girls, kids as young as three and four.

It was stomach-turning stuff, but as a piece of evidence, this was more than enough to hold him. By the time Peter Lindley arrived, straight from LX1 in Langley, adrenaline was running high in the observation room.

'What have we got here?' he said, taking a file from one of the assistant special agents in charge.

'George O'Shea,' the ASAC told him. 'He's the head of maintenance at the Branaff School — '

'I know who he is, for God's sake. What have we *got?*' Lindley said. He seemed to be in his usual bad mood. Several other agents stepped out of the way to make a space for him at the one-way glass.

On the other side, O'Shea was sitting with the Bureau supervisor from the Child Abduction Unit, Ken Mugatande. They'd been talking for two hours straight now.

O'Shea was slumped forward, with his head resting on his clenched fists.

'He's ready to admit the porn's his,' I told Lindley. 'But he swears up and down that he doesn't know anything about Ethan and Zoe's disappearance.'

'He's begging for a polygraph,' the ASAC said.

Lindley turned and glared at the agent. 'This is the guy whose office is twenty-five feet from that tunnel under the school?' Nobody answered. It was a rhetorical question. 'So what the hell are we doing here? Let's get him down to the polygraph room — *now!*'

68

The Field Office's polygraph room looks a lot like the other interview rooms — small table, two chairs, plain white walls, and a big one-way mirror. If anything, the observation space is smaller. A dozen of us squeezed in there to watch the interview.

'What is your name?'

'George Luther O'Shea.'

'What is your address?'

'It's 1109 Edgewood Road, Riverdale, Maryland.'

O'Shea had asked for this, but he looked even more miserable than before. He was wired up with pneumographs around his chest and abdomen, a blood pressure cuff on his arm, and two finger clips, all feeding into a laptop on the table.

The polygrapher was Sue Pilgrim, a forensic psychologist out of the Hoover Building.

Sue sat at a right angle to O'Shea and just behind him, where he couldn't see her during the test. Her first several questions were a standard opening battery, mostly lie-proof stuff like name and address, to establish a baseline. After that, she moved on to the meat of the interview.

'Have you ever knowingly downloaded a pornographic image of a child to your own computer?' Pilgrim asked.

'Yeah,' O'Shea said, after a shaky sigh.

'Have you ever knowingly uploaded a pornographic image of a child from your computer to the Internet?'

'No,' he said.

Both times, Agent Pilgrim nodded. As far as she and her machine were concerned, he'd just told the truth.

Then she asked, 'Have you ever conspired with any group or individual from another country to commit an illegal act here in the United States?'

'*What?*' O'Shea swiveled on his seat to look at her. 'What in God's name are you talking about?'

She was talking about Al Ayla. This was the other possibility we had to confront. O'Shea could have had some tie to The Family, if they were in fact behind the kidnapping. Maybe he was their contact at the school. Maybe they had paid him off to be their 'inside' person.

Agent Pilgrim responded to the outburst with quiet professionalism. 'George, I just need you to answer the questions as simply as possible. Do you want to take a break before we go on?'

'No,' he said, turning back around to face front. 'I just . . . I don't understand where you're going with this. What do you mean . . . contact with other countries?'

'I'll ask again,' she said, and repeated her question verbatim. This time, O'Shea answered with a simple no, and again, Pilgrim nodded.

Next, she opened a file and set an eight-by-ten photo on the table in front of him.

It was a mug shot of Ray Pinkney, the

drugged-out van driver from the morning of the kidnapping.

'Do you recognize this man?' Pilgrim asked.

I watched O'Shea's face as he looked at the photo. There was no lateral movement in his eyes, no physical signs of evasion or lying that I could see at all.

'I've never seen him before in my life,' he said.

'Do you know where Zoe Coyle is right now?' Pilgrim asked.

'No,' he said.

'Do you know where Ethan Coyle is right now?'

'*No!*'

Every one of his answers got a nod from Agent Pilgrim. It was starting to add up.

It's not that polygraphs are foolproof. They're a guide, and nothing more than that. But even so, we seemed to be heading toward an unwanted conclusion here. You could feel it in the room.

George O'Shea wasn't our guy. He didn't have anything to do with the kidnapping.

69

They were just finishing up with the polygraph when I got an unexpected phone call. There weren't many people who could have pulled me out of that room just then, but here was one of them.

'Detective Cross, it's Nina Friedman from the White House. Could you please hold for the First Lady?'

Just like that — a direct call from Regina Coyle. Sure. Happens every day. Of course I could hold for the First Lady.

I stepped out and into one of the empty interview rooms. Just as I was pulling the door closed behind me, Mrs. Coyle came on the line.

'What can I do for you, ma'am?' I asked.

'I'm wondering what you can tell me about this George O'Shea person,' she said.

The question caught me off guard. I wasn't completely surprised that she'd already gotten word on O'Shea, but still, this put me in a tight spot.

'Excuse me for asking, Mrs. Coyle, but how much do you already know?' I said.

'I know who he is. I know that he's been arrested. And I know the reason why. What I'd like to know is what *you* think of him.'

'I can tell you he just passed a polygraph test,' I told her. 'But that's not impossible to fake. I've seen it happen before.'

'Yes, but what do you *think*, Alex? You're my eyes and ears on this. I'm not looking for absolutes,' she said. 'Just . . . anything to give us hope.'

The more I knew Mrs. Coyle, the more I found myself relating to her, parent to parent. I probably said more than I should have.

'I don't think he knows where Ethan and Zoe are. I'm sorry.'

'I see,' she said.

There was a long, silent moment on the phone. I could hear people out in the hall, leaving the observation room. Presumably O'Shea would be transferred to the U.S. marshals' custody and taken to the arraignment courts from here. Then over to the central cell block after that. The pornography charge alone would put him in jail.

'Mrs. Coyle?' I said.

'I'm still here.'

'As long as I have you, I'd like to ask a question about the morning of the kidnapping. If it's all right.'

'Of course,' she said. I think any distraction from the disappointing news was welcome at this point.

'Do you know if Zoe brought her phone to school that morning?' I asked.

'Her phone?'

'There's been some talk among the kids about a texting incident last year. Involving Zoe. I just wondered if — '

'Zoe doesn't have a phone,' Mrs. Coyle said. 'Not as far as I know. Even if Secret Service

212

would allow it, her father and I wouldn't. And believe me, we've had our battles about this one.'

My mind started turning over everything I'd heard that day. Everything I'd learned about Ethan and Zoe from the beginning.

'Is it possible she could have gotten a phone on her own? Something she kept secret?' I asked.

'Of course. This is Zoe we're talking about,' she said. 'She knows how to get what she wants. Honestly, everyone likes to talk about how brilliant Ethan is, but if you ask me, my daughter's the one with a future in politics.'

I liked that word right now. *Future*. It was a good thing to keep in mind.

'I trust you're going to look into this,' Mrs. Coyle said.

'Absolutely,' I told her. 'I already am.'

70

At eleven fifteen that saturday night, Ned Mahoney and a handpicked team of HRT agents set out from the MPD Third District Heliport in an unmarked FBI van. Mahoney preferred to run his ops in daylight — ultimately at dawn. But this detail was what it was and it had to happen now.

His order had come in to Quantico ninety minutes ago. The arrest plan described four suspects, all Saudi, holed up at a motel just south of Silver Spring, Maryland. Presumably they were Al Ayla, but there was nothing about that in the fax Mahoney had received.

He rode shotgun and looked over the motel diagram as they drove north, at full speed, through the city.

The motel room, number 122, was fairly straightforward: large bedroom, alcove, closet, bathroom. The only way in or out was the door at the front, accessible directly from the parking lot. The FBI entry team would be small, just four agents.

'Command, this is Red Team. We're on Sixteenth, heading north,' Mahoney radioed over to the command center, set up at an old taxi dispatch a few blocks from the target. 'What's the visual you have on the motel?'

'Copy that, Red Team,' the unit commander came back. 'We're all go on this end. It looks like

214

everyone's tucked in for the night.'

Advance had already come through and quietly cleared guests out of all the adjacent rooms. SWAT had the perimeter held down, with tactical teams on three different rooftops around the motel. MPD and emergency services were both on standby.

HRT would go in first, as always.

Once the van came into range, Mahoney flipped his goggles down. He gave a thumbs-up to the three agents in back, who flashed the same sign. Samuels, Totten, and Behrenberg were all good to go. The unit was outfitted in full battle uniform — black Nomex flight suits, load-bearing vests, Kevlar helmets, and MP5s. It was heavy gear, enough to slow you down, but the adrenaline would more than compensate.

Before the vehicle even came to a stop, the doors were open and they were out. The team hit the ground running in a single-file beeline for Room 122.

'This is Red Team,' Mahoney radioed on the fly. 'We're going in!'

This had to be Al Ayla.

71

'FBI! open UP!' Mahoney shouted.

At the same time, a forty-pound battering ram took out the motel room door in one swing. That was the extent of their 'knock and announce.'

Before Mahoney was even inside, he saw the bathroom door slam closed at the far end of the otherwise empty room. He went for it, with Samuels at his back.

Totten and Behrenberg fanned out, checking the beds, the closet, the pile of luggage in the corner. A string of white laundry was suspended across the alcove. These people had been living here for a while.

Mahoney's boot heel was all he needed to obliterate the cheap bathroom lock. The door flew open and he found them there, all four, cowering inside.

It looked a hell of a lot like a family to him. There was a mother, father, and two teenaged boys. The parents barricaded the younger two with their bodies, while the boys squatted in the tub.

All four of them had trickles of blood running down their chins. Oh, Jesus God!

'Hands! Show me your hands!' Mahoney screamed, waving his MP5 in their faces. Samuels repeated the order in Arabic, but nobody moved. They clutched at one another, watching with dark eyes that were wide, but not

216

scared. These people were ready to die.

'Command, this is Red Team. We've found all four suspects in the bathroom. I can't say for sure, but I think they just downed suicide capsules. Cyanide, probably. Requesting immediate medical assistance.'

'We need these people alive,' the unit commander came back.

No shit, Mahoney thought. The whole operation was worth only as much as the intel it uncovered. He motioned Samuels farther inside. 'See if you can get some vitals.'

The mother and one of the boys started to convulse first. When Samuels tried to reach them, the other two scrambled over to get in his way. All four were wheezing badly, as if their breath was coming through the tiniest of straws.

'Where are the damn EMTs?' Mahoney radioed.

But then Totten called out from the other room.

'Hold that thought, boss,' he said. 'We've got another problem.'

Mahoney turned around to see Totten on his stomach, looking at something under one of the beds.

'I've got eyeballs on some kind of gray brick,' he said. 'Looks wired. I think we need to get the hell out of here pronto!'

Mahoney didn't wait. 'Totten, Behrenberg! *Go — now!* Samuels, grab one of these people. Whoever's going to make it.'

Samuels reached for one of the boys. When he did, the mother put her hand in his way. She smiled, her teeth stained bright cherry red with oxygenated blood. In her shaking fist was a small cylindrical detonator.

'Oh, Jesus — '

Instinct took over. Mahoney shoved Samuels farther inside and swung the door closed behind him — just as the blast went off.

The door came right back at them, off its hinges, and knocked both of the agents down.

In the small space, they fell on top of the family in a blind tangle of bodies. Plaster shook down from the ceiling. A long crack ran down the wall, as water began shooting out from the showerhead connection.

Mahoney struggled back to his feet. The bedroom was in flames.

He couldn't see Totten or Behrenberg anywhere.

Hopefully that meant they were already clear, and not — gone. The explosion had blown out the entire front of the room, picture window and all.

'Go, go, go!' He pulled Samuels off the floor and shoved him out the door.

A quick triage showed him that only one of the four suspects was still moving. It was the boy Samuels had been trying to extricate just a few seconds ago. His eyes were barely open, and his face was almost purple. Mahoney hooked his hands under the kid's arms and started pulling him out.

In the bedroom, the heat was intense. He could feel his exposed skin prickling as he dragged the kid along, keeping as low as

218

possible. It was painfully slow going.

Too slow. All at once, the boy coughed up some blood, and he spasmed hard, one last time. That was it. Before Mahoney reached the door, he knew he was dragging a dead body.

Book Four

NECESSARY EVILS

72

'Get on your toes! That's it. Shoulder front. Good. That's perfect. Now pick up that can of Coke.'

Ava reached out and took the Coke off the shelf where I'd put it.

'Good. Now put it back,' I said.

She set the soda can down, but then dropped her arm in frustration. 'I thought boxing was about punching,' she said.

'What do you think you're learning to do?' I said. 'Now go again. But keep your elbow in this time.' I showed her. 'Keep it tight. Close to your side.'

'Gotta keep the box closed,' Ali said, mirroring the stance for her. He was loving this, being able to tell a thirteen-year-old what to do. Ava didn't seem to mind. It was me she rolled her eyes at.

'How am I supposed to learn anything if you won't let me wear gloves?'

'You'll get the gloves when you're ready,' I said. 'Now pick up that can again.'

I honestly wasn't sure if boxing was a great idea for Ava, or a terrible one. But she'd expressed an interest, and that was enough for me to give it a try.

'How do you like your new school?' I asked, motioning her and Ali into the center of the floor. They knew the drill and turned to face each other.

Ava kept her elbows in as she put her hands up, left foot in front. Ali did the same.

'It's a'ight. I like Ms. Hopkins,' she said.

It probably doesn't sound like much, but this was about a thousand percent more than Ava had been giving me so far. Kids off the street can go one of two ways. It's either no boundaries at all, and they share way too much, too fast. Or they clam up tight. That was Ava. So far, we had our good days and our bad days.

There were still plenty of questions I wanted to ask. Like what happened to you out there on the streets? Did you know your mom was going to die? What makes you feel safe, Ava? Who are you?

The questions would come, eventually. For now, I stuck to small, tangible stuff like school, meals, movies — and boxing.

I ran the kids through some balance drills, did some more mirroring, and then let them play at dodging the heavy bag. That one was Ava's favorite. She gave up a few rare smiles while she and Ali swung the bag, feinting and weaving on the balls of their feet. At least the two of them were bonding.

After a while, Jannie came down the basement stairs and poked her head under the banister.

'Hey, Daddy? Mr. Mahoney's here to see you. And Nana says enough with the roughhousing. It's time for bed.'

I looked over at the clock radio on the windowsill. It was quarter to ten and a school night. Oops.

What was Ned Mahoney doing here at the house this late?

'All right, guys, that's it. Gym's closed for the night,' I said.

Ava stood holding the bag with both hands. 'Just a little more,' she said.

'Nope. It's already past your bedtime. Ali's too. Let's go.'

A nasty scowl came onto her face. 'I don't need no goddamn bedtime,' she said. She swung the bag hard and caught Ali off guard. It knocked him right to the floor. While he burst into tears, Ava started stomping up the stairs.

That was, until I made her come back and apologize — first to Ali, and then to me.

'No more boxing this week,' I said. 'You need a break. This isn't the way it's going to work in this house.'

'Whatever,' she said, in that really charming way adolescents can have. Then she turned to go.

Like I said, good days and bad days. Sometimes all at the same time.

73

Ava was still sulking when we got upstairs. She walked right by Mahoney, who was waiting in the front hall. Ned pointed at the kids as they went by, counting on his fingers. 'Three?' he mouthed at me.

'Don't ask,' I said. 'Also known as Ava.'

'Good night, Also Known as Ava,' he called up the stairs.

'G'night,' Ava said without turning around. But at least she talked.

'Good night, Mr. Mahoney!'

'Good night, Jannie. Good night, John-Boy. Good night, everyone!'

Jannie and Ali liked Ned just as much as I did. Once they were gone, though, he dropped the 'Uncle Ned' act and his face turned serious again. I hadn't spoken with him since the raid at the motel, three nights earlier. I think this was the first time I ever saw him when he wasn't clean shaven and raring to go.

'How are your guys doing?' I asked.

'They've been better. Totten's already home, but Behrenberg's going to be in the burn unit for at least two more weeks,' he told me, shaking his head.

'How about you?' I said. 'You holding up?'

Ned shrugged. 'I've been spending most of my forced time off at the hospital with Behr's wife. But they're putting me back on tomorrow,' he said.

'Is that a good thing?'

'Sure. Nothing worse than sitting on the sidelines. I need to be in on this, or I'm going to go crazy.'

I could have guessed Ned would feel responsible for what happened. I'd probably feel the same way, for better or worse.

'Listen, Ned, if you ever need to talk about — '

'Thanks,' he said, 'but I'm already seeing one of the Bureau shrinks. She's pretty good, actually. A lot better-looking than you, too.'

I was glad to see the trademark sense of humor wasn't dead, anyway.

'Well, how about I pour you a drink, then? I've got some good Scotch I think even you could appreciate,' I said.

'Actually — ' Ned took a step toward the door. His keys were still hooked on his finger, and he had *that look* in his eye. The one that said he'd never really left work behind.

'I was wondering if you wanted to go for a ride,' he said. 'I've got something you might be interested in seeing. This is good. You *want* to see it.'

I nodded. 'Of course I do.'

74

Half an hour later, Mahoney and I showed up at a four-story, red-brick building on the corner of Sixth and P streets, across from Masjid Al-Qasim mosque. We parked in the back and took the stairs to a third-floor railroad apartment.

Inside, it was mostly empty. Just a few lawn chairs and long folding tables, loaded up with listening equipment. Two agents sat in the chairs, both of them with headphones on. Another was at the kitchen counter with two laptops in front of her.

I didn't know any of these agents, but Mahoney's kind of a rock star with the surveillance crews. He introduced me to Cheryl Kravetz in the kitchen, and pointed out Howard Green and Andrew Landry with the headphones.

'Thanks for calling,' Mahoney told Kravetz. 'We'll try to stay out of the way.'

'No problem.' Kravetz worked while they talked. She had half a dozen different camera views up on two screens and scrolled through them with an external keyboard hooked up to both computers.

Most of what I saw didn't look like much — an empty hallway, a classroom of some kind, a dark alley.

'Isha prayers let out about an hour ago,' she told us. 'I'm not sure what the holdup is.'

'And nobody's going in after them?' Ned asked.

'When was the last time you took someone down in a mosque?' Kravetz said. 'Or any church, for that matter. It's too damn complicated. Besides, we've got this covered.'

I listened but didn't say anything. This wasn't my op. All Mahoney had told me in the car was that intel from the Bureau's Al Ayla informant had been coming in fast and furious. Tonight was supposed to be some kind of takedown. As for who they were going after, he had no idea.

It was another hour before anything significant happened. Ned and I were talking quietly in the corner when one of the listening agents put up a hand and snapped his fingers several times.

'Here we go,' Kravetz said. We went over and stood behind her, where we could see. She had pulled up two full-screen views. It looked like the front and back entrances of the mosque.

A second later, one of the double front doors opened from the inside, and a woman in a *hijab* and long coat started backing out onto the front walk.

'What the hell — ?'

It took a second to see the man in the wheelchair. Once they'd cleared the door, the woman did a 180 and started pushing him down toward the street.

'That's *them?*' Mahoney said.

They looked to be in their sixties, both of them heavyset. The man had a thick, almost nonexistent neck and just a few wisps of hair. The woman walked with a slight limp. Actually, she hobbled more than walked.

Kravetz manipulated her controls to follow them on camera.

'Wait for it,' she said. 'Wait for it . . . '

As soon as they turned onto the sidewalk, two unmarked cars were there! They pulled up to the curb, and half a dozen agents jumped out. One of them took control of the wheelchair. Another cuffed the woman immediately.

I could hear the man in the chair shouting now, but I couldn't make out what he was saying.

It all happened very fast. They'd barely gotten the woman into one of the cars when a handicap-accessible van pulled up. The Bureau was clearly ready for this. They loaded up their mystery man and everyone took off, leaving the corner just as quiet as it had been sixty seconds ago.

I looked over at Ned when it was done. He was still staring at the screen, but his eyes looked blank. If I had to guess, I'd say he was thinking about that terrible scene at the motel from the other night. Was this couple responsible? Were they the planners?

'Where are they taking those two?' I asked. 'Any idea?'

Mahoney shrugged. 'To hell, I hope.'

75

The name of the man in the Wheelchair was Faizal Ahmad Angawi. According to the prevailing intel, he went simply by 'Uncle' within the organization.

When they reached their destination, he was unloaded from the van, and his blindfold was removed.

'You maniacs! Where in God's name have you taken me?' he screamed at the FBI agents. 'You are breaking your laws.'

They'd arrived in a vast, unheated garage bay. Nothing too specific to clue him in to his exact whereabouts. There was a loading dock and a long row of empty steel shelving units along one wall. Several fluorescent light fixtures hung from the girdered ceiling, far overhead. Also, it was quite cold.

CIA interrogator Matt Sivitz stood in front of Angawi. His hands were clasped behind his back, while the seated man ranted on and on.

'I have my rights! You can't do this. I demand to see my attorney immediately!'

'Absolutely,' Sivitz told him. 'Just as soon as we're back in the real world, you can see a lawyer, Mr. Angawi. Or should I call you Uncle?'

The man squinted up at him while the corners of his mouth turned down. 'Uncle? What's that supposed to mean?'

'Don't be insulting. You know exactly what it means.'

Sivitz walked over and took a folding chair off the dock. When he set it across from the wheelchair and sat down, the two men were face-to-face.

'Here's how I see it,' he went on. 'I think you're stuck in the middle of something here. You answer to your people back in Saudi. You pass orders to your operatives. But you don't control anything. Not really. You've got all the knowledge but none of the power — and that's what makes you vulnerable. Am I close?'

'Close to what?' Angawi shouted. 'This is an outrage! I'm a law-abiding man. Look at me!' He reached for the wheels on his chair and found them locked.

Sivitz held up a finger, which was also clearly a warning. 'Actually, we've been watching you for a while.'

He unfolded a slip of paper from his pocket and glanced down at it. 'Does the number 20852409 mean anything to you?' he said. 'No? Maybe you didn't memorize the account numbers. How about Trinity Bank, in Washington? Saudi British Bank, in Riyadh?'

Angawi was having none of it. 'You can't intimidate me like this,' he said between clenched teeth. 'All of my accounts are perfectly legal.'

Sivitz nodded. 'All of Faizal Ahmad Angawi's accounts are legal. That's true. But not the ones you've created under Muhammed Al-Athel. Or Charity of Hope. Or Chesapeake Properties.' He watched the man while he spoke, gauging his expression. 'That's where Al Ayla's money is coming in, isn't it? Please correct me anytime here. Just in case I have any small details wrong.'

The detainee didn't even show a glimmer of recognition. Just pure, seething hatred.

'I have a right to an attorney,' he said again. 'I insist you take me back to the mosque *this instant! Right now! Do you hear me? Are you recording this?*'

Sivitz stood up fast. His chair slammed back onto the concrete floor.

'Listen to me,' he said. 'Listen very carefully. If you ever want to see your wife again, you're going to drop this pathetic act of yours and start talking to us. Who is your contact in Saudi Arabia?'

'Are you threatening my *wife?*' The man was shaking with rage now.

'No, Faizal. *You are.* What I'm saying is that you're both going to spend the rest of your lives in separate American prisons at the rate you're going. So tell me, who's running your ops in the District?'

'This is illegal! Racist! Outrageous — '

'Where are Ethan and Zoe Coyle?'

Angawi reeled back then and spit in the agent's face.

Sivitz saw red. He cocked a fist and came at him until Angawi was cowering with his hands up around his head. This meant he wasn't immune to pain. Good to know.

It took another breath for Sivitz to pull himself back from the edge. He wasn't going to hit this cripple. There would be no bruising. No physical proof of anything. Instead, he reached down and took Angawi's chin in his hand.

'Look at me,' he said.

Slowly, the man's eyes came up to meet his.

'You want to keep wasting your people the way you've been doing, you go right ahead. Put your wife on that list while you're at it. Doesn't make any difference to me. But just so you know — we're not leaving this place until you give me something I can use. And — I *will* hurt you.' Sivitz stepped back and let go of his face. He looked visibly shaken now. 'Names, Faizal. Places. Targets. You know what I want.'

Angawi took a deep breath. For the first time, it was hard to tell which direction he might go in. Maybe they were making some progress here, after all.

'I . . . demand . . . to . . . see . . . my . . . attorney,' Angawi said. It was so slow as to be mocking. Then he folded his hands on his lap and bowed his head, either at rest or in prayer. It was hard to tell which.

Sivitz watched for a minute, then turned away. He took out a pack of gum and unwrapped a piece as he headed for the door. 'Goddamn, I miss cigarettes,' he growled to no one.

It was going to be a long night.

76

The hallway off the loading dock had been cleared of all personnel except for a lone armed agent at the far end. The guard pushed the elevator button for Sivitz as he approached.

'How's it going in there?' he asked.

Sivitz ignored him and got onto the elevator without a word.

He rode to the sixth floor, where another agent was on post. Continuing down the hall, he passed a long row of dark offices until he came to the last one, with a light showing under the door. The placard next to it had his name engraved in block letters beneath a small rendering of the CIA seal.

Sivitz knocked twice, then opened the door with his key.

Inside, Mrs. Angawi was sitting at the conference table with a female translator from Langley. Peter Lindley was there as well, and Evan Stroud from the Directorate of Intelligence, who had jobbed Sivitz in for this one. All four had Styrofoam containers of sandwiches and chips in front of them and bottles of water from the kitchen down the hall.

'How are we doing in here?' Sivitz asked. 'Everybody nice and comfy?'

The translator quietly relayed the question to Mrs. Angawi, who came back in a torrent of Arabic.

''I want to leave this building, this city. It's a cursed place,'' the translator said, speaking for the woman as she went. ''I shouldn't be here anymore. It's not safe for me.''

'Tell her she'll be in a hotel tonight, perfectly secure. Once we have everything we need, other arrangements can be made,' Stroud answered.

Sivitz kept his thoughts to himself. The woman seemed a little simple to him. It was amazing that the Bureau had put this much stock in her. Although, by the same token, all of her intel had been good so far. Maybe her own people had underestimated her, too.

He also noticed that her *hijab* was down around her shoulders, even with these strange men in the room. That spoke volumes about her.

''I want a new life,'' she went on through her translator. ''My husband is not the same man that I married. I can't stand by and watch this happen anymore. I have friends here. American friends, do you understand?''

'Yeah, yeah, I've got it,' Sivitz said.

Somewhere in there, she'd turned her attention on him. Maybe she felt like she wasn't getting anywhere with Stroud and Lindley. But he was no baby-sitter. 'Ask who her husband reports to in Saudi Arabia. We need to know who's giving the orders here.'

'We've been trying, Matt. You do know that, right?' Stroud said.

'Pretty please?' Sivitz's adrenaline was still high, and he didn't give a shit whose pay grade was up the scale from whose right now.

Stroud nodded at the interpreter, who posed

236

the question to Mrs. Angawi.

''I don't know,'' she translated.

'What about the Coyle kids?' Sivitz asked.

''My husband says that The Family is responsible. He said as much to two of our people just the other day. The ones who are in charge now, I think.''

'And who are they? What are their names? What do they look like? Where are they?'

Sivitz tried not to rush, but he was finding it difficult. Time was short.

''I believe she is a doctor. The man is somewhat plain — in his looks, but also maybe in his head. I think it's the wife who controls things. She's very strong.''

'And you don't know their names?' Sivitz tried again.

No.

'Or where they are?'

No.

'Jesus.'

He turned and walked to the window. The Capitol dome loomed just a few blocks away. The needle of the Washington Monument stood tall in the distance. It was a great nighttime city, really. Not that he ever got to enjoy it.

Again, the woman spoke up, followed by the interpreter. What the woman had said seemed important. Her voice had risen.

''What I can tell you is where the next attack will be. Also maybe when it is scheduled.''

Everything in the room seemed to go still. When Sivitz turned around, Mrs. Angawi's expression had changed. Was she smiling? The corners of her mouth looked curled.

'Tell me,' Sivitz asked. Lindley was already dialing his phone. 'Give me a location. A time. Whatever you've got. Then you'll get what you want.'

She sat back then. Yes, she was definitely smiling. She was just as smug as her husband when she wanted to be, wasn't she?

Taking her time now, the woman picked up the uneaten half of her sandwich and carefully wrapped it in a paper napkin. She tucked it into the purse on the table next to her and then put the purse on her lap, speaking quietly through the translator as she did.

''As soon as you get me out of this godforsaken city, I'll tell you what you want to know.''

77

First thing the next morning, I was back on the trail of Zoe Coyle's cell phone. The number I got from her friends traced to a prepaid Firefly flip model. It was the kind of thing you could pick up at any convenience store — no calling plan, no subscriber information required. Zoe had obviously gone to some trouble to keep this thing a secret.

Fireflies were especially popular with school-kids, since they were so small and easy to hide. Even their advertising campaign played it up — *Where's Your Firefly?*

I hated to think about where Zoe's might be right now. Buried underground somewhere? In pieces at the side of the highway? Sitting in some maniac's glove compartment? None of the images that flooded my mind were good ones.

As soon as I had the signatures I needed, I faxed off an administrative subpoena for records to the phone company down in Jacksonville, Florida. I gave them exactly one hour to respond.

When I didn't hear back, I called and left a message for their director of security: another subpoena was on the way. He could bring those records up and present them to the grand jury himself, if that's how they wanted to play it.

Five minutes later, my phone rang.

'Detective Cross, it's Bill Shattuck with

Essential Electronics. How can I help you?'

'What don't you already know?' I asked, cutting through the bullshit.

'Well, I've got the records for the number you requested right here in front of me. Should I e-mail you a copy?'

'Please and thank you,' I said.

Shattuck cleared his throat. 'There's one other thing. I can send you the transaction logs for text messages and voice calls, no problem, but we just don't have the kind of data storage you get with an AT&T or a Verizon. The actual content of any texts drops off our system after seven or eight days, and the last transaction on this phone was . . . let's see. Twelve days ago. An incoming text on September ninth.'

No surprise there. Just a little punch to the stomach. That was the day of the kidnapping.

'Just send me what you've got. Thanks again,' I told him, and hung up.

The report came through a minute later. As soon as I got it, I scrolled down to the bottom and looked at September 9. The text in question was the only entry for that day.

It had come into Zoe's phone at 8:05 a.m., right in the middle of Branaff's homeroom period. That was also about fifteen minutes *before* Ethan and Zoe disappeared.

It took me only a few keystrokes to run a reverse lookup on the incoming phone number. It was registered to a Cathy Allison, with an address in Foggy Bottom. And in fact, I knew the exact house. I'd been there on Saturday to interview Ms. Allison's daughter Emma, one of

Zoe's inner circle of girlfriends.

I looked up at the clock. It was 10:15 a.m. Emma would be in class right now — third period.

If I left right away, I could be there by fourth.

78

Emma Allison's eyes went wide as she stepped out of the science lab and into the hall, where I was waiting for her. So was the headmaster.

'Emma, Detective Cross is here to ask you a few questions,' Mr. Skillings told her.

She seemed like a scared little girl to me, but in a fourteen-going-on-thirty kind of way. She had too much dark liner around her eyes and a pair of half-shredded leggings under her school uniform. The thick-soled boots looked just like the red ones Zoe had been wearing the morning she disappeared.

'Did they find Zoe?' she blurted out. 'Oh please. Please, please, *please*.'

'No, I'm sorry, Emma,' I said. 'Actually, what I need is to get a look at your phone.'

'My phone? But why? What's going on?'

'Do you have the phone with you?'

'I hope not,' Skillings said pointedly. 'The students aren't allowed to have any electronics in class. Isn't that right, Emma?'

'It's in my locker,' she said.

The headmaster motioned her up the hall, not even trying to hide his impatience. I'd already spent a good fifteen minutes in his office, tracking down Mrs. Allison and getting permission to speak with Emma in the first place.

We followed her outside and across a breezeway, into one of the campus's several

242

redbrick annex buildings.

Halfway up another hallway, Emma stopped at locker 733 and twirled the combination on the lock.

She reached inside, took out an iPhone in a zebra-striped rubber case, and held it out for me.

Her eyes flared again when I pulled on a pair of latex gloves to take it from her.

'Emma, when we spoke on Saturday, you said that the last time you had any contact with Zoe was the afternoon before the kidnapping. Is that right?' I asked.

'Yeah. We have eighth period social studies.'

She craned her neck, trying to see what I was doing. I'd powered up the phone and navigated over to her Sent messages.

Sure enough, there it was, September 9, 8:05 a.m.

'*Z — Quik ciggie b4 assembly? Ditch if you can — pleeeez?? I've got major dirt to share . . . . . . xoE*'

'And there were no calls between you two on the morning she and Ethan disappeared? No texts?' I asked.

'That's right,' Emma told me. 'I got to school, put my phone in my locker, and went to homeroom, like always. Why?'

'You're positive about that? This is important, Emma. This is extremely important.'

'I swear!' She fiddled nervously with the purple ribbon around her wrist. Most of the students and staff had started wearing them since the kidnapping.

'Am I in trouble?' she asked.

'No,' I said. 'But I am going to have to hold onto this phone for a little while.'

A minute later, I was double-timing it back down to the visitors' lot and my car. Finally, we had some kind of pattern to work with — or at least, the suggestion of one. Could that earlier text from Ryan Townsend's phone have been a test run of some kind? Were there others?

And most of all, if Emma Allison's phone was in her locker that morning, and she didn't send this latest message — who did?

The caller had to be the kidnapper. Who else could it be?

79

Suddenly a lot was happening, even more than I realized. I was shuttling back over to headquarters, when I got a call from Ned Mahoney.

'It's your better half,' he said, and snorted out a laugh.

'Well, you've got Bree, Nana Mama, and John Sampson ahead of you on that one,' I said. 'But what's up?'

'Those two arrests from last night. The dude in the wheelchair and the sixty-something accomplice? I don't know what kind of black op hole they fell into, but one of them must have coughed up some serious intel. Joint Terrorism Task Force is standing up another whole operation for tomorrow night. They've already got full surveillance going on some parking garage in Chinatown. That's all I have so far, but it's going to be big, Alex, and I'm not talking about just standing around watching this time.'

I could barely process what Ned was telling me. My mind was overflowing with the details of everything I'd just learned at the Branaff School.

'Thanks, Ned, but my plate's a little full here,' I said. 'Isn't that what I have you for?'

'Actually, buddy — old friend, old pal — I was calling to get in on *your* team. This takedown's going to be all SWAT, but they're pulling people from the kidnapping side for the investigative unit. I'm thinking this time *you* bring *me* in.'

'Ned, I don't even know what we're talking about,' I said.

'You will. I wouldn't be surprised if your captain's leaving you a voice mail about it right now. There's a briefing, two o'clock today. It's at the police academy in Southwest.'

'Why all the way down there?' I asked.

'They need the room. They're going to be staging this thing all into the night. Like I said — *mucho grande*. Tell me you'll let me tag along.'

'You don't need my permission for that,' I told him.

'Actually, I do this time.'

This was unbelievable. I thought about everything I still had to get done — the things I wanted to do myself and the few things I could hand off. There were dozens of calls and texts on Zoe's phone to track back. I also had to try and reach the First Lady, if I could.

'Let me make this easy for you,' Ned said, cutting into my thoughts. 'You're coming to the briefing. You know it, and I know it. Can we move on now?'

I swear he's got caffeine instead of blood. The guy's one of the Bureau's locomotives.

And he was right. If this had anything to do with the kidnapping, I wanted to be in on it — whether I had the time and energy or not.

'Yeah,' I said. 'All right. Police academy, two o'clock. And where's this parking garage you're talking about, anyway?'

80

That Thursday evening at six o'clock exactly, Hala and Tariq's attack team convened on the upper level of the Chinatown municipal parking garage on H Street.

There were eight of them in all, four couples who arrived separately and would also travel in their own vehicles to the target site. Everyone wore Western business dress, as they had been instructed to do. The men's jackets and women's tops were specially cut to conceal the identical Sig Sauer pistols they'd all been issued.

Only Tariq was unarmed. He'd resisted his part in the assignment, but Hala had insisted he be there. He handed around earbuds, transmitters, and laminated conference badges while she began the briefing.

'I'll make this as fast as possible,' Hala said. 'The U.S. secretary of the interior, Justin Pileggi, is scheduled to address the World Alternative Energy Expo at seven thirty tonight. Pileggi will have a full security detail, of course, and they'll keep him moving around the convention center. His remarks may or may not start on time. We need to keep ourselves just as unpredictable,' she said. 'Anyone watching out for an assassin will have seven of us to contend with. No one can stop us.'

There were a few approving smiles around the circle. A few nervous expressions as well. But they all got the plan.

'If at any time you have a clear shot, you're to take it,' Hala went on. 'At that point, the rest of you should know what to do. Escape, if you're able. And if not — '

She held up the cyanide capsule from her pocket in one hand and her Sig in the other.

'Those are the options. Any questions?'

No one was smiling now.

'I have a question,' one of the men said. He was the tallest in the group, with a heavy brow and an aggressive stare. 'What about the arrests at Masjid Al-Qasim the other night?'

Hala kept her face expressionless, but the question surprised her. She hadn't realized anyone even knew about the mosque, much less Uncle's disappearance.

'What about them?' she said.

'Well, it's troubling, isn't it?'

The rest of the group remained perfectly still, their eyes darting between Hala and the man. This one wasn't just obnoxious, she realized. He was dangerous. He'd have to be dealt with accordingly, but now was not the time.

'There were arrests, it's true,' she said. 'There have been murders and suicides as well. Bombings, too. We're at war, *if you haven't noticed.*'

'But who's in charge now?' he asked. 'Who is the leader here in Washington?'

'*I am,*' Hala said without hesitation. 'This is how The Family works. One falls, and another is there to take his place. Washington *will* be brought to its knees, make no mistake about it.

248

Where's your loyalty, brother?'

'Don't preach at me, sister,' he shot back. 'My loyalty is to Allah, and to The Family. Not to you. Do you even know if this assignment is meant to proceed?'

The truth was, Hala didn't know. There had been no word either way.

But she never got to answer the insolent man's question. Before anyone realized it was happening, three stun grenades skittered across the cement floor and went off in a shattering volley of noise.

Suddenly men in gas masks and dark uniforms were streaming out of the stairwells, carrying M16s and AR15 assault weapons.

Two more flash bangs went off almost right away. One of them detonated at Hala's feet, and she was completely deaf before she'd even started to run away.

81

It was a huge, coordinated operation. Swat units from three different agencies made up the first line of attack. Mahoney and I were pressed into the parking garage stairwell, waiting for our go-ahead from the unit commander. Once the suspects were contained, we'd go in as part of a second wave and take it from there — arrest, transport, and questioning.

I heard three flash bangs go off like giant firecrackers!

Then a rush of pounding footsteps and shouting as the SWAT teams moved in. The whole idea was to catch these people off guard and contain them before anyone could reach for the cyanide. If there was one thing we knew about Al Ayla by now, it was that they had no regard for human life — including their own people. These operatives were just disposable garbage to them.

A second round of stun grenades echoed off the concrete walls, ceiling, and floor. Even in the stairwell, the sound hurt my ears. My heart was thudding.

Mahoney was champing at the bit, waiting to go like a horse at the starting gate. It wasn't in his nature to hold off at times like these.

Then suddenly I heard the distinct, percussive pop of gunfire. A single shot came first.

Then a fast double tap.

'Suspect down!' someone shouted.

Two people flew by the stairwell door, sprinting away from the action.

It was a man and woman in American business dress.

Mahoney didn't hesitate. He was out after them. And I was right behind.

The couple raced down a long row of parked cars toward the circular ramp at the far end of the garage. The woman had a pistol in her hand and fired blindly back over her shoulder as they went. Even firing like that, she was accurate, skilled.

We took cover behind the nearest parked car, an Audi A6. A bullet ricocheted off the hood and took a divot of shiny silver paint and metal with it. Too close.

Gunfights are never fair game for the police. The bad guys have no rules whatsoever. We have to know exactly what we're shooting at *and* what's beyond it. The best strategy is to stay as unpredictable as possible.

I kept to a low crouch and ducked around the back of the car. Once I reached the far end, I popped up, squared my feet, and got off one fast shot before they even knew I was there.

My vision tunneled around them like a spotlight. There was a flash of red.

I'd caught the man in the right hand. He yelped, but they didn't slow down. The woman returned fire, pushing him ahead of her now. She was very good with a gun.

They cut between two cars and scrambled over a concrete barrier. A second later, they'd dropped down to the level below and disappeared.

Already, Ned Mahoney and I were up and running again.

'Careful, Ned, she can shoot lights-out.'

82

I threw myself over the parking barrier after our two runners and jumped maybe ten feet. The cement landing was a vicious jolt to the bones. I had to drop and roll before I got up again, just to save my legs.

There were several dime-size red blotches on the ground where I landed, but nothing to indicate which way they'd gone. The guy might have wrapped his hand.

All I could see from here were lots of parked cars, concrete, and a dozen ways out.

'What the hell?' Mahoney came running up behind me. Several more SWAT officers were sprinting down from the level above as well. 'Where'd they go?'

'Any sign of them?' Command radioed down.

'Negative,' I said. 'Get all the exits covered. And shut down the block if it's not too late.'

We all fanned out, checking the adjacent rooftops, throwing open doors, looking under cars with any kind of clearance. But it was no good. They were gone. Somehow, they'd gotten past us. The woman was a professional. She didn't panic and she could really handle a gun.

There was still a chance someone could pick them up on the street. Their faces were a matter of record now, and every unit in the city would go into high alert.

Homeland Security could even shut down the

bridges and put checkpoints on the highway if they wanted to, but that wasn't my call.

By the time Ned and I got back up to the top level, everything on that end had been contained. One of the SWAT sergeants, Enrique Vaillos, was sitting on the bumper of the same Audi where we'd taken cover. The back of his hand was up against his mouth. It looked like he'd gotten a nasty pop in the face during the takedown.

'What's our status up here?' Ned asked.

'Five in custody, one dead,' he said, 'and two — ?'

'Still missing,' I said.

Farther up the row of cars, a tall Saudi man in a gray suit was laid out flat on the ground. His head was turned our way so you could see the open, glassy eyes — also, the perfectly round black hole in his forehead. Even now, it sent a chill rolling down my back.

'What happened?' I asked.

Vaillos shook his head. 'It was the damndest thing. That chick? The one who got away? Just before she ran, she turned and put a fast one in the guy's head, point-blank. I don't know why she did it, but I'll tell you what. It's all she had time for. Probably saved one of my guys' lives.'

He turned away and spit a mouthful of red on the cement.

'Whatever. I ain't going to lose sleep over it. These people want to act like a bunch of cannibals, I say let 'em. Just makes our job easier.'

I was thinking about the woman again, and how she wasn't going to make our job easier.

83

The 'Al Ayla Five' were transferred to a U.S. Marshals holding facility at the DC Jail on Massachusetts Avenue. A wing of eight-by-ten soundproof interview rooms was cleared, and the suspects were brought in one by one. Above all, there would be no exchange of information between them.

We worked in teams, rotating from suspect to suspect. I was with Mahoney, along with a forensic psychiatrist from the CIA, a ranking rep from Homeland Security, and an FBI field office supervisor, Corey Sneed, who took the lead. That was fine with me. I kept my focus where I needed it — on the Coyle kids.

Presumably, these people were Saudi nationals, but none of them was carrying any identification, and none of them would talk to us. Nothing. Not even to ask for a lawyer, though we suspected they spoke English.

Our strong assumption was that the whole eight-member group had been composed of four couples, given Al Ayla's m.o. up to this point. If that was true, then one of these women had just lost a husband. Maybe that was something we could use.

After two hours of getting nowhere, I took my best guess and asked to speak privately with the one woman who had seemed most on edge.

'Go for it,' Sneed told me. It almost seemed like a dare.

I stopped at the vending machines on my way back in and bought a bottle of water. It wasn't much, but I wanted to bring something in with me besides files and questions.

When I opened the interview room door, the woman's head jerked up as if I'd caught her off guard. Her dark hair was pulled back in a French braid, and her magenta silk blouse and gray pinstriped skirt looked wrong on her somehow, like someone else's idea of American dress.

I came around and unlocked the cuff securing her to an eyebolt on the metal table.

She rubbed at the red mark around her wrist as I sat down but ignored the bottle of water I'd left for her.

'I've got something I want to show you,' I said. 'You should look, at least. Just look.'

I opened one of my files and took out a screen capture from the night's surveillance video at the parking garage. The image was grainy, but the eight of them were easy enough to make out, huddled next to a couple of SUVs.

When I slid the picture around to show her, my finger was on the woman at the center of their group.

'This is the one who shot and killed your husband,' I said, watching her face.

I wasn't positive about the husband part — not until her eye twitched, and her lips tightened over her teeth, like she was holding in a scream, or maybe a curse.

'Do you want to tell me who she is?' I asked.

To my surprise, the woman answered.

'I don't know,' she said in a thick Saudi accent. 'Her, I would help you find, if I could. Evil bitch. Controlling. Hard.'

'Is she running Al Ayla's Washington cell?' I asked, but already, she'd retreated back into silence.

'Let me ask you something else,' I said. 'It's about the kidnapping of the president's children. Do you know if Al Ayla's responsible?'

All I got there was more of the same. Silence, and she wouldn't look at me.

'You know, it's not too late to cut a deal here,' I said. That got her attention. It even got me some minimal eye contact. 'The first one of you to talk is going to be on a plane back to Riyadh when this is all said and done. The rest are going to be here for a long, long time.'

'A *deal?*' she said then. 'Do you think I am absolutely stupid?'

The question spoke for itself. If she wasn't interested, she wouldn't have asked.

I shrugged. 'Believe what you want. This offer stands only as long as nobody else comes forward. If I get a knock on that door' — I thumbed over my shoulder — 'then you and I are done here.'

I didn't want to give her too much room to think, so I leaned in and kept talking, a little faster now, whatever came into my head.

'If your husband had been martyred, I might understand all this silence. Or even if he'd been allowed to take his own life. But that's not what happened, is it? He was killed by one of your own. By Al Ayla. *The Family*. I can't imagine that's what either of you signed up for,' I said. 'What do you owe them now? What do you owe your husband's murderer?'

She was seething but still watching me. I took it as a green light.

And then slowly, without even the slightest change of expression, she said, 'There have been rumors.'

'What kind of rumors?' I said.

'Talk. Among some of the others. They say Al Ayla kidnapped those children. That your president got what he deserved.'

'Do you know if the children are still alive?' I asked. 'Just tell me that.'

'I don't know.' She slumped in her chair, maybe hating herself for doing this, for even talking to me. This was against all her beliefs, wasn't it?

'Do you know where they were taken?' I pressed her.

This time she only shook her head. I was starting to wonder where this was going, if anywhere. Did she know more than she was telling me? Probably.

'How about this?' I said. 'Do you believe those rumors are true? Do you think Al Ayla has those kids?'

Her expression muddied. It was like I could see the gears turning. Her defenses were down now, clearly weakened, and she was easier to read.

'Of course I believe them,' she said — about two seconds too late.

She'd just put herself in a corner, and we both knew it. She wanted to believe those rumors, even *needed* to believe them. But she didn't. Now she had nothing left to give me. No currency to buy her freedom.

'I think we're done,' I said. Then I counted to ten in my head. When she didn't say anything, I stood up to go.

'And just so you know,' I told her, 'the secretary of the interior wasn't going to be anywhere near that expo tonight. Your mission failed before it even started. The plan you were given was a bad one. Your husband died for nothing.'

I left the room with a clear conscience. The fact was, we'd both lied to each other. There was no deal. Never had been, never would be. I hadn't even cleared the idea with my team.

Some days are just like that. You do whatever you need to do to get the job done. Anything at all. By tomorrow, maybe my conscience wouldn't be so clear.

84

The Major Case Squad Office was a twelve-cubicle circus that morning. Staff were coming and going, phones were ringing off the hook, detectives were swapping information across the room — all the usual, but it was nonstop chaos these days. A thousand clues and rumors were being chased down. At least that many leaks. Way too many.

I barely noticed any of it. I was hunched over my desk with a stack of Branaff personnel files spread out around me.

Whatever had or hadn't been achieved the night before, it remained true that we had seventeen Branaff faculty and staff unaccounted for during that homeroom period when *someone* used Emma Allison's phone to set a trap for Zoe Coyle.

I'd also started to wonder if Ethan had been an unintended second victim in this kidnap plot. Had Zoe's fight with Ryan Townsend thrown a monkey wrench into the plan? Was she the sole target to begin with?

I was up to my eyeballs with all of it when I got a knock on my cubicle wall.

'Uh, Detective?'

It was Dennis Porter, one of the research team members. Porter was fresh out of the academy, and still green, but eager and fairly bright, I thought. The bags under his eyes and day-old ginger fuzz on his face were a testament to his hard work.

'What's up, Denny?'

'Well, maybe nothing, but I just found this,' he said, and laid a copy of a death certificate on my desk.

It was from the Department of Vital Records in Dauphin County, Pennsylvania, dated November 10, 2006. The name on the certificate was Zachary Levi Johnson-Glass.

'Glass?' I said. 'As in — '

'I think so,' Porter said. 'There's no obit that I can find, but I did pull the birth certificate. The parents are listed as Rodney Glass and Molly Johnson, Harrisburg, Pennsylvania. The poor kid was eight years old when he died.

'And I found a 1998 lease agreement from Harrisburg with the same Social Security number as Glass's file at Branaff. Like I said, maybe it's nothing, but I thought you should know.'

Glass, the school nurse, was one of those seventeen names on the list. I was already pulling his file to the top of the mess on my desk.

'I want you to start from scratch on this guy,' I said. 'LexisNexis the hell out of him. Check NCIC again, and Interpol while you're at it. I want to know where he's lived, every job he's ever had, every parking ticket, every itch he's ever scratched. Pull in whoever you need, I'll sign off on it. Don't take any crap from anybody on this. Just get it done.'

Porter still looked a little tentative. 'Don't you already have all that on file, sir?'

261

I picked up the death certificate and waved it at him. 'You would have thought so, right?'

He smiled for half a second before he seemed to remember how serious this was. 'I'll get right on it,' he said, and went off at a trot.

I wasn't going to get too excited . . . yet. It's easy to be blinded by circumstantial evidence. But that didn't stop me from putting a whole new lens on Rodney Glass.

One thing I kept coming back to over and over on this case was how *personal* the kidnapping felt. There had been no indication that Ethan and Zoe might be returned to their parents under any circumstances. Just like Rodney Glass had lost his own child forever? There wasn't anything more personal than that, was there?

I also thought about the last time we'd spoken. 'Ethan's my little lunch buddy,' he'd told me. There would have been plenty of opportunities to gain Ethan's confidence. Maybe enough to have learned about Zoe's secret cell phone while he was at it.

Not to mention that someone had gotten Ray Pinkney high as a kite on the morning of the kidnapping. And someone had also very likely drugged Ethan and Zoe into unconsciousness before pulling them off campus. The fastest way to do that is by injection. Not that you have to be a nurse to know how, but it doesn't hurt.

By the time I'd run through it all in my mind, I was ready to move on this, pronto.

85

Molly Johnson was the closest thing to immediate family I could find for Rodney Glass. She'd never taken his name when they were married, and the two had been divorced for over four years now — since about six months after the death of their son. She agreed to meet me at the end of her lunch shift, hostessing at the Fire House Restaurant in Harrisburg. I left DC right away and was waiting for her in the parking lot by the time she came out. We spoke right there in my car.

'I don't know how much help I can be,' she said. 'I didn't even know Rod was back in the States. A friend told me he'd gone into the Peace Corps.'

'He's been living in Washington for three years now,' I told her.

'Gosh, really? Time flies.'

She stared out the window and absently fingered the gold crucifix around her neck. I could tell she was nervous. All she knew so far was that I wanted to ask about her ex-husband. So why was she so jittery?

'So I'm guessing you two didn't part on very good terms,' I said.

'No. After our son died — Zachary — it got . . . pretty bad between us.'

'Can I ask how he died?' I said.

She smiled, the way people do when they're

263

trying not to cry. 'The actual cause of death was severe malnutrition,' she said. 'But in terms of why his organs started shutting down, we never did get an answer. They just kept passing us from specialist to specialist.'

'That must have been a nightmare for you, for both of you. I'm sorry,' I said.

Without any prompting, she took a red leather wallet out of her purse and opened it to show me a school picture of a very cute little boy. He had Rodney Glass's same dark hair and pale blue eyes. I felt a pang of hurt for the parents.

'He wanted to be a doctor, like his dad,' she said. 'Or at least, like his dad was going to be. Rod was in med school when Zach got sick. The nursing thing was supposed to be temporary. Funny how life turns out.'

'And you said things were difficult between you afterward?' I asked.

She nodded as she put away the picture. 'Rod changed. I mean — to be fair, we both changed. But he just got so . . . paranoid. And so angry, angry, angry. I think on some level, he blamed himself. Like he never got to be the doctor who could save his own son, you know? But on the outside, he blamed everyone else.'

'And when you say everyone — '

'I mean everyone,' she answered. 'The doctors, the hospital, the whole messed-up healthcare system. We didn't have any insurance at the time, so you can imagine. If you'd asked him then, he probably would have said it was the system's fault that Zach got sick in the first place.'

Molly stopped suddenly and turned to me, as if something had just occurred to her. 'What's he done, anyway? Is Rod in some kind of trouble?' she asked.

I'd been gauging her carefully the whole time, trying to figure out how much was too much to say here. I didn't want to leave without getting everything I could, so I went ahead and took a calculated risk.

'Molly, I told you before that Rodney's been in Washington for the last three years. But what I didn't say was that he's been working at the Branaff School for most of that time.'

She looked at me blankly. Apparently, the name didn't mean anything to her.

'It's where Zoe and Ethan Coyle are enrolled. It's where the kidnapping occurred.'

'Wait,' she said. 'Are you saying Rod's a *suspect* in that kidnapping?'

'Technically, anyone who works at the school is on our list,' I said. It was the kind of answer I had to give, but she understood perfectly.

Now her whole demeanor changed. Suddenly she seemed twice as shaky and nervous as before. Her hand treaded back up to the crucifix and her eyebrows knitted together.

'I just can't believe that. No. I mean . . . he couldn't possibly . . . could he?'

'I don't know, Molly,' I said quietly. 'Could he?'

It took her a long time to answer. She bowed her head and closed her eyes for several seconds. Her fingers were all over the cross and I wondered if she was saying a prayer. And also if she was involved herself.

When she looked up again, she was trembling all over.

'There's something I have to tell you,' she said. 'Maybe something important.'

86

'It was a few months after Zachary died,' Molly Johnson started in. 'Things had gotten pretty awful between me and Rod. But then one night, out of the blue, he came home and said he wanted us to go for a drive.'

She was still staring off into the distance, not really focusing on anything — except maybe the memory of that night. We'd obviously opened some kind of Pandora's box. I kept my mouth shut for the time being and just listened to her.

'Honestly, Detective, the last thing I wanted at that point was to go anywhere with him, but we'd been fighting so much, it just seemed easier to say yes. So I got in the car and he started driving.

'After a while, Rod took out this thermos he used for work. He told me he'd filled it on the way home, at this place where I always liked the hot chocolate. It seemed like he was trying really hard to be nice, so I went ahead and drank some. I didn't even think about it until later, but he never had any of the cocoa. Just me.'

It seemed pretty clear where this was headed now. I could feel the dread climbing up my neck, thinking about Molly, but also about Ethan and Zoe.

'Pretty soon, I started feeling sleepy,' she went on. 'Like weirdly sleepy. It came on so fast, I didn't even get to wonder what was happening.

'The next thing I knew, I was waking up in this . . . place. Like a basement, or a cellar. I don't even know what it was. I remember it smelled like dirt, if that makes any sense.'

'Molly, do you have any idea where this was?' I asked. I couldn't hold back my questions anymore. 'Do you remember where he took you? Anything about the ride there?'

She shook her head. 'Believe me, I've wondered, but that whole time is just a foggy dream in my mind. He left a cooler with sandwiches, and some water, and I'm sure the food and water had more of whatever was in that hot chocolate. But it was like I didn't even care. I barely remember any of it. Sometimes I even wonder if it happened at all.'

'I think it did, Molly. Please go on. How long were you there?' I asked.

'Three days. I was in and out the whole time. Then, at some point, I woke up again and I was just . . . back home. In my bed. There was a note from Rod, trying to apologize, and all of his things were gone.'

She took a long, deep breath and looked over at me for the first time since she'd started her story. She was still shaking, but not as much as before.

'That was it. A week later, I called a lawyer and filed for divorce. Rod didn't contest it.'

'And you never pressed charges?' I asked.

'I never told anyone about this,' she said. 'Not a soul. I know how that must sound, but . . . I don't know. After losing Zach and everything else that happened, I just couldn't stand to look

268

back anymore. Like I'd go crazy if I thought about it too much. All I wanted was to move on.' She smiled again, sadly, down into her lap. 'You must think I'm pretty pathetic.'

'No,' I said. I reached over and took her hand, fighting back my own tears. 'Just the opposite. I think you might be a hero.'

87

On the way back to DC, I got Bob Shaw, the captain of MPD's Homicide Unit, on the phone and started lining up an immediate mobile surveillance team on Rodney Glass. This detail needed to be as covert as possible. That meant pulling cars out of the pool that weren't Crown Vics or Impalas — makes that screamed 'undercover cop' to the informed eye.

I also gave Shaw a list of names from Narcotics and a few of the warrant squads — guys I knew had the look and skills to go unnoticed on the street. What I didn't want was anyone who had been anywhere near the Branaff campus since this investigation had started.

That included myself. Glass knew me. I was going to have to stay on the fringes of this surveillance for the time being.

By four o'clock that afternoon, I was back in the city, and we had three cars positioned strategically around the school neighborhood, just as Glass was leaving for the day.

All of my team were carrying GPS locators so I could use a single laptop to track them from a distance in my own car. We had radio communication set up on an alternate, nonrecorded channel, which was as private as we were going to get on short notice. I parked several blocks away and listened in.

'This is Tango. He's out the south gate. Green

270

Subaru Forester, turning north on Wisconsin.'

'Go ahead, Tango. This is X Ray. I'll cut around and get you somewhere after Thirty-seventh Street.'

'No problem. Bravo, hang back if you can.'

'Copy that.'

We had just enough units to run a floating box, with one car following for a while, then dropping off while another came in to take its place. I gave them some time to get ahead of me, then pulled around and brought up the rear from about half a mile back.

'Who's got eyes on him?' I asked, once I was headed up Wisconsin the way they'd gone. 'What's he doing?'

'This is Bravo. He's just driving. Listening to music, it looks like, tapping his hands on the wheel. Guy doesn't seem like he's got a care in the world.'

'Yeah, well, I think maybe he does.'

Glass stayed on Wisconsin for a couple of miles. It seemed like he might be headed into Maryland, but then I got word he was stopping in the Friendship Heights shopping mall. He parked in the lot outside Bloomingdale's and walked over to the Mazza Gallerie mall.

I sent two guys inside after him and kept one circling the block, then parked myself just past the lot, where I could see Glass's empty car.

For the next forty-five minutes, it was the usual kind of boring minutiae you get on ninety-nine percent of surveillance details. I sat and listened while Glass went to McDonald's. Got a burger. Sat at one of the tables, reading a paperback copy of Sebastian Junger's *War*, which I'd read myself. He didn't seem to be in any kind of hurry. Nothing special about the day.

When he finally got up again, they followed him into Neiman Marcus, leapfrogging around the store while he looked at shoes and men's shirts. It almost seemed like he was deliberately killing time for some reason.

And then suddenly he was gone.

'Tango, you got him?' I heard.

'Negative. Hang on a second. Hold on. I think he went into the bathroom.'

Another fifteen seconds ticked by. *C'mon, c'mon, c'mon!*

'What's going on there?' I said.

'This is Tango. It's not him in the bathroom. I think we might have lost him.'

'Lost him?' I said, trying not to rip anyone's head off — yet. 'Or he gave you the slip?'

'I really don't know,' he said. 'But we're going to want some more eyes in here.'

I resisted the urge to run inside myself. I didn't want to lose my head and blow this thing. But I sure as hell didn't want to lose Rodney Glass, either.

88

This was pure misery. A disaster — and I'd been in charge. I was so angry at myself, even if I couldn't have done anything differently now.

I was going crazy, watching Glass's Subaru from the confines of my own car, and listening to nothing but radio silence while my guys scoured the neighborhood.

Both malls.

The parking lots.

Side streets.

Then, just after seven o'clock, I spotted Glass.

He came sauntering around the corner from the front of the mall and cut diagonally across the parking lot. That son of a bitch!

'I got him,' I radioed. 'He's headed back to his car. Get out here, and get yourselves ready to go.'

It was dark by now, but the parking lot was well lit. I used a small pair of binoculars to try and see what Glass was carrying. He'd been empty-handed on the way in.

The shopping bag he had in one hand was from Anthropologie, I saw. The kind of place where my kids might shop. Or the president's kids, for that matter. Nothing in there for someone like him. He was a tall, strapping guy — a grownup, for starters. He favored L. L. Bean and Carhartt, as far as I could tell. Not the trendy fashions of this place. What was that about?

In his other hand, he had a tall cup with a straw sticking out the top. The logo on the side said AMC. That meant the movie theater, not the food court.

Jesus. Had I been tearing out my hair for three hours while Rodney Glass had taken himself to a *matinee?*

Or was that just what he wanted us to think? Was this all for show? Where else might he have been all this time?

As I watched him throw his bag into the back of the car — casually, maybe *too* casually — I started to get a horrible, sinking feeling. It was nothing I could prove to myself either way, but my gut was starting to tell me what my head didn't want to know.

He knew he was being watched, didn't he? He knew.

Book Five

RUSH TO
THE FINISH

89

Hala kept her head down, her face averted, as she walked up First Street.

She crossed K Street and then cut left into a narrow alley near the bus station.

It was well screened at the front by several large, gray dumpsters, with stacks of wooden pallets, abandoned furniture, and old bags of garbage at the back, where Tariq was waiting for her.

He was even paler than when she'd left him. It looked like he'd lost a good deal of blood. Tariq was becoming a liability.

'Did you get it?' he asked.

'Some of it,' Hala answered, and knelt down where he was sitting propped against the brick wall. From inside her shirt, she pulled out a small bottle of Tylenol, a roll of gauze, and an Ace bandage. It was as much as she'd been able to lift at the drugstore without being seen.

'Let me see your hand,' she said. 'Please. *Let me see.*'

She pulled away the strip of shirt cloth she'd used to wrap Tariq's wound the night before. It was in horrendous shape. The bullet had passed right through, probably shattering the metacarpal of his right thumb as it did. He had no flexion, no extension at all. If they didn't get proper medical attention, and soon, she was going to have to start cutting away the dead and dying flesh.

That part, she kept to herself.

He moaned as she rewrapped it, using the gauze first, then the Ace bandage. Pressure was the only tool she had at her disposal for now, but she could see the agony it put him in.

When she held out several of the Tylenol, he shook his head.

'Hala, please,' he said. 'It's not enough. You know what I want.'

She did. That was exactly why she'd taken the cyanide from him. Both of their capsules were now in her pocket, where she intended them to stay.

The only other thing they had left to their name was Hala's Sig Sauer pistol. Everything else — their passports, money, computer, all of it — was back at the Four Seasons. It might as well have been locked in a vault. Even on her quick trip to the drugstore and back, Hala had seen her own grainy image gracing the cover of several newspapers.

They didn't even have the means to get themselves out of Washington. This godforsaken city had become their prison — and Tariq knew it. The empty, defeated look in his eyes said everything she needed to know.

'Please, Hala,' he tried again. 'There's no dishonor in this. We've done all we can.'

She pressed the Tylenol into his hand. 'Take them,' she said. 'Trust me, my love. We're not done yet. Not even close.'

There was still one possibility she could think

of. It was a risk, but less extreme than the option at the bottom of her pocket.

When she got up to leave again, Tariq reached after her like a child who couldn't bear to be left alone. 'Where are you going?' he moaned.

'Not far,' she said. 'Just wait here. I'll be back for you. I promise.'

90

Hala left Tariq at the back of the Alley and crossed the street to the bus station.

There was every reason to feel terrified right now, but she wasn't. The more Tariq seemed to be giving up, the more determined she became. Their backs were against the wall, and so what? They'd been there before. They had trained hard for just this eventuality.

And, if the worst did happen — if the capsules proved necessary in the end — there were still nine rounds left in her gun. That meant nine more Americans who would die before she did.

Inside the mostly deserted bus terminal, she crossed the waiting area to a small bank of battered and heavily graffitied pay phones at the back. Surprisingly enough, the first one she picked up gave a dial tone, and she pressed zero.

It took an irritating amount of time to place the call — overseas, collect, to Saudi Arabia. The American operator was virtually useless.

But then all at once a familiar voice was there on the other end of the line, accepting the charges.

'Hala, darling, is it you?' her mother said in Arabic. 'Where are you?'

'Still in America, Mama,' Hala said. It was strange, using her native language after so many weeks of English. 'Our business isn't done here

280

yet. Tariq and I are staying on First Street. Between K and L.'

'I don't know what that means, Hala. K and L?'

'It's where we're staying right now,' she said.

'But when are you coming home?' her mother wanted to know. 'Fahd and Aamina ask about you every day. They miss you so much.'

Hala squeezed her eyes shut against the tears that wanted to come. She mustn't do anything to draw attention here, she knew. Not even the smallest thing. She would not let herself cry, or show any other weaknesses.

'Give them my love, Mama,' she said. 'Please.'

'But they're right here,' her mother said.

'No! I can't stay on the phone,' she tried, but too late. A moment later, Fahd's sweet voice was in her ear.

'Mama! I miss you!'

'I miss you, too. Are you being a good little man?' she asked. Her own voice was thick. She hoped the boy wouldn't notice. It was nearly overwhelming.

'Yes, Mama. We're learning about geology in school. Do you know what sedimentary rock is?'

'I do,' she said. 'But, Fahd, I can't talk right now. Mama has to go.' She could hear poor little Aamina clamoring for a turn in the background. 'Back to First Street, between K and L. Across from the bus station.'

'What, Mama?'

'I have to go,' she said quickly. 'Tell your sister that Papa and I love her very much. We love you, too. You are the best children in the world.'

'Will we see you soon?' he asked.

Hala gave the only answer she could bring herself to give. 'Yes,' she said. 'Soon. Very soon.'

Hanging up the phone on Fahd was as difficult as anything Hala had been called upon to do in America. But also just as necessary. Every second she spent in public here was a large risk. As soon as she'd gathered herself, she turned and walked quickly back the way she'd come.

Now all she could do was pray that the right people — and none of the wrong ones — were listening in on her parents' telephone calls. The Family was very thorough that way, but so much had changed in the past few days.

Whether or not they'd heard what she said, and whether they'd come for her and Tariq, only time would tell.

Inshallah.

91

I woke up to a text on my Blackberry the next morning. It had been sent by Peter Lindley's office assistant: '8:30 AM Liberty Crossing, vital meeting with AD Lindley. Pls confirm.'

The last thing I wanted now was to be pulled back out to LX1. I'd tripled the surveillance on Rodney Glass and had three teams keeping an eye on him around the clock in eight-hour shifts. If he made any more odd moves, I wanted to be close by when they happened.

So I was feeling more than a little anxious by the time I got all the way out to Langley. What I expected was a full meeting of our CIA work group, but when I came into the conference room, it was just Lindley and half a dozen of his own case agents and team leaders. Two stories below, through the glass wall, I could see the command center bullpen, buzzing away.

'You're here. Good,' Lindley said, waving me inside. It looked like the rest of them had been at it for a while. Ties were loose, sleeves were rolled up, and the table was littered with files. Most of those had the Bureau's seal stamped on the front.

'First of all, we've got a credible line on another accomplice to the kidnapping,' Lindley said.

One of the agents dropped a file in front of me.

I opened it to see a small photocopy of a mug shot, bulldog-clipped to what looked like several arrest reports. The name on the photo was Deshawn Watkins.

'What about him?' I asked. 'Who is he?'

'His girlfriend came in through one of the hotlines,' Lindley said. 'One of a million calls, of course, but she had a few interesting things to say. Namely, that Mr. Watkins was recruited online and paid five hundred dollars for his services, plus a hit of some kind of high-grade smack.'

'Just like our van driver, Mr. Pinkney,' I said.

'Our *first* van driver,' Lindley said. 'It seems now that maybe there were two.'

I started flipping through the file. Watkins had a mile-long record of misdemeanors and a few felonies, including some jail time for armed robbery when he was sixteen. He'd also done a couple of court-ordered stints in rehab.

'The girlfriend says Watkins was instructed to pick up a vehicle on the morning of the kidnapping, then back it up to the groundskeeping shed at Branaff and wait for some kind of package to be delivered. After that, she says, he drove it out to Reagan National, long-term parking, and walked away. The back of the van was locked from both sides, and he never got a look at what he was transporting.'

'Or who put this 'package' into the van,' I said.

'That's right.'

'Smart. Jesus.'

It was starting to add up . . . to how Rodney Glass could have gotten Ethan and Zoe off campus and still be around for the aftermath. Then all he'd have to do was drive out to the airport, maybe stop to sedate the kids again, and continue on to wherever he wanted to take them. If anything had gone wrong in the meantime, Glass had a fire wall of anonymity for himself. Pinkney and Watkins couldn't finger him if they wanted to. They had no idea who he was. None at all.

'Where's Watkins now?' I asked.

I saw a few smirks around the table. 'That's what the girlfriend wants to know,' one of the case agents told me.

'Apparently, Watkins skipped town two nights ago — along with this woman's younger *sister*. Sounds like she ran out of reasons for protecting him. She came in with a lawyer this morning and struck up a pretty quick deal.'

'We've got his name out on WALES, and every field office in the country's looking for him,' Lindley said. 'But quite honestly, Deshawn Watkins is not our number one concern right now.'

I looked up from the file. Lindley was just picking up a steel briefcase from the floor.

He set it down in front of him with his hands on the double combination lock. Then he nodded to the half-dozen other staff around the table.

'Excuse me, everyone. Could we have the room, please?'

92

As soon as we were alone, Lindley opened the case. The Toughbook inside powered up automatically, and he entered a long string of characters to access whatever it was he wanted to show me in private.

'What you're about to see is a video that came into the Richmond field office this morning. A copy, anyway. The drive it came on is at the lab, but the First Lady asked personally for you to see this.'

That might have explained why I was the only non-FBI personnel here. Mrs. Coyle trusted me, for better or worse. So far, I felt like I was letting her down.

Lindley turned the case around so the screen was facing me, then hit the space bar to start the video.

At first, it didn't look like anything was happening. Then I noticed some kind of vague movement, like someone was carrying a camera through a dark room.

My pulse ticked up a notch, anticipating what I was about to see.

A light of some kind came on, wobbly, like a handheld flashlight.

I saw the folds of a dark blue blanket. The camera kept moving, and a hand came into the frame.

Then Zoe's face.

She seemed to be sleeping. Probably under heavy sedation, I thought, given what Molly Johnson had told me. The shot was too close up to show Zoe's surroundings — but could this be the basement Molly had described? The one that smelled like dirt? Where the hell was it?

'The date stamp on the video file is for two days ago,' Lindley said. 'Not that you can't fake something like that, but it's the best sign we've had so far that they're alive.'

In fact it was the only sign we'd had, but I didn't say anything.

The camera stayed on Zoe for another ten seconds or so. Then there was a blur of movement, and Ethan was there. His face was just as filthy as Zoe's, and just as gaunt. At least there was no blood or scars, nothing to suggest they'd been beaten.

'The son of a bitch is starving them,' I said. My eyes welled up. I couldn't help it.

Finally, I had to look away from the video.

Lindley cleared his throat. 'There's twenty-three seconds in all,' he said. 'And then . . . this.'

The screen went dark. This time, it looked like the camera had been turned off.

When it came on again, we were looking at a plain white piece of paper with something printed there, in a small, plain font.

As the image slowly zoomed in, the words on the page became clear.

'*Believe what you want, Mr. President.*'

'It's more of the same,' I said. 'He's turning up the torture. He wants Coyle to watch his kids waste away, just like Rodney Glass had to watch his own son die.'

Lindley nodded sedately. He took back the

computer case and shut it up tight.

'I'm inclined to agree,' he said. 'That's why we think it's time to put everything on the table.'

I wasn't sure I liked the sound of that. 'What does that mean?'

'It means if we're lucky, we've got one last chance to save Ethan and Zoe. We're pulling Glass in for further questioning.'

'*What?*'

'I know it's a risk,' he said. 'But all we have is circumstantial evidence — at best. We need him to think he's cornered. A confession's our only shot.'

'Hang on. Did we just see the same video?' I said. 'What do you think happens to Ethan and Zoe if you take him out of commission?'

Lindley didn't like to have his authority questioned. I could see it in the way he set his jaw when he looked at me.

'What are you suggesting, Cross? We do nothing about this? We wait him out?'

'I'm saying let's consider all our options while we still can.' I got up and started moving, trying to think clearly. After weeks of walking through molasses on this, it was all happening too fast. 'Maybe we create a false story. We say we have his print on the videotape. Something to let Glass think he's got no room to maneuver.'

But Lindley wasn't even listening anymore. His phone had just buzzed. He looked down to check whatever message had come in.

'Too late,' he told me. 'Glass is already here.'

93

Rodney Glass was a damn good actor. He seemed genuinely perplexed about why he'd been pulled in for another interview. But he didn't fool me for a second. He'd been to medical school. Of course he was bright.

'How many times do I have to say this?' he asked, less than a minute into the interview. 'I was treating Ryan Townsend for a bloody nose just after Ethan and Zoe went missing. I've got Ryan himself, not to mention at least one Secret Service agent, to back me up on this. So can someone please explain what I'm doing here?'

He had a cocky, almost adolescent quality to him, all the way down to his NBA kicks. Was that part of the act, too? Just another way to get the kids at Branaff to trust him? I also had the impression Glass had taken something, maybe even just a Klonopin, to keep himself loose while he was here. He certainly knew his way around pharmaceuticals.

'What about just before Ethan and Zoe disappeared?' I asked. 'Where were you then?'

'Isn't this already in your files, or whatever?' he asked.

'Humor us,' Lindley said. After our initial argument, Peter and I had agreed on one thing. Now that Glass was here, we needed to hit him with everything we had. And maybe some things we didn't have.

'I was in the faculty restroom, okay? Taking a dump, if you really want to know.'

Lindley scribbled something in his file.

'And how long does it take to walk from the faculty restroom back to the infirmary?' I asked.

Glass shook his head and frowned. 'I don't know. A minute and a half? You tell me.'

'Just about a minute and a half,' I said. 'But you weren't coming back from the restroom, were you?'

'And that's not really a question, is it?' he said.

'It also takes about a minute and a half to get back from the tunnel under the school, if you hurry,' I told him. 'I timed it myself.'

'Yeah, good for you,' he said.

I hated this guy. I really did. The stakes couldn't have been higher, and I was feeling edgier by the second. I didn't care anymore that he'd lost a son. That didn't excuse what he was doing now.

'Before that, you were using the phone from Emma Allison's locker to send Zoe Coyle a text. One that would get her down into that tunnel just after homeroom,' I went on. 'I guess the only thing I'm wondering is whether you planned for Ethan to be there, too, or if you had to improvise.'

Glass actually grinned and looked around at everyone else in the room. There were five of us, including two of Lindley's agents, recording the interview with a camera and a laptop.

'Why do I feel like I'm being set up here?' he said right into the camera.

Lindley put down his pen and closed the file

in front of him as if we were just getting started.

'Mr. Glass, was there some sort of incident, between you and your ex-wife in March of 2007?' he asked.

Glass did an exaggerated double take, looking back and forth between Lindley and me. 'I'm getting whiplash in here. What are you talking about? I'm lost.'

'She says you drugged her and held her hostage for three days, shortly after the death of your son.'

'*What?*' His face dropped. For the first time, he actually seemed surprised. 'So this is how you want to play it? The dead-kid card? Are you joking?'

I stood up. I couldn't sit still for this anymore. 'Do we look like we're joking?' I said.

Lindley went on in the same monotone. He stayed in his seat. 'Would you be willing to show us where you took her?' he asked.

'*I can't!*' Glass shouted at him. 'I can't — *because it never happened!* Did you even bother to check Molly's medical records? She had a complete breakdown after Zach died. I'm talking clinical. So if she *thinks* I held her hostage, or whatever, that's her problem, not mine.'

'You know, your compassion's a little under-whelming,' I said.

'Yeah, so's your police work,' he shot back. 'Jesus. If Ethan and Zoe do wind up dead, at least we'll all know whose fault it is.'

That was it. I snapped. The next thing I knew, I was halfway across the table with two handfuls of Glass's shirt.

291

'Where are they?' I yelled.

'Alex!'

'*Where are they?*'

It was a moment of pure adrenaline. If I could have split open his head for the information, I might have done it.

'Get him out of here!' Lindley shouted behind me.

'This isn't going to bring back your son!' I told him. 'Give it up, Glass — for God's sake! Don't let those kids die!'

I was still yelling as they pulled me out into the hall. The last thing I saw before they closed the door was Rodney Glass, raising a hand my way to wave good-bye.

Jesus. What had I just done? He'd gotten exactly what he'd wanted, hadn't he?

I'd risen to the bait.

94

I was crouched down in the hall, trying to regroup, still angry but also embarrassed about what had happened with Glass, when I realized someone was standing over me.

'Take a walk?'

I looked up from a pair of black steel-toed boots to see Ned Mahoney, holding out a hand.

'How'd you know I was here?' I said.

'After that little scene? I think everyone knows you're here,' Ned said. Several other people had stopped and were still staring. 'Come on. Let's go breathe some air.'

'You didn't answer my question,' I told him.

'That's true,' he said, and headed up the hall. So I stood and followed.

We wound our way down to the ground floor of Liberty Crossing and out through the west lobby. The whole place is a huge X-shaped complex, with one of those sterile concrete plazas in the crook of the two main wings. We stopped there and took a seat on one of several empty benches overlooking the parking area down below.

The dropping temperature outside didn't do much to cool me off while I told Ned what had happened. In fact, talking about it only made me feel worse.

'I screwed up, Ned. Glass is probably going to be home in his own bed tonight, while Ethan and Zoe . . . ' I shook my head. I couldn't even finish.

'That would have happened whether you went off the deep end with him or not,' Ned told me. 'You said so yourself. He's too clean, too smart.'

'Clean as dirt,' I said. 'Goddamnit. But I know we can get him.'

Mahoney was uncharacteristically slow to respond. Usually his brain has a direct line to his mouth. Then finally he said, 'You're sure Glass is the one?'

I nodded. 'I'm sure.'

'And you can't prove it?'

'I can prove it,' I said. 'Just not fast enough.'

'So maybe it's time to think about some alternatives,' he said.

I felt a chill down my back, and not because of the stiff breeze blowing up from the parking lot. I let Ned go on.

'Listen, I'm a company man when I need to be one,' he said. 'If the system didn't work at least some of the time, I couldn't do this for a living. But guess what, Alex? It's not working. Not on this one. It's not even coming close to working.'

'Hard to disagree. Glass is unusual, smarter than most.'

I couldn't get Ned to look at me. He just stared down at the pebbled concrete between his feet while he talked. This was Langley, after all. You never knew which bush had eyes, or which bench had ears.

'Ned, you're talking about — '

'I'm not talking about anything,' he said. 'But if I were, I'd tell you that I could pretty easily put my hands on some things you might need. Also, that I wouldn't leave you hanging on this, if you're interested.'

I wanted to say, interested in *what?* But I was sure I already knew. Before I could say anything else, Ned got to his feet.

'Go home, Alex. You've got my number if you want to . . . you know. Talk.'

'Talk,' I said. 'Right. I do have your number.'

He hunched his shoulders against the wind and blew into his hands. 'Should have worn a jacket out here,' he said. 'Cold as hell.'

Then he turned and walked away.

Cold as hell for sure.

95

Record.

'After I left Cross, I was almost overwhelmed by my own emotion. I'd done it, I'd won. I'd beaten all of them and I was still winning every single battle. Every one.

'And yet I felt a subtle change in myself. Was I so filled with guilt ... that I was someone different now? Why hadn't I struck out at Cross?

'The honest truth: I wasn't as impressed by him as I thought I might be. But was he *playing* me? Setting me up for the kill? He was certainly physically imposing, and smart, I suppose. He's definitely passionate about what he's doing.

'But I don't believe he's going to catch me, to stop me, to put me away for what I've done, the awful things.

'I'm not afraid of Cross.

'But that's not what my feelings are about. This isn't about the detective; it's about me. I know that to be perfectly safe I should do nothing about him. I'm clever enough to figure out something deadly. I'm good enough to execute it, and get away with it.

'So why haven't I acted? What's stopping me? Is it guilt? Remorse over what I've done to the children? Maybe something got to me — something about Cross's kids, or his wife, or Cross himself? His passion is inspiring.

'Or is it this: I know I can't stop myself and I want Cross to do it for me?

'No. I don't think so. I don't believe I want to be stopped. I've won . . . and I rather like that.'

96

When I got home that night, I could hear the kids going at it down in the basement. Ever since Ava had come to stay with us, the three of them were getting on like a house on fire, and they'd turned the downstairs into their own makeshift all-in-one clubhouse, boxing gym, and movie theater.

Bree and Nana were in the living room, stuffing envelopes for Southeast Children's House. That was the name of the charter school Sampson and Billie were still struggling to start up . . . without much help from me these days.

I flopped down on the couch with my plate of leftovers and a Budweiser.

'What's the good word?' Bree said, sliding me a sideways kiss, then another. She smelled good, felt even better. I'd missed her.

'All bad,' I finally told her. I couldn't get Mahoney's offer out of my head, but this was not the time or place to talk about it. I was home now.

I reached down and picked up a tattered paperback copy of *Precious*, which someone had left on the floor. It was the movie tie-in version, with the amazing lead actress, Gabourey Sidibe, on the cover.

'Is Jannie reading this for school?' I asked. 'Tough story. Good one.'

'Actually, I got that for Ava,' Nana said. 'I told

her she needed some meat and potatoes to go with those comic books she's been gobbling down.'

'Speaking of Ava,' Bree said. 'We got a call from Anita at Child and Family Services today. Just checking in to see how things are going.'

'I guess that means they don't have a placement for her,' I said, forking up a mouthful of meat loaf and sweet potato.

'I think Anita's hoping they have one,' Bree said. 'She thinks Ava's going to make it.'

I looked up from my plate to see both of them staring at me.

'Don't look so surprised, Alex,' Nana said. 'You knew they'd push for this.'

'Let them,' I said. 'We still need to get Ava into a real foster home before she gets too settled here. Or too attached.'

Nana threw down the flyer and envelope she was holding. 'Well, isn't that just typical!'

'What?' I asked.

'Apparently, it's obvious to everyone but you that Ava is *already* attached to this family,' she laid into me. 'And most of us are attached to her!'

I set down my plate and rubbed my eyes. The last thing I needed right now was a lecture from my grandmother. Or a fight. *I was home.*

'Nana, I can't tell you how bad the timing is.'

'And, Alex? I can't tell you how little I care what you think right now. Why do you suppose Ava never smiles at you?' she said. 'Why do you think the conversation always drops off when you come into the room? It's because you're never

299

here! You think she's that way with everyone?'

'Excuse me, but I'm trying to help bring two kids home to their parents,' I said, barely holding onto my temper.

'Oh yes, because nobody else is working on that one. Excuse *me*, but those Coyle children have thousands — *thousands* — of people looking out for them right now. What does Ava have? She's got us, that's what.'

'That's not fair,' I said.

'Well, someone let me know when everything gets *fair* around here.'

She snatched the copy of *Precious* off my lap like she didn't even want me touching it and she left the room. A second later, I heard the basement door open.

'Who wants ice cream?' she called out, like nothing had happened, and a small army of feet started up on the stairs. 'I've got Chunky Monkey, Mint Chocolate Chunk, Cookie Dough . . . '

I took a deep breath. Then I took another.

'What a great day,' I said.

Bree gave me a sympathetic smile. I could tell whose side she was on, but she wasn't going to beat me up about this. Not right now, anyway.

'Come on, tough guy,' she said. 'Let's go put some Mint Chocolate Chunk on it. You deserve it.'

97

Sleep was apparently out of the question that night. With Bree off working another graveyard shift, the bed seemed way too big and I was left alone with my thoughts. Including thoughts about poor Ava.

Every time I closed my eyes, I saw Ethan and Zoe's dirty, emaciated faces. And every time I opened them, I thought about what Ned Mahoney had said to me after my encounter with Glass. Or rather, everything he hadn't said. I could feel the idea of it taking shape like a heavy ball in my chest — half dread, half adrenaline.

If I'd understood Ned correctly, we were talking about something I'd resisted ever since I became a cop, a line I'd never crossed. But then again, maybe that was only because I'd never had to.

What if this was the one night — the hour, the minute — that might make a difference for Ethan and Zoe? Could I live with that? And what if it was my own kids out there, I thought, or Ava, for that matter? Would I even be lying here wondering what to do?

Of course not. In a strange way, my fight with Nana only drove that point home. I would do almost anything to save those kids.

Finally, just after midnight, I couldn't stare at the ceiling anymore. I sat up fast. In the dark,

there are two things I always know how to find
— my phone and my Glock. I reached for the
phone. Dialed Sampson's number.

'Hullo?' he answered in a thick voice. 'Alex?'

'Sorry to wake you,' I said. 'I need to talk,
John. Actually, I need your help on something.'

'No prob, sugar.'

'Put on a pot of coffee. I'm coming over.'

'See you in a few.'

I threw on some clothes, splashed water on my
face, and left the house.

On the way to Sampson's, I called Ned
Mahoney, too.

He answered on the first ring. 'I thought you
might call,' he said.

98

Sampson was on board the minute I told him what I wanted to do. He knew I couldn't ask outright, so he volunteered, and I was just desperate enough to accept. John is six nine, with the kind of arms Michael Vick might wish for. Plus he had exactly the skill set I needed to back me up.

And Ned Mahoney had the tools. He was carrying a small messenger bag when we picked him up at a Park and Ride in North Fairlington.

With twelve years on Hostage and Rescue, Ned was the break-in expert of our group. For the rest of the ride, he did most of the talking. Planning. I just drove and listened.

By two thirty a.m., the three of us were huddled around the back door of Rodney Glass's condo in Alexandria. It was an attached duplex with a well-lit shared driveway in front, but a lawn and pool area in the back that was all dark and closed up for the night.

I held a penlight for Ned while he unrolled a leather kit of picks and tension wrenches, each one in its own pocket. Usually Ned's all about the forty-pound battering ram, but he knows how to do small and quiet, too.

Less than ten seconds after he'd angled the first pick into the dead bolt, it turned with a soft click.

The lock on the doorknob went even faster.

I took it from there and led the way inside. It was dark and quiet on the first floor. We stopped there to pull the black balaclavas down over our faces. Honestly, it wasn't a good feeling. Seeing Ned and John in their masks really drove home for me what we were doing. This was nowhere I ever thought I'd be, but there was no turning back now.

For that matter, I didn't want to. I wanted to save those kids if they were still alive.

We went in a line up the hall to the front of the house. The stairs were carpeted, and therefore no problem. It didn't take long before we were standing outside Glass's open bedroom door. I could hear him snoring and saw his outline, sleeping on his back with one arm thrown over his head.

I signaled John to take one side of the bed. I hurried around and took the other. Mahoney stayed at the foot with his first syringe uncapped and ready.

Then I counted it down for them on my fingers.

Three — two —

All at once, Glass roared awake. He rolled toward me and reached for something under the mattress, but John was already there to pull his arm back. I stuck my hand into the same place and felt the contours of a pistol. He was an avid hunter, I knew, with several legally registered firearms in his name. I left the pistol where it was.

As soon as Sampson had him, I tore off a length of duct tape and pressed it over Glass's mouth. Then I pushed him facedown into the mattress while John slapped a pair of speed cuffs onto his wrists.

Mahoney was next. He knelt on the bed, flipped back the covers, and jammed a needle into his hip. Glass tried to scream from behind the tape. Then his whole body went rigid like he was being Tasered.

The rush of adrenaline made him even harder to handle, but that didn't last long. Within a minute, his limbs started to go slack. Every sound he made got a little weaker, until they'd ebbed into a kind of lazy, constant hum. He shuddered the way we sometimes do at the edge of sleep. He wasn't completely out, but he was completely useless, for the time being.

'That's it,' Ned said. 'We're good to go.'

We hustled him into some pants and down the stairs, holding him up, dragging his legs. At the door, I threw a jacket over his shoulders to hide the cuffs. Then we walked him out to the car in a tight group.

As we took off, I had no doubt in my mind that, ultimately, we were doing the right thing. Rodney Glass knew where Ethan and Zoe were. *He had to know.* But God help us if I was wrong, I thought.

In fact, God help us, period.

We were kidnapping Glass.

99

'Wake up. Wake up right now!'

It all happened very fast. Hala hadn't meant to fall asleep. Now someone was there, shining a bright light in her eyes. By instinct, her hand went straight to the Sig in her lap. Before she could reach it, the point of another pistol came out of the light. It stopped just short of her forehead.

'Don't, sister!' the other woman said. 'Please. We're from The Family. We've come to get you. We're only here to help.'

'Hala?' Tariq was just stirring. The infection in his hand had left him feverish and bleary. 'What's going on?'

'I don't know,' she said. 'Someone is here. They say they're from The Family.'

'We have to hurry,' a man's voice said. 'And I'll take that weapon.'

Her finger tensed on the trigger. 'I don't think so,' she said.

'Sister, listen to me.' The woman took a step back now and lowered the light. Her voice was calm. *Sisterly*. 'You placed an overseas call. One that you meant to be intercepted, isn't that so?'

Hala stared up at the two strangers, but it was impossible to gauge their faces in the dark. It was also hard to think clearly. They hadn't eaten or even had a sip of water in over twenty-four hours. Still, it was hard to argue with the

306

information these people had. And what option was there, anyway?

'All right,' she said, and put the butt of the Sig into the man's outstretched hand. 'But I'm going to want that back.'

'Of course,' the man said.

The Al Dossaris were made to stand and lift their shirts next, to show there were no wires or listening devices of any kind. Then they were each frisked.

'Just a precaution,' the woman assured them. When her hand passed over the pocket in Hala's skirt, she took the two cyanide capsules as well. 'You won't be needing these anymore,' she said. 'You're heroes. Both of you. Everyone in The Family honors your name and what you've done.'

For the first time in days, Hala smiled.

A black Toyota 4Runner was waiting at the top of the alley. In the streetlight, Hala saw that the two strangers both had olive skin and dark eyes. The woman's hair was bleached blond, and the man's head was shaved to a rough stubble, his scalp tattooed with an Arabian falcon at the back. In their tailored black clothing, they looked as if they could have just come from one of Washington's trendier clubs. For all Hala knew, they had. She pushed Tariq into the backseat, then got in beside him.

'My husband's been shot in the hand by the American police,' she said as soon as they'd pulled away. 'I'm going to need antibiotics, disinfectant — '

'Here.' The woman handed a plastic grocery

bag over the seat. 'This will have to do for the moment. We need to get you out of Washington before we do anything else.'

When Hala looked inside the bag, she almost wept with relief. There were bottles of water, chocolate bars, a jar of almonds, a first-aid kit, and a small pharmacy bottle of amoxicillin. Two weeks ago, she might have wondered how all of this was even possible, but she'd learned — just like the Americans — never to underestimate the power and resources of The Family.

She took Tariq's good hand in hers and gave it a reassuring squeeze. If he'd had his way back in that disgusting alley, she knew, he would have been dead by now.

'Thank you,' she said to the two in front.

'No,' the other woman said. 'Thank The Family. And thank Allah.'

100

Mahoney Drove. Sampson sat in front. I took the backseat with Glass, who was as high as a kite by now. His eyes occasionally rolled up into the whites.

I waited until we were out on the Beltway. Then I reached over and pulled the silver tape off his face.

'Wha' the *hell*'s goin' on here?' he started right in, running his words together like a drunk. 'You assholes are in *so* much trouble — '

Sampson reached right across the seat and popped Glass hard, upside the head. It must have hurt because it immediately stunned him into silence.

'You listen first, dumbass,' John said with a finger in his face. 'Then you talk.'

Glass hunkered down, trying to get away, but he seemed more pissed off than scared. That was the scopolamine, doing its thing.

'Wha'ever,' he said.

'Rodney?' I said. 'Listen to me. I'm going to ask you about Ethan and Zoe Coyle. That's our only subject here. Do you know where they are?'

He smacked his lips a few times. His eyes fluttered. 'Wha'd you gimme? Is this thiopental? My mouth's like a sandbox.'

'Glass! Where are Ethan and Zoe?' I said. 'They're in a basement somewhere, right? There's a dirt floor. What else?'

'I dunno know . . . what you're talking about,' he slurred.

It's not that scopolamine is a truth serum, per se. But cognitively speaking, lying is a lot more complex than telling the truth. The drug just makes it that much harder to do. My best bet was to keep coming at him with simple, direct questions. Eventually he might slip up.

'Ethan and Zoe are in a basement somewhere,' I said again. 'Isn't that right, Rodney?'

His head lolled back and he swallowed several more times.

'Why should I tell you?' he said. John reached for him, but I put up a hand to stop him.

'Are they in a basement, Rodney? Or is it some kind of a cave?'

'I, um . . . '

'Are they? Tell me. Right now.'

'Nah,' he finally said, and my heart lurched. 'I mean . . . yeah. But not a basement. It's a, uh . . . you know. More like a root cellar.' His head fell back again, and he let out a bizarre, low chuckle.

'What the hell's so funny?' Sampson asked him.

'You are, man,' he said, and laughed again. 'I mean . . . you're all cops, right? But now you're the ones who're goin' to jail. That's funny, man. That's fuckin' classic.'

101

It took a second injection and a lot of wrong turns to tease some more details out of Glass. The closer we got to the truth, the funnier he seemed to find it. It was everything I could do to keep from knocking that smile right off his face — or letting Sampson do it.

After two long hours, we found ourselves on a dark secondary road somewhere south of the Pennsylvania border and Michaux State Forest. The middle of nowhere, basically.

Mahoney kept our speed low and the high beams on. The result was — we were going nowhere. We had no final destination yet.

'Hang on,' Sampson said suddenly. 'What's that?'

Ned stopped and angled the car at the side of the road. A wall of high grass and brambles was broken in one spot, like it had been trampled and bounced back. On the other side, it looked like an old ATV trail, or maybe a driveway, running into the woods.

Glass let out another long, drunken laugh.

'I'll take that as a yes,' Ned said, and pulled in.

As we drove on, a single set of tracks showed itself in the dirt. Someone had been here recently, but the trail wasn't well traveled.

Had Glass been coming in from more than one direction? I wasn't sure what to make of it.

About a hundred yards off the road, the trees

cleared and I saw an old farmhouse straight ahead. It was falling down all around itself, barely holding onto the clapboard.

Beyond that was a three-story barn, standing a little straighter in the dark, and my stomach knotted right up. It looked like just the kind of place where you might find an old root cellar.

Ned pulled around and stopped, with the headlights shining inside the barn. Everything about this was eerie and scary, even though we were the ones supposedly in control. But Glass still was, wasn't he?

'What the hell's that?' Mahoney said.

A half-decomposed animal carcass, or maybe more than one, was piled right in the center of the open barn doorway.

'Nice welcome mat. *That's* supposed to keep us out,' Sampson said. 'I think we're in the right place.'

'Cuff him to the door handle!' I was already out of the car. This thing had me in its own slipstream now.

I ran straight inside the barn, past an empty tack wall on one side and a row of stables on the other.

'*Ethan! Zoe!*' I shouted at the top of my lungs. '*Anyone here?*'

The only sound that came back was Glass's obnoxious giggle from the car.

At the back, the barn opened up all the way to the beams overhead. Vines and saplings had worked their way in through the walls, but those were the only signs of life I could see.

'You got anything?' I shouted to the others.

312

'Nothing over here,' Sampson called back.

'Nothing,' Ned said.

'There's got to be a way down. Stairs, or a ladder, or something.'

I came back and stood in the alley between the tack wall and the stalls, shining my Maglite in every direction. What were we missing? Were the kids even here?

As I came around again, I noticed that all but one of the stalls were empty. The one farthest from the door was piled high with junk. It looked like someone had taken everything they could find and dumped it in one place. Why?

'Hey!' I yelled. '*Hey!* Give me a hand!'

By the time Ned and Sampson found me, I was already throwing splintered wooden pallets and loose lumber out of the stall. There was a truck axle, a few bundles of rusted wire mesh, some concrete pilings, and an old corn shucker — the kind of thing I hadn't laid eyes on since I was a little kid in North Carolina.

As soon as the space was clear, we dropped down and started brushing away the dirt and gravel and old remnants of hay.

While I did, I noticed some of the debris was trickling down through a crack in the boards. Right away, it showed itself as a straight line — and then a definite rectangle in the floor.

'It's a door!' John said, and we dug our fingers into the gap.

We heaved straight up and flung open the whole panel. Then we picked up our flashlights and shone them down into the space we'd just opened.

'Oh, my God,' Mahoney said. 'Oh, no.'

Sampson and I stood there, speechless.

Just below floor level, there was a layer of dirt. It was dark, and moist, and looked like fresh earth to me. Like someone had only recently filled this hole.

The only other thing to see was the top of an old wooden ladder, just breaking the surface.

It looked like a grave.

And behind me, I could still hear Rodney Glass laughing in the car.

102

By six thirty a.m., the old abandoned farm was a full-blown federal crime scene, and it was lit up like Nationals stadium on a game night. The tension was unbelievable. I could see it on every face. I'm sure the others could see it on mine.

A military excavation crew had been driven up from Fort Detrick. Peter Lindley sent a team from the Crisis Management Unit in DC to supervise the logistics, including security.

Even the Frederick County Sheriff's department was kept out on the road. And word was that the Bureau director himself, Ron Burns, was on his way to the scene. I didn't doubt it for a second. I wondered if the president or First Lady would come here. I hoped not, for their sakes.

The toughest part was not knowing what to expect. Nobody was calling this a recovery mission yet, but no one was calling it a rescue, either. The feeling on the farm was incredibly intense. I've never seen such a huge operation get under way so quietly, and with so much mystery.

After a fast consult with an engineering unit from Quantico, it was decided that all the digging would be done by hand. There was a rotating auger and mini excavator parked in the yard, but this root cellar was a complete question mark. We couldn't risk the machinery, or the vibrations it would cause.

Three soldiers in fatigues and headlamps got right to it. They worked with sawed-off shovels, taking shallow scoops as quickly and as carefully as possible.

Even the soil itself had to be loaded out, bucket by bucket, for transport to the Bureau's forensics lab.

Ned, Sampson, and I split up. John helped haul equipment at first, and then dirt, as the digging got under way. Mahoney ran interference on Rodney Glass, who was sleeping off the last of his scopolamine in the back of a Bureau car. As for what Glass would say, or even remember, when he woke up, I couldn't be bothered right now. I had other things on my mind.

I spent my time with two of the Bureau's witness-victim specialists, Agents Wardrip and Daya. Both of them had extensive backgrounds in child and trauma psychology and knew a great deal about the impact that something like this could have on a kid. Survival was just the beginning.

I told them everything I knew about the case, but it was a tough conversation. We needed to be ready for the best and worst possible outcomes at the same time. The longer this went on, the harder it was to stay optimistic.

But then around seven thirty, everything changed.

I was outside with Wardrip and Daya when word started circulating that the crew had found something. We dropped everything and ran inside.

As I came to the edge of the stall, I saw one of

the three soldiers, up to his waist in the hole. He was conferring with the special agent in charge from DC, while the other two were crouched down under the floorboards, furiously pulling dirt away from one side with their hands.

So far, the digging had exposed only an old stone and mortar wall under the barn. But now they'd come to a wooden frame of some kind, and beneath that, the beginnings of a steel panel. Or maybe a door.

I could hear the first soldier talking with the SAC now. He was excited, and his voice carried above all the other chatter around me.

'Sir, I don't think we've been digging out the root cellar all this time,' he said. '*I think we just found it!*'

103

Everything intensified as our focus narrowed. Nobody said much while the crew cleared material out of that hole faster than ever. A bucket brigade went up, passing the dirt out of the barn, hand to hand.

Several times, the digging stopped and the soldiers pounded on the door with a shovel.

'Anyone there? Ethan? Zoe?'

So far, there was no answer.

As soon as they'd cleared enough space to cut a hole, two of the crew scrambled out and another soldier climbed down with a reciprocating saw.

A couple of seconds later, the barn filled up with a grinding, squealing sound as he drilled straight in. Then he changed direction and started slicing right through the steel.

It didn't take long. Once most of the panel was cut, the soldiers used a pry bar to pull it back into the hole, rather than letting it fall through.

Then they cleared out and two EMTs took their place. I was less than six feet away from the digging. Several more medical staff waited nearby with a crash cart and two gurneys. There were also three ambulances in the yard, and two Sikorsky helicopters with aeromedical teams waiting out on the road.

One EMT got down on his belly and crawled

straight back into the dark. The other handed through a medical field kit and then followed behind.

Everyone else seemed to hold their breath at the same time. In the silence, I said a prayer.

God, let them be there. Please. Let them be okay.

104

Then almost right away, one of the EMTS called up to us. His voice was hoarse — and excited. 'Someone's in here,' he said.

We waited. Everything was silent now. Everyone hopeful . . . yet afraid.

'We've got 'em. They're both here.'

The rescuer kept his voice low, maybe for the kids' sake, but I don't think anything could have stopped the cheer that went up in that barn.

There were handshakes, and hugs, and tears on more than a few faces. The feeling of relief was indescribable. Mahoney gave me a hug. Then so did Sampson. Then even Peter Lindley did.

Agents Wardrip and Daya took over from there. They had the work lights turned way down, and they excused the military crew. Then they climbed into the hole to help bring Ethan and Zoe up themselves. A few minutes later, word came that the kids were ready to be brought out.

Zoe came first. It was a moment of true joy mixed with heartbreak to see the young girl, trembling all over and clinging to Wardrip as he carried her up the ladder.

Her clothes were just filthy rags, and her eyes were wide and glassy. But they weren't vacant. She knew where she was.

They got Zoe onto a gurney and started

oxygen and a saline drip right away. Then they covered her with a heavy blanket all the way up to the shoulders, until you could barely even see her anymore.

Wardrip stayed right there, speaking softly to her while they brought Ethan out.

He looked about the same as his sister, but smaller, more vulnerable if that was possible. As he came up from that prison where they'd spent the last two weeks, he was mumbling something against Daya's shoulder, over and over.

I could see his dry, cracked lips moving, but I couldn't hear him.

The second he was on his own gurney, Zoe reached out from under her blanket and took Ethan's hand. Nobody tried to stop them or separate them.

They stared at each other like no one else was there, and her mouth started moving with his.

It was only as they were wheeled out past me, still holding hands, that I heard what they were saying.

'*Thank you, thank you, thank you. Oh, thank you.*'

The words couldn't have been simpler, or more eloquent.

105

I wasn't thinking about anything but Ethan and Zoe when I came out of that barn. I wasn't even thinking about Rodney Glass until I realized they'd already taken him away.

The car where he'd been held was gone, and somewhere in the confusion, I'd lost track of Mahoney and Sampson, too.

Then I saw Ron Burns. Or more specifically, he saw me. 'Cross!' he yelled, and wagged a finger.

As I came toward him, he turned and walked farther off, away from the hustle and bustle in the yard. The rescue mission was winding down while the investigative crews were just kicking into gear.

Evidence Response Teams had already started unpacking their vans, photographers were snapping everywhere, and a couple of total-station techs were setting up their equipment — the little black shoebox, I call it — to start a 3-D rendering of the entire farm.

I caught up to Burns at the foot of the porch stairs at the old ruined house. I could see he was already steaming.

'Rodney Glass tells us he has no idea how he got out here,' the FBI director started right in. 'He also maintains he knows absolutely nothing about the kidnapping.'

I wasn't sure where to start. Burns and I have

some history together, not all of it good. But all in all I'd always trusted him.

'Ron, I — '

'Not a word,' he said. 'The less you say right now, the better off we'll both be.' He pushed the tail of his jacket back with both fists. I was a little surprised to see he was armed.

'Whatever it was you got from Rodney Glass, and however you and your little A-team got it, none of it's going to be admissible. You do understand that, right?'

I knew better than to answer.

'As it stands right now, we've got nothing substantive to hold Glass on. We'll be able to detain him for twenty-four, maybe thirty-six hours, but unless something new turns up here, he's going to be out by tomorrow night.'

I couldn't hold back anymore. 'Ron, I'm not done with Glass,' I said. 'We'll get him. I've already got a surveillance crew up and running. We can put a GPS on his car — '

Burns put a hand up. 'Seriously, Alex. Does anyone ever tell you that you talk too damn much?'

He took a deep breath then. It seemed to let a little of the air out of his tires, and his tone came down as he went on.

'No one's pretending this is just cut-and-dried,' he said. 'It's likely those kids wouldn't have survived if it weren't for you, and you're going to have the gratitude of some very powerful people. Obviously. So I'm not too inclined to start turning over any rocks that don't need turning over, understand? As long as

Glass doesn't file a complaint — and he'd be a goddamn idiot if he did — I'd say this was your chance to shut up and walk away.'

He pointed over to where someone had moved my car. I saw Sampson was there, too, leaning against the fender and watching us.

'I don't want to walk away,' I told Burns.

He just shook his head like he felt sorry for me and started back toward the barn. 'Yeah, I know,' he said over his shoulder.

106

As the sun slowly rose over the Horizon, Hala could see that they had arrived at the ocean, the powerful, very gray Atlantic. They were in Massachusetts, maybe. Or this could be Connecticut. Once they'd gotten off the highway, it had been much harder to track the road signs.

A row of shuttered cedar cabanas sat along the beach. Beyond that, waves broke onto an empty shore in the early morning light.

Actually, the beach wasn't quite empty, Hala realized. A man was there, bent toward the water — toward Mecca — in prayer. She could see only the figure of him, no distinguishing characteristics. Presumably, it was his silver Mercedes parked next to their 4Runner. The rest of the dusty lot was deserted.

Tariq raised his head from her shoulder. His hand was still badly swollen, but he was at least hydrated, with a fresh bandage and the first course of antibiotics in his system.

'Where are we?' he asked.

'We're . . . here,' Hala said. It was as much of an answer as she had. For that matter, *where* seemed less important than *who* they were here to see right now. Whoever this man was, they'd driven all night to get here.

Neither of the two in the front seat spoke. They waited for the stranger to finish his prayers and only then opened their car doors to get out. Hala and Tariq followed.

The four of them came around and stood by their vehicle while the man walked slowly up from the beach, shaking the sand from his prayer rug as he came.

He was elderly — older than Uncle had been, but fitter. His snowy hair was brushed straight back over his head, and he wore the kind of tracksuit an American businessman might wear on the weekend. Dark blue with a single white stripe. His feet were bare, and he carried a pair of Adidas scuffs in one hand.

Hala could feel the excitement rising in her chest. Before they'd come to America, no one had even suggested that advancement within The Family was possible. But that was before they'd met Uncle. Now, it seemed, anything was possible.

She grinned at the ground. America really was the land of opportunity, after all. The irony in this amused her.

The old man smiled as he came close. He walked right up and embraced Tariq, kissing him on each cheek. Then he shook Hala's hand warmly but respectfully.

'It is good to meet our famous warriors from Washington, DC,' he said in a thick Najdi accent. 'The Family owes you a tremendous debt of gratitude for what you've accomplished.'

'Thank you for the opportunity,' Hala said. She'd learned not to appear too proud. 'And thank you for saving us. It was more than we deserved.'

'*Psh!*' The man waved a hand in the air. 'You were clever to make that phone call. A risky move, yes? But here we are. It is good.'

He was even more ingratiating than Uncle had been, Hala thought. The fact that he addressed her more than Tariq said quite a bit about what he must already know.

'Excuse me,' she said, 'but if I may ask — who are you, sir?'

'I would have thought someone as clever as you might have guessed,' he answered. 'In any case, it is not important who I am. In this country, we are all just nameless, faceless monsters. Isn't that so?'

Hala allowed herself to laugh. And before the man spoke again, she realized all at once who he was.

'You may call me Jiddo if you like,' he said.

Jiddo. It was the first word of Arabic any of these strangers had spoken to them, and exactly what she'd expected to hear.

It meant Grandfather.

107

'I love the ocean,' Jiddo said. 'As close to a view of home as we have here, yes?'

Hala and Tariq stood with him at the edge of the beach, looking toward the water. The air was cold, but the sky was a brilliant blue with just a few wisps of cloud floating near the horizon. Seagulls rode the breeze over their heads.

'I've never seen the Atlantic before,' she said.

'Ah. Well, now you have,' he said, in a way that told Hala the topic was about to turn back to business. Tariq took hold of her hand and stayed quiet. It was unusual for him to take the lead, but that's what he did now, signaling for her not to talk anymore.

'Our Washington operations are over,' the old man said. 'Rather, I should say they've been suspended for the time being.'

'I'm sorry to hear that,' Hala said honestly. 'We would have liked to have gone much deeper.'

'Don't be sorry. You are invaluable, an impressive soldier. We trained you quite well, it seems.'

'Yes,' she agreed.

'The jihad is not over. America is only just beginning to kneel. While they lick their wounds on one side, we will attack them from another. It will be like that until they are defeated.'

Hala smiled again. It excited her to hear him

speak this way. 'I hope there will be a role for us,' she said.

'Of course,' he said right away. 'In fact it begins right here.'

Hala turned to see the younger man pulling a familiar case from the trunk of Jiddo's Mercedes. It was the laptop computer she and Tariq had brought from Saudi Arabia. The one she'd been forced to leave behind at the Four Seasons.

She stared. 'How did you — '

'*Psh!*' Jiddo said again. 'Please don't be surprised. That would disappoint me.'

The assistant carried the computer over and opened it on the hood of the car.

'We created a very secure system for ourselves,' Jiddo told them. 'Perhaps too secure. With the man you know as Uncle out of circulation, our access to certain information has been . . . somewhat restricted.'

Hala understood immediately. 'You need for me to open my files,' she said, to an approving smile. She stepped over to the laptop, where a flashing cursor waited on the blank screen. It took only a moment to still her racing mind. Then the sixteen characters she needed flowed out of her fingers as if by muscle memory: 23EE4XYQ9R21WV0W.

The screen blinked once, then repopulated itself with a familiar series of icons. Hala scanned through them quickly, making sure everything was as she'd left it — target names, home addresses, public schedules, maps, security contacts.

'I believe it's all here,' she said.

'Very good,' Jiddo said. 'And now — '

Tariq spoke up all at once, in a voice that was oddly grave. '*Hala!*'

She turned around and saw the other couple standing behind them. The man had his hand out. In his palm were the two cyanide capsules that had been removed from her pocket earlier.

The woman stayed to the side, covering them with her Sig from the opposite angle.

'And now,' Jiddo said again, 'we must ask for one last act of dedication to The Family.'

108

Hala stared at the old man, understanding everything — and understanding nothing at the same time. The Family was supposed to be smart, wise.

'You can't be serious,' she said.

'I believe you're familiar with the terms,' he answered. 'It is preferred that your deaths be deemed a suicide by the authorities.'

The words hit Hala like scalding water. And the reversal of it all. She remembered the night at the Harmony Suites Business Hotel, when she'd said virtually the same thing to the other couple. The ones she'd thought were traitors.

The ones she'd been *told* were traitors.

'How can you do this? After all of our service? All we went through?' she said.

Jiddo was unperturbed. 'You came to this country prepared to die at any time, isn't that so?'

'*For the cause!*' Hala spat back. 'Not for this! Not for The Family's convenience.'

'And how exactly are those different?' he asked. 'Please make the right choice. If I'm not mistaken, there are . . . two little ones at home? Is that correct?'

'You wouldn't!' she said. But of course, she knew that they would.

'Hala.' Tariq was there now, and as he spoke, there was more clarity in his voice than she'd

331

heard in days. Maybe ever. 'We have to, Hala. Fahd and Aamina will be taken care of. Your parents — '

'This can't be happening!' she said.

'I won't warn you again,' Jiddo told them.

Like something out of a waking nightmare, she watched as Tariq reached over and took the capsules from the other man. He pressed one into her shaking palm and closed her fingers around it. Then he kissed her, unapologetically. There were tears in his eyes, but love as well. So much love.

'We'll see each other again,' he said.

'Tariq, no!'

109

But it was too late. He shoved the capsule into his mouth and bit down on it. She saw him wince, as the glass cut into his gums. Then the trickle of blood from his lips. Now it was just a matter of time before he was dead. Her Tariq was already dying.

Hala turned to face the old man. She looked from the suicide pill in her hand back up to his pathetic, wrinkled face. The arrogance in his eyes.

'There was one thing you said before,' she told him. Her voice broke more than she would have liked, but she pressed on. 'One thing, anyway, that was true.'

'Yes?' Jiddo said solicitously. 'And what was that, my child?'

'I was very well trained,' she said.

Hala turned all at once and landed a grip on the other woman's wrist. She snapped it easily with one clean motion. The woman screamed.

When the gun dropped from her hand, Hala was right there to catch it. Her finger found the trigger, and she shot the woman. Point-blank. In the face. No hesitation.

There were no idle or slow thoughts now. Only intentions. And fast actions.

She fired again, into the younger man's chest as he came at her. Jiddo had started toward the cover of his car, but Hala put a round into the back of his head before he could get there.

He sprawled onto the hood, sending the laptop flying, then he slid off the Mercedes's expensive finish to land next to it on the dusty ground. Only a broad paint stroke of red was left behind.

By the time Hala turned back to Tariq, he'd already sunk to his knees. The convulsions had begun. His head hitched with every attempt at a full breath.

'Go!' he wheezed at her. 'Go . . . now!'

'I can't!' She knelt next to him. For the first time since their so-called mission had begun, she was frozen, unable to act.

Then something moved behind her.

Tariq's eyes went wide. 'Hala!'

She rolled and fired instinctively. The bullet caught the younger man in the temple.

Blind rage took her. Hala was back on her feet. A wild, animal scream sounded in her ears as if it were coming from someone else while she emptied her magazine into their bodies.

Then she kicked and railed at their torsos, their limbs, their heads — even their faces. There was no amount of damage she could do to pay them for their sins, but still, she didn't stop. *They would arrive in the afterlife looking nothing like themselves.*

Finally, she fell back to the ground, panting and sobbing as she took Tariq up in her arms.

He lay half on his side where he'd gone down. His wide eyes seemed to be focused on the sky. It was as if he were still regarding the heavens, and it struck Hala that maybe God had been the last thing he'd looked for before he died.

Time slipped away. Later, Hala wouldn't be able to remember how long she had stayed there with Tariq, but slowly, her senses came back to her.

She had to keep moving now. That much was clear. Grief was one thing, but weakness was quite another. Hala was anything but weak. She was trained to be a warrior — to survive at any cost. That's what she would do.

Without even standing, she moved over to the others on the ground. She ran her hands through the young man's pockets until she found the car keys. She took everything else they had, too — cash, credit cards, even the dead woman's long black coat.

Jiddo's pockets were empty. The only thing Hala took from him was the laptop computer. There was no knowing when or if the information it held might prove useful. Maybe it could be used to ransom her children.

Finally, she stood up again but felt like she was moving underwater. Everything seemed to flow slowly by as Hala climbed into the 4Runner, backed it up, and pulled out toward the road.

Drive slowly, Hala. Do nothing out of the ordinary.

Coming to this country, she'd been prepared to die at any time. And in a way, she realized, she just had. Hala Al Dossari's life was over. Another one would have to begin.

Somewhere. Somehow. Her life as a warrior would continue.

But who, Hala wondered, will I fight?

110

When I received permission to interview Ethan and Zoe, it came from the same place as my last invitation to the White House — straight out of the East Wing. It had been a week since the rescue, and the media circus was going full tilt. I'd never seen so many reporters outside the White House, and that's saying a lot, for Washington.

Security on the other side of the fence was something else again. It took forty-five minutes for Mrs. Coyle's deputy to get me from the East Visitors Gate up to the residence.

When we reached the second floor hall, Mrs. Coyle was there to greet me herself. She came right up and took both of my hands.

'It's good to see you, Alex,' she said. 'I'm not even sure how to say what I'm feeling. There are no words.'

'Thank you for having me' was all I said. Getting this interview had been no easy thing. I don't imagine anyone *but* the First Lady could have gotten me here.

She walked me up the hall in the opposite direction as the last time, while two Secret Service agents followed at a respectful distance.

'Zoe will probably be a little reticent,' she told me, 'but Ethan's actually been eager to talk about the kidnapping. I've gone over everything with them, and with their care team. You can ask what you need to.'

We passed the famous Yellow Oval Room and came to a large, sunny den, with a view of the South Lawn. Ethan and Zoe were sharing one of the couches, watching *Despicable Me* on a huge wall-mounted TV. I recognized the president's mother, knitting by the window. She smiled and nodded but didn't get up.

'Ethan? Zoe?' Mrs. Coyle said. 'Can you turn that off, please? This is the detective I told you about. This is Alex Cross.'

111

The kids both looked over their shoulders at me. Interested, but not too much.

'Hi,' they said together quietly.

'Come in. Please.' Mrs. Coyle motioned me farther inside and we came around the couch to sit down.

I started the interview slowly, asking closed-ended questions at first, then opening it up to whatever they might remember or want to tell me.

Zoe was as quiet as her mother thought she might be. She pulled her feet up under her and drew little circles with her finger on the arm of the couch, mostly with her eyes down.

Ethan was nearly the opposite. He watched me closely, and always answered first, with the kind of quiet clarity you get from kids sometimes after a crisis.

'We just kept talking to each other,' he told me at one point. 'I knew we had a chance since we were still . . . you know. Alive.'

The blessing, if there was one, was that neither of them remembered a whole lot about their time in that cellar. Given the levels of Rohypnol in their systems after the rescue, that was no surprise.

Neither of them could say much about their captor, either. Everything they'd been given to eat or drink came through a sliding panel in the door. There had been no conversation at all.

'He just ignored us the whole time,' Ethan

said. 'Like we weren't even there.'

'You knew it was a man, though?' I asked. They hadn't been told a word about Rodney Glass, particularly the fact that he'd been released from custody for a lack of evidence.

'I saw his hands a couple of times. Man's hands. And sometimes, I could hear him talking on the other side of the door,' Ethan said.

'Talking?'

He nodded. 'I think he thought we were asleep, and sometimes we were. But sometimes I'd only pretend.'

'Did you ever hear what he said? Or recognize the voice?' I asked.

He shook his head. 'I tried, but it was too soft.'

Ethan seemed to stop short then. His chest sunk in a little and he looked up, like he was remembering something.

'There were these clicking noises, too,' he said. Zoe looked over at him.

'What kind of clicking?' I asked.

'It was like — ' He held up his hand and bent his thumb back and forth. 'Like Dad used to use.'

'The tape recorder?' Mrs. Coyle said suddenly.

'Yeah. Back in Madison.'

'Ed used to dictate briefs from home when he was practicing law,' the First Lady told me. 'All the time.'

'I heard it, too,' Zoe said quietly, and we all looked at her. She was mimicking the same hand gesture that Ethan had just been making. 'It was like . . . click on, click off.'

'Yeah, exactly,' Ethan said, nodding enthusiastically. 'Like he was always recording himself.'

112

Record.

'I've been a good boy for a week now. Not that there's much choice, is there? The only way I could have more cops watching me these days would be if I was actually in jail. Now it just feels that way.

'At least I can get out here, stretch my legs, and get my thoughts down.

'This is probably the last private place I'm going to have for a good long while. And even this is going to get ruined, with people coming around, and gawking, and wanting to know what really happened here.

'It's kind of depressing. I mean, just because everyone knows *what* happened, it doesn't mean they know *why*. Which of course is the whole point.

'All my new little friends at the FBI and Metro Police think I'm just some sadistic bastard who got away with the crime of the century. Well, I've got a news flash for them. As far as I'm concerned, I didn't get away with anything. We're all just right back where we started. And I know what I'll do next. I will kill Alex Cross.'

Stop.

He looked down from the ridge at the old farm. The police and FBI had packed out by now, but you could see how the place had been picked over. There were still some shreds of

340

yellow tape on a few trees, and a few stray pink flags in the dirt.

It was tempting to go down there and have a look around, but not yet. It was still too fresh.

Not that they could arrest him for being curious, but this was close enough for now. In fact, it was getting late. He took one last look, then turned and headed back into the woods.

Record.

'I don't know. Maybe I should have just killed them while I had the chance. At least if Ethan and Zoe had died, it could have stood for something.

'But instead, all this did was prove my whole point. We live in this world where some kids are more valuable than others, I guess, and the average Joe on the street is just fine with that, so long as it's not his kid getting screwed over or dying.

'Well, guess what? I'm no average Joe. I'm no kook, either. I've got a valid story to tell. People need to hear this, and I'm not going to stop until it's done.

'You will not be forgotten, Zach. That's a promise, my man. I'm going to make you proud if it's the last thing I do. Your death will mean something by the time I'm finished.'

Stop.

He pocketed the recorder and kept the bow in hand as he walked the rest of the way, but even the rabbits seemed to be keeping their distance these days.

Whatever. He was too distracted to do any real hunting, anyway.

It was just getting dark by the time he came out of the woods and onto the old fire road, where he usually parked. His head was so full of angry thoughts, he didn't even see the other car until he was practically on top of it.

That's when he saw the cops, too. There were two of them standing there. One, he recognized by sheer size — the guy was closer to seven feet than six.

The other had a face that Rodney Glass would never forget. Not since they'd been nose to nose in that interview room in copland. He was a detective with the Washington police, and his name was Alex Cross, and he would be defeated too.

113

'*Put down the bow, Glass,*' I said. 'Put it down right now!'

He had a recurve on his arm, with the arrow pointed down at a forty-five-degree angle. It's a weapon I've never fired before, never gone up against. I wasn't sure what it would take to get a shot off. That's why my Glock was out and pointed at his chest.

One reason, anyway.

Glass froze, but only for a split second. Then his face broke into a wide grin. It shouldn't have surprised me, but it did. This guy was cocky all the way to the final buzzer. It was impossible not to hate the man, no matter what had happened to his son. He was a kidnapper, with the heart of a murderer.

'Well, look who it is,' he said. 'Are you going to shoot me out here in the woods? So nobody will know?'

'Is that what you think?'

'You heard the man,' Sampson said. 'Put the bow on the ground and step back away from it. Do it now.'

Something flashed in Glass's eyes. I'm guessing it was the memory of Sampson's right hook on the car ride. In any case, he crouched down slowly, still watching us, and set the bow next to his car. Then he carefully slid the quiver of arrows off his shoulder.

'What are you doing out here?' I asked. 'Seems like a strange choice, all things considered.'

He shrugged nonchalantly. 'Just curious. People have been telling a lot of lies about me. I figured I might as well come out here and see what all the fuss is about.'

'Jesus,' Sampson muttered next to me.

'You know, we've been a little curious, too,' I told him. 'Mostly about that tape recorder of yours. The one you keep in your glove compartment.'

Glass stood with his head cocked to the side, keeping his hands where I could see them, but stealing glances at my gun.

'I like to get my thoughts down sometimes,' he said. 'That's not illegal, is it?'

'Not at all,' I said. 'You want to know what else isn't illegal? Putting a transmitter the size of a match head in that little recorder of yours. Not with the right warrant, anyway.'

I reached into my pocket and took out my own recorder. Mine was a little nicer than his. It was a gift from Ned Mahoney and his technical people at the Bureau.

Then I pressed play.

' . . . *maybe I should have just killed them while I had the chance. At least if Ethan and Zoe had died, it could have stood for something. But instead . . .* '

Glass blinked. That's all he did. He was as cocky as ever.

'This doesn't prove anything,' he said.

'Rodney Glass, you're under arrest for the kidnapping and attempted murder of Ethan and

Zoe Coyle,' I said. 'Get down on the ground and put your hands away from your sides.'

'We got you, Glass,' Sampson said. 'We finally got you. And *that's* fuckin' classic.'

114

Glass stayed where he was. The grin stayed on his face. 'You know, there is just so much wrong with this picture. You guys are way out of your jurisdiction. Go back to Washington where you belong.'

Sampson's Glock was out now, too. 'Oh, we're going back to Washington,' he said.

'Yeah, I don't think so.' Glass rolled his eyes at us and turned halfway around like he was walking away.

'Glass — '

But it was only a cover. He swung back around fast, and as he did he pulled something out from under his jacket. A pistol in his right hand.

'Glass, don't!'

'Glass!'

The words came out at virtually the same time that I fired. Sampson, too. Glass's own shot went wide as he took two bullets high in the chest. We weren't messing around. These were kill shots, and he went down hard.

I kept both hands on my gun and sited him as I stepped closer. He was out flat, with both eyes closed. There was no discernible movement. *Was this finally over?*

'Check him,' I told John. 'Careful.'

Sampson kicked Glass's gun away first. Then he ran his hands down Glass's sides and each leg to check for other weapons. He put two fingers to Glass's carotid artery. 'There's a pulse,' he said, and turned toward the car. 'I'll call it in.'

Glass groaned weakly.

'Rodney?' I said. 'Can you hear me? Hang on. We'll get you help.'

He didn't say anything. But he wasn't grinning anymore.

I used my knife to cut up the middle of his sweatshirt. There were two dark burn holes in his chest. As far as I could tell, neither of the bullets had passed through.

I could hear John on the radio phone. He sounded urgent. 'This is Detective Sampson with Washington PD. We need immediate medical assistance. We're on an unmarked fire road, just off of Hampton Valley . . . '

Even as John was talking to dispatch, he handed me a plastic take-out bag from the car. I pressed it over Glass's chest, trying to seal the two wounds and keep them from sucking air.

Glass shook his head. He reached up with a hand on my wrist and tried to stop me.

'Doesn't matter,' he gutted out. 'No use.'

He'd obviously punctured a lung, if not both. A fine mist of blood was coming out with every labored breath. Essentially, he was drowning, and he knew it. Glass was a nurse, after all.

'My boy . . . shouldn't have died,' he said. And then, unbelievably, that awful grin of his returned. '*You* should have died. You ruined it.'

Then, before Sampson was even off the phone, Rodney Glass let out one last, long hiss of air, and he was gone. Bizarre turnarounds happen sometimes. One second, you're trying to stop someone from killing you, and the next you're doing everything you can to save his life.

I'd like to say I felt something when Glass died, but the truth is, nothing came. I wasn't glad, and I wasn't sorry, either. After everything that had happened, it all seemed to be over incredibly quickly — just like the story Glass had been trying to tell all this time, in his own deluded way.

He never did get the ending he wanted so badly, but he got the one he deserved.

Epilogue

FAMILY TIES

115

'Let's go, Let's go, Let's go! I'm ready. Let's go, everybody!'

Ali was already in his shirt and tie, and as far as he was concerned, that meant it was time to leave. The sooner we got out of the house, the sooner he could be back home and out of that cursed silk noose around his neck.

'Just sit tight, little man,' I said. 'Maybe your big brother will do a little wakeboarding with you.'

I did what I used to promise myself I never would, and plopped Ali in front of a video game to distract him. Damon, who was home from boarding school for the Thanksgiving weekend, picked up the other Wii controller.

'It's good to have you here, Day,' I said. 'We miss you like crazy.'

'And I miss kicking Ali's butt,' Damon said, jumping into the virtual water with both feet. 'Let's do this, little man.'

The ladies of the house were all still in their rooms. I ran upstairs and knocked on Jannie's door, where the sounds of Jennifer Hudson's latest were playing at full blast.

'Don't come in!' she yelled over the music.

'Ten minutes, Miss Cross.'

Ava was already dressed. Her door was open and she was sprawled on the bed, reading Nana's latest assignment — *Twilight*.

'How's the new book?' I asked.

She gave me one of her trademark shrugs. 'S'okay. Kind of weird.'

'I'm glad you're reading anyway,' I said. 'It's good to see.'

She just nodded and turned the page. Another scintillating conversation between the two of us, but I had to keep moving.

The foster parenting application, meanwhile, was working its way through the system. Bree and I had done the required twenty-seven hours of training with Child and Family Services, and it looked like Ava would be staying with us for the foreseeable future. Damon would bunk with Ali while he was home, and then next summer — well, we'd figure that out next summer.

I was running way behind. Still, I was determined to get a quick shower. The fact that I found Bree already in there was what you call a lucky break.

'Mind if I sneak in?' I asked, rattling the curtain.

'You're going to have to ask my husband about that,' she said. 'And grab a washcloth, please.'

Fifteen-plus minutes later, everybody was finally assembled downstairs. Nana was fussing over the bow tie she'd gotten me for my birthday, and Bree was still fixing Jannie's hair even as the coats were going on.

'Why are you smiling like that?' Jannie asked, eyeballing me in the hall mirror.

'I'm just glad to have all of us together,' I said. 'It doesn't happen often enough.'

'*Mmm-hmm*,' Nana said pointedly. Then she

gave my tie one last adjustment and patted my chest to let me know we were finally good to go.

With that, the Cross family tornado was out the door.

'You look cute in that tie.' Damon got in a last little dig.

'Adorable,' said Jannie, piling on.

116

The auditorium at St. Anthony's was filled to overflowing that night. We'd already moved the event over from the cafeteria when word got out that Regina Coyle would be speaking.

I had the pleasure of introducing the First Lady, and I'm pretty sure I impressed a few patriotic biddies in the audience when she stopped to kiss me on the cheek as she came to the podium.

Then she spoke beautifully, all about the importance of quality neighborhood schools. She talked about her admiration for what a lot of charters had been able to accomplish in Washington — mentioning Arts and Technology Academy and Booker T. Washington specifically — and told the room how she just knew that the Southeast Children's House was going to be a huge success when it opened its doors.

'And with your help, it *will* open. I have no doubt about that,' Mrs. Coyle said. Her husband may not have exactly swept the District in the last election, but we were all on our feet when she finished, applauding like crazy. As Nana put it later, politics stayed home that night. For once, thank goodness.

Afterward, we had a few minutes with Mrs. Coyle, and I got a chance to introduce our family to her.

'I'm sorry the president couldn't be here

tonight,' she told us. 'I know he would have liked to have come.'

'Maybe next time,' Nana said with a wink. 'I'd just love to talk to him about his education funding proposals.'

'This is my wife, Bree,' I said, moving things along. 'And my two oldest, Jannie and Damon.'

'I think very highly of your father,' she said, shaking the kids' hands.

'We do too,' said Jannie, 'most of the time, ma'am.'

Mrs. Coyle laughed, and I imagined that Jannie reminded her a little of Zoe.

'And this is Ali and Ava. They'll both be going to SCH when it opens.'

'Wonderful,' she said. 'Does that mean you'll be able to walk to school?'

Ava looked up at her, awestruck. She barely nodded before she turned away, but I caught a little smile, too — and with all due respect to everyone who was there, it was the highlight of my night. If I wasn't mistaken, I'd finally just managed to impress Miss Ava. All it took was an introduction to the First Lady of the United States.

So I rode that wave. I spent the rest of the night feeling good about myself, and pretending for just a little while longer that I was someone important.

But don't ever tell Nana I said that.

117

'Sir, it's been two months since the bodies were found at the beach in Truro. Since that time, there have been no known attacks from or by Al Ayla that we're aware of. All of our intercepts and intel from the Kingdom indicate that their Washington operations have shut down for the time being.'

President Coyle looked across his desk at the dozen high-ranking men and women gathered in the Oval Office. The events of the last few months had left these people exhausted. He could see it in their eyes.

But it had also brought a renewed sense of unity to the intelligence community. The breadth of knowledge and experience in the room this evening was not insignificant.

'What about those bodies? Any progress there?' Coyle asked.

'Still no luck identifying three of them, sir,' answered Norma Tiefel. 'The fourth was Tariq Al Dossari, the husband of the woman we believe was in charge of the Washington cell just before everything died down.'

'And she is — ?'

'Unaccounted for. It's like she disappeared. We believe she might have killed the others.'

Coyle twirled a sleek gold pen over his thumb like a propeller. It was something Zoe had taught him to do on the plane to China last summer.

That seemed like a very, very long time ago now.

'What about elsewhere? New York, Chicago, LA?'

'All quiet, as far as we can tell,' FBI Director Burns told him.

'Of course, it's possible that they're just regrouping,' Evan Stroud from the CIA put in. 'But none of the major agencies anticipate any kind of resurgence without some kind of advance chatter giving us a heads-up.'

'Right. Because we've never been surprised before,' the president said.

'I'm sorry, sir, I don't mean to oversimplify anything. I'm just saying that these moments of quiet between the United States and the Kingdom are getting harder to come by.'

'Which is just another way of saying wait and see,' Coyle grumbled. He sat back and took stock of the room. 'Well, it will come as a shock to no one that I'm not one to duck and cover in the meantime,' he said. A few polite smiles showed on the group's tired faces. 'I intend to carry on with the business of this country, and I suggest you all do the same.'

'Yes, sir,' they said in chorus.

'Let me rephrase that. I *expect* you to do the same.'

Then everyone stood with the president as he rose and left through the West Colonnade doors.

Certainly there had been any number of mixed opinions in the room, Coyle thought, as he headed back toward the residence. He had no delusions of lockstep agreement on these matters, or even the desire for it.

But what he did have was confidence where it mattered most. Every man and woman in that meeting, he had no doubt, carried an unwavering respect for the country they served, for the presidency itself, and for the job before them all. To lead.

Books by James Patterson
Published by The House of Ulverscroft:

WHEN THE WIND BLOWS
BLACK MARKET
CRADLE AND ALL
THE JESTER (*with Andrew Gross*)
THE LAKE HOUSE
SAM'S LETTERS TO JENNIFER
HONEYMOON (*with Howard Roughan*)
JUDGE AND JURY (*with Andrew Gross*)
BEACH ROAD (*with Peter De Jonge*)
SUNDAYS AT TIFFANY'S
(*with Gabrielle Charbonnet*)
SAIL (*with Howard Roughan*)
THE MURDER OF KING TUT
(*with Martin Dugard*)
SWIMSUIT (*with Maxine Paetro*)
WORST CASE (*with Michael Ledwidge*)

THE ALEX CROSS SERIES:
CAT AND MOUSE
POP GOES THE WEASEL
ROSES ARE RED
VIOLETS ARE BLUE
FOUR BLIND MICE
LONDON BRIDGES
THE BIG BAD WOLF
MARY, MARY
CROSS
CROSS COUNTRY
I, ALEX CROSS
CROSS FIRE